BRIDGE
of
SOULS

T0321436

BRIDGE
of
SOULS

BLOOD OF ZEUS: BOOK FOUR

MEREDITH WILD
& ANGEL PAYNE

For Angel,

for all the magic you've brought to this journey.

— Meredith

For Meredith.

You are magic!

I'm so grateful for your friendship, partnership, and unending support.

Thanks for teaching me so much and for the privilege of being on this journey with you.

— Angel

"Who in the world am I?
Ah, that's the great puzzle."

— Lewis Carroll,
Alice's Adventures in Wonderland

CHAPTER 1

Kara

L IFE CAN CHANGE WITHIN SECONDS.

I learned that one from the moment Maximus Kane first touched me. And tonight, from the way his hand tightened around mine as Hecate, the goddess of the moon and magic, invoked a string of stunning words.

You're a bridge now, Kara. The gift of magic flows in you . . . and through you.

The statement, so serene, flowed from her, even as she faced off with Hades himself and saved the city in which I grew up. Los Angeles is still wrapped in a smoky pall far behind Maximus and me, but the memory of Hecate's voice lingers like a steel girder on the air, making me feel like the cabin of the truck is the safest place to be right now.

I'm still reeling with disbelief.

How am I supposed to believe that her powers run in *my* blood too? Blood that already belongs in part to my demon *and* human ancestry. Still, Hecate showed up at our family's villa and fought for me to stay on *this* side of hell when I needed it most. Without her, I'd be on my way back to the castle in the middle of the underworld right now. I'd be miserable, alone, and facing a lifetime of Hades's whims. Instead, Hecate brokered a deal my heart will never stop aching over.

A soul for a soul. My freedom in exchange for my grandfather's. Despite my protests, Gio Valari returned to Dis instead of me.

I clench my hands in my lap, trying to accept that I'll never see him again. Trying to move on anyway. Feeling as if it'll be impossible. Gone are the days where I could seek out Gramps to be a mental and emotional barometer on hard days—days like today, when my mind is still battling to process all that's happened.

Like the fact that Gramps will no longer be just a car ride away.

Like the fact that Hades's antics had Kell dragged into a human emergency center—with her half-demon blood nearly exposed to a lot of people who'd never understand.

Like the fact that Jaden is probably still trying to escape from Rerek, the demon who's smitten with him.

Like the fact that I can't do one thing about any of it. Not yet.

Not without Hecate's help.

Maybe that's why I'm so willing to follow her directions, scribbled in old-world feminine script on the piece of paper I'm holding in my hand.

But unlike the last time Maximus and I were on this part of Pacific Coast Highway, we're not heading to a casual party. Hecate's hest was clear: drop everything and come now. Maximus and I are still dressed in what we had on when we left his apartment so many hours ago, after a massive earthquake hit the area. A catastrophe caused by the very god Hecate defied for me.

"Are you sure we're going the right way?" Maximus's tight tone betrays his anxiety.

"It's all pretty clear. She wants us to continue up Topanga for two and a half miles."

I leave the reply at that, refusing to give voice to my own anxieties. Though Hecate's driving directions are seemingly leading us nowhere, I search inside for some extra faith. It's not overly hard when her earlier words are still so entrancing, echoing in my heart. Reminding me of when they blew open my mind...

Kara Valari. You are of the earth. Your blood sings with the fire of the underworld, but your soul declares the words of the high spirits.

"Well, we did pass a few houses back there," he states in the thoughtful baritone that zings along every inch of my nervous system. "But past this point, there's a lot of nothing for a bunch of miles, unless you count some hiking trails and a lot of wildlife."

I shake my head. Hecate's voice lingers in my mind like a spell in its own right.

"I don't think she'd have any reason to lead us astray."

A frown crinkles his bold profile. "I'm still puzzled

3

about why we're driving at all. We both know that gods can travel a lot more efficiently."

His jaw joins the expression, stiffening into a visible blade beneath his beard. He peers over the steering wheel as if his brilliant blues are enough to pierce the thickening darkness.

"Not too much farther now," I assure him.

As the miles pass, I imagine Hecate occupying an off-the-grid cottage somewhere out in the canyon. A cozy little place where she'd be able to privately tutor me on this crazy new aspect of my DNA. The Virgil to my Dante, with better hair and shoes.

"Are we getting close?"

I blink out of my closet fantasies and glance at the paper, then up to the road.

"Just ahead you'll see an open iron gate on a dirt road to the left. Pull in there."

"Here we go, beautiful." He reaches over and squeezes my fingers with determination. I return the pressure, acknowledging how desperately I need the contact, while watching him use his free hand to crank the wheel into the turn. "Guess a guy *can* trust an Olympian from time to time."

I flash a quick smirk. "You know that Hecate's an Olympian in name only, right?"

"Of course I do. She had to earn it, too. As far as goddesses go, she's one of the hard-working ones. And as I recall, she's as much a ballbuster as a soul protector."

We both jostle as the truck tackles the bumps and ditches

onto which we've turned. In another part of the world, this road would likely be labeled as a cart path. Fortunately, the big harvest moon provides extra light. The taller brush thins out as we climb a small hill. At the gently sloping crest, the path veers slightly right.

We descend and drive along the base of another foothill and then another. The terrain becomes starker, with shadows the moonlight can't reach. But the breeze is crisp, still touched with tang from the ocean. I recognize most of the flowers and shrubs in the glare of the truck's headlights. We're not in a totally different dimension.

So I keep hoping.

Or maybe that's just a way to keep my mind off the anxiety.

The mind-set that takes over anyway, gripping harder as another turn reveals lights in the distance.

"You weren't wrong, little demon," Maximus utters. "There really is a cabin in the woods."

But it's so much more than a cabin, we realize while closing in on our destination. Soon, the lights are joined by others, which illuminate a complex of buildings that look like a Mykonos villa took a detour through Taos on its way to this Southern California canyon. The buildings, though shaped like boxes, are given personality with hanging plants, colorfully painted doors, and twinkle light drapes between the rafters.

I peek in at spacious gardens and take note of a pretty creek that feeds a kidney-shaped lagoon. To one side, there's a small farmhouse with chickens, goats, and a pair of horses outside. Looks like there might be more critters inside too. On the other side, a small slope has been planted with prospering grapevines and fruit trees.

Maximus presses his foot to the brake pedal for the first time in what seems like several miles, easing our approach. "Do I cue the theme to *Little House on the Prairie* or *The Blair Witch Project*?"

I want to laugh but don't. "Wow. Both of those in the same reference. Nice work."

"You think I'm only good for mythology quotes and Dante trivia?"

I return his tease with a gentle smack to his sizable shoulder. "What I think is that you'll never be a boring date, Professor."

Though he brings my fingers to his lips, his sightline doesn't veer from its careful angle out the windshield. "A date? Is that what we're still calling this?"

Desperately, I yearn to make him stop so I can kiss the air out of his lungs. The very oxygen he risked by diving into hell on an insane rescue mission for me. The life that he might be putting on the line once more, by driving me into the middle of nowhere to—

Where exactly *have* we arrived? Are we in the right place at all? There are still no signs of life in the little complex near the parking space, such as it is, that Maximus guides the truck into. Only a couple of goats and chickens declare their noisy greetings before he kills the engine.

"Stay here," he instructs. "Let me come around for you. God knows what's out here."

After helping me down from the cabin, he maintains his protective grip on my waist. I'm grateful, since a shiver takes over the rest of my form. I'm not sure if it's from noticing ours is the only car parked here or because of the chilled wind that suddenly races down the ravine, but neither explanation will manifest the jacket I badly need.

I'm still dressed in nothing but a pair of Kell's pool slides and the baggy clothes I borrowed from Maximus back at his place—cinched sweats and a T-shirt he's affectionately nicknamed Mr. Fluffy.

But I'm feeling the opposite of fluffy right now, as the wind picks up and the hairs at my nape transform into skittish needles. Hecate made such a big deal about it being safer to travel here ahead of us, but where is she now? Where is *anybody*? Did we make a wrong turn? How could we have?

Just walking into this place doesn't seem right.

"Why do I feel like we should be soaking in the rain and staring at a fifty-foot castle door?" I mutter for his ears only.

Or so I think.

"Because of all your preconceived notions?" comes the humor-tinged answer—though definitely not from Maximus.

The voice is filled with other qualities. Elements I remember so vividly from when they soothed my ears an hour ago, next to the pool in Mom's backyard—the one a goddess materialized over, so mesmerizing in her otherworldly finery.

There's no regalia like that now.

No more windswept gown, layers of necklaces, or star-strewn hair. Still, even my mortal side would recognize Hecate as the complete goddess that she is.

Her approaching steps, beneath her dark-green broom skirt, are steady and strong. Her posture, outlined by a yellow formfitting blouse with emeralds along the sleeves, is straight and regal. Though her honey-colored hair is piled atop her head, it descends across her high forehead and prominent cheekbones like wispy, shiny vines.

She's incredible.

The air escapes my chest just like before. For long moments, her very aura steals my ability to form words.

But already, a beautiful certainty crashes through my chest and soothes every inch of my soul. *We're going to be okay.*

As it resounds in my mind, a smile grows across Hecate's graceful lips. Her eyes start sparkling with every color at once, a brilliant contrast to her silken sienna skin.

"No looming castle," she says with a musical lilt. "Just our humble retreat, here to be your refuge."

Maximus lifts his head with a quizzical frown. "*Our* retreat?"

"My apologies, dear prince." Hecate bows her chin toward her prayerful hands. "Where have my manners fled? The evening must have tired me more than I thought."

Despite her statement, the glimmer doesn't fade from her serene gaze. But I'm not given any longer to contemplate the contradiction. The next second, the atmosphere seems to quiver and change. From the midst of that disruption, six more females emerge and fan to either side of their queen.

Witches.

I already know it as fact, as certainly as there are stars in the sky and a sharper wind in the canyon. A breeze as firm but comforting as their gazes on me, each glowing with the same multicolored light as Hecate's.

"These are my *ministras*," she declares. "They are all eager to meet you and to join me in welcoming you to Iremia, where your journey to your own power begins."

CHAPTER 2

MAXIMUS

IREMIA IS MUCH BIGGER than it looks from the figurative curb. The complex is more like a luxury hotel, not that I have a ton of experience in that arena. The few academic conferences I've attended as a representative for Alameda were at places close to airports, with beds in which I had to sleep diagonally while listening to my neighbors through cardstock walls.

But this...

Well, it's not the *Blair Witch* cabin. Or even the big, brooding castle from Kara's reference.

I could actually get used to all this.

Beyond Iremia's front entrance, which is weirdly bare of any guard gate or security apparatus, there's a wide courtyard with various fishponds and picturesque bridges. One of the larger pools empties down some rocks and becomes a sizable stream that disappears around a bend. Cradling two sides of the courtyard, like a wide V, are long stone buildings. Their brightly lit interiors reveal a community room with worn leather furnishings, a dining area with communal tables, and a library that has me thinking of Recto Verso rebooted, the British decor accents replaced by mandala prints, Moroccan lamps, and sherpa chairs.

Ahead of us, positioned in the open side of that V, are a dozen freestanding cottages of different styles and sizes. They're all accessed by connected wooden plank paths, enhancing the bohemian feel of the complex.

"We've arranged some welcome treats for you out in the grove," the goddess says with a serene spread of her arms. "But first, some introductions."

I'm not opposed one bit to that idea. Even without Kara's empathetic skills, I'm aware of the keen curiosity from the others. Their glances say as much, like visual lasers at us both. But the blasts aren't hostile so far as I can tell, conveying needs to illuminate instead of decimate. I attempt to breathe easier, sensing that Kara knows that too. Still, her lips are taut as she attempts an encouraging smile at Hecate.

"Thank you," she says. "I think I'd like that."

"I can start." The words are almost ironic, since they come from the most easily identifiable female in the bunch. The iconic witch practically announces herself with a mother-of-pearl complexion and red curls that extend past her waist. "I am called Circe."

"You're kidding," Kara sputters. "I—I mean I *know*." And then she turns an adorable shade of red. "It's so awesome to meet you."

In that trying-but-not way of hers, my woman has put

everyone at ease. The laser glances fade to friendly smiles. One of them widens on the face of a petite olive-skinned woman to Circe's left.

"I am Aradia of Italy, and I am so happy to welcome you," she says while approaching with graceful steps.

The striking brunette next to her is cooler about her presentation. "Morgana of Camelot. Charmed."

I'm not too sure about her finishing statement but shrug it off as the others take turns offering similar greetings, delivered with musical inflections from their origins. Marie's voice has Creole influences. Kiama speaks with gentleness that strikes me as original to an African nation. Liseli's voice is the same as her Native American accessories, bold and noble.

After everyone is done, Hecate clutches her hands at the middle of her chest and swishes her long skirt with her joyful swaying. "Thank you, everyone, for working so quickly to ensure Kara and Maximus's warm arrival. I know the circumstances were sudden. Now let us proceed and celebrate!" She turns back to us, nose scrunching from her strange little smile. "This is also a little unorthodox, but after everything you've already been through, the *sala* might be a bit…overwhelming."

My Greek isn't always polished, but sala is simple to figure out. The main meeting room we just passed was warmly decorated and appeared comfortable. Not an inch of it was overwhelming.

Instead of explaining, Hecate beckons my attention ahead by sweeping her arm toward one of the plank paths between the cottages. Soon, we're stepping off one toward a crushed gravel walkway that leads into a stand of eucalyptus trees. Their refreshing smell is joined by a minty tinge from a pair of willows that droop over a wider part of the stream I noticed earlier.

Through the gentle curtains of branches, there's a glow from swooped strings of soft white lights illuminating a long banquet table. It's adorned with colorfully patterned cloths that are accented by gold fringe and bronze bells. I look around, wondering if we're going to be joined by a small army of exotic warriors—because there's enough food on the table to feed all of them and then some.

"Sit. You must be hungry from the journey," Hecate offers in her soothing tones.

"Wow." Kara conveys the surprise for us both.

I'm grateful, because while I'm still trying to narrow down an ulterior motive for the world's biggest charcuterie board, she's emitting grateful moans that already dissolve our hostesses into enchanted grins.

"This is …I mean, *wow*," she repeats.

"The meat was cooked in my own spice blend," says Marie.

"And we designed the cheese flowers." Kiama lifts Liseli's hand in a triumphant gesture.

"They're beautiful," Kara says with genuine awe. "I mean it. Is that a bleu cheese hydrangea?"

A proud smile emerges from Liseli. "Tastes better than it looks."

"But who could be heartless enough to eat it?" Kara

asks, nearly breathless as she clearly considers the idea.

"Me." I lean over and buss her cheek. "Sorry, my love. *I'm* that merciless. And hungry."

"Oh, I like him."

The compliment is from Circe, swishing forward in her filmy green gown. The famous sorceress seems perfectly at home in her toga-like attire, as do all the others in their moderately updated wardrobes.

Hecate's the only one who still looks trendy in her bohemian ensemble, thanks to the permanence of the comfortable fashion style.

"I'm hungry too," Circe declares.

"But guests first, of course," Aradia intones.

Circe holds up both hands. "Calmness, sister. I will leave enough for them."

"You will leave enough for *everyone*." Hecate definitely has a gift for decrees that sound like flattery. The remark seems to mollify the whole group, even an obviously irked Aradia.

In the end, the quibble doesn't matter. There is more than enough for everyone to eat their fill while we sit around the impressively outfitted table. It doesn't feel as bizarre as I thought to be the only male in this bunch. Not that I haven't been the only guy in the room before, being in an academic field that's crowded with women, but this imbalance is markedly different.

Every attendee at this late-night mixer is a formidable magus—if, in fact, they're real. The conclusion has me gazing around again, on the verge of awestruck. Aradia and

Morgana are supposedly nothing but folklore, and I'm still not sure if Circe has ever been authentically identified like this. All three of them have temperaments with gray areas, if the classical texts are to be believed. I know nothing about Kiama and Liseli but decide to err on the side of caution and consider they might possess some of the same.

But so far, I'm breathing a little easier overall. It seems Kara is too. Her hand, clasped casually in mine, isn't clenched so hard around my fingers. She even accepts a glass of white wine when Kiama uncorks a bottle, and she manages to laugh as the conversation circles around to a recent action movie that everyone is prioritizing, apparently because of the swarthy hunk as its lead.

"I tell you all this, even after centuries of evaluating the finest males on earth, he measures up," Aradia declares, earning herself a round of girlish giggles.

"Now, now," Circe chides. "Let's be respectful of our gentleman guest." She sees my no-offense-taken shrug but hardly blinks about it. "Besides, he's probably got a stunt double for those fancier moves."

"Speaking of dazzling actions..." As Liseli leans forward, her gaze is velvet-dark with intent. "Did you really escape from Hades's library, and then hell itself, in the space of one spell?"

Kara's lips twist. "I...um...I have no idea. A spell? Was that what it was?"

Morgana arches a brow. "You mean you don't know?"

Kara isn't ignorant of the additional reactions around the table. Kiama's silent-mouthed *wow*. The exchanged glances between Aradia and Liseli, communicating the same thing.

"I mean…I guess that's what it was, now that I think about it. There was a lot going on…"

"Of course," Hecate breaks in with purpose. "We all understand where your thoughts and instincts were in the moment." She rakes a pointed gaze up and down the table. "Though some of our memories are dimmer than others, we all started from the exact same place."

Kiama and Liseli shrug in unison, but it's Aradia who speaks up for the group.

"You are correct, Goddess," she says solemnly. "We are simply…surprised."

"It's all right," Kara replies. "But I have to know…why? Did I do something wrong? Or in the wrong way?"

Hecate pushes out a gentle huff. "Abolish both those thoughts at once. If anything, what you did was extraordinary. Now, we are here to help you tap into all that power, in all the proper ways."

"Exactly." Circe picks up that cheerful mood with some happy bounces against her seat cushion. "And it's going to be fun. So. Much. Fun."

For the first time since we sat down, Marie inserts a reaction into the conversation. "Ahhh, *oui*. Be certain to drink your morning elixir." Her dark eyes gain some distinct twinkles. "I suspect you may need the extra nutrients."

"Agreed," Morgana says. "Who wants to wager on how fast our little prodigy climbs the levels of legerdemain?"

Marie shakes her head. "Last time I went in for one of

your wagers, I lost a crystal ball."

"And me a Pompeiian goblet," Aradia adds.

The others chime in with more good-natured banter, but I'm not listening anymore. Kara's crawled back into a tension-lined shell and stays there for the rest of the gathering, which ends mercifully soon.

I don't have to look at my watch to know we're closer to dawn than midnight by now, confirmed by everyone's discreet yawns as they embrace Kara on their way out from the willows.

Morgana and Aradia, who hung back to cast cleanup spells, have cleared most of the clutter by the time Hecate beckons to Kara and me with a graceful wave of fingertips, summoning us toward another pathway out of the grove.

The packed-dirt trail closely follows the stream's curves, and I can't say I'm complaining about the peaceful break from one of the most chaotic nights of my life. Even my insomniac side doesn't want to be conscious for the stroke of four a.m.

"You two need some rest. Your cottage isn't much farther."

Right now, I can't think of ten better words in the world. I'm pretty sure Hecate already sees that, her smile radiating kindness as she stops and motions us toward an offshoot path.

Ahead, with soft amber light in its rustic windows, is a picture-perfect dwelling that belongs more in the hills of Umbria or Tuscany. All the hallmarks of the vibe are here, including the vines along the stone walls, the front porch with exposed beams, and the rustic iron chandelier over a sturdy pine picnic table.

"Hecate…" Kara murmurs as the goddess leads the way up a small incline, past well-kept flower beds and a scallop-edged fountain, to a flagstone walk that ends at the cottage's arched front door.

Hecate stops and casts back an inquisitive look. "Hmmm? Is everything all right?"

"Oh, yes." Her voice is tired, but there's a defined purpose in her gaze. "This place… It makes me think about the stories Gramps used to tell me, about the summers during his boyhood when he visited his grandparents in Perugia. This is exactly how he described it."

"So it is to your liking?" the goddess inquires with a gentle look.

"Oh, definitely. It's lovely."

"Inside, the refrigerator is stocked with cold drinks. You'll find some new apparel in the bedroom wardrobe and toiletries in the bathroom. But if we've forgotten anything—"

Kara's laugh is instant and sincere, evoking a surprised look from Hecate. Seems the goddess has bought into a few impressions from the outside world—at least about Kara being a Tinseltown princess expecting regular white-glove treatment.

My sweet woman doesn't waste any more time in dispelling that one.

"Are you kidding me? We couldn't ask for anything better."

Hecate's smile is fast and full. "Then I am pleased. The others will be too. It was a real group effort for the conjurings, since we had no idea you'd be arriving so soon."

Kara's cheeks are taken over by a flush. "None of you had to fuss over me."

"Don't be ridiculous. We have waited so long to call you our guest. We are honored to have you."

To this, Kara can't even drum up a proper gush. It's an awkward moment for her but one I understand. Hecate's banter is a denial of everything Kara's learned as her personal identifiers. The dutiful daughter. The careful line follower. Even, in Hades's terms, the *fascinating* prize trophy, there to meet family obligations and nothing more.

Hecate fills the pause with a scrutinizing stare around at the stylish furniture. "I hope you'll be comfortable here for the duration."

"Duration of…?" I say it with careful calm but don't disguise my questioning undertone.

"Kara's enlightenment, of course."

I tighten my gaze. "You make it sound like training."

"*Enlightenment* is the word, Professor."

I sense this is just an issue of semantics, but there's something in her tone, an insinuation of sorts, that rattles my patience.

"For the record, Kara is already rather enlightened. She's one of the brightest students at Alameda. On top of that, she's grown up with grace and humility in an unforgivable spotlight. But she's hardly just a piece of red-carpet candy. None of the Valaris are. They're strong and smart and—"

"Part demons," Hecate finishes. "An aspect they have, remarkably, kept hidden from every member of the Hollywood media. That's extraordinary in and of itself." She pulls in a long breath, gaining an inch of height with the regal shoring of her spine. "But none of them are *you*, Kara. None of them will be able to share your journey now. But here, after our guidance and tests, you'll be so much better prepared."

"Prepared," Kara echoes, her palpable exhaustion and tension matching my own. "And tested. For what? A journey to where?"

"I know it's confusing." The goddess loops her fingers with her others, linking them at her middle like a new-age abbess. The comparison isn't my favorite, right up there with triggers like creaky pews and votive candles, but I can't escape the calming influence of her overall impression. "But you're safe here. Both of you. Things will become clearer, I promise. Deep inside, I think you know that. Once you've had some rest, we can begin."

"Begin *what*?" Though Kara visibly reins herself back, her eyes are desperate and pleading. "Hecate, it's not that I don't trust this ... process. Or whatever it is. But—"

"Maybe Hecate's right." I can't believe that's just spilled out, but I quickly latch on to the underlying logic. "We've been through the wringer, Kara. The last twenty-four hours ..."

She cuts in with a rueful laugh. "You mean the last *week*?"

"That too." I smirk, but even that's painful. "It's been a

lot. Almost too much." I swing my head up, arching a brow toward Hecate, hoping it looks more jovial than skeptical. "I'm hoping those double doors lead to a bedroom?"

Before I'm done, she's sweeping fingertips through the air and waving the portals back.

"Perfect," I mutter with a relieved sigh.

Kara groans. "You can say that again, but please don't. Let's just get in."

I'm aware of Hecate's indulgent laugh but nothing else. At some point and in some way, I'm sure the goddess has let herself out of the cottage, because as soon as I strip off my clothes and climb between the cool sheets with Kara, I'm lulled to sleep by a night filled with nothing but crickets chirping around a peaceful stream.

CHAPTER 3

WHEN I WAKE UP, it's not willingly. Even with Maximus's heartbeat under my ear and his solid muscles beneath my flung thigh, my mind craves nothing but several days' worth of dreamless nothingness. Sleep won't prevent my soul from continuing to know he's here. In some ways, my body will know it too. He's holding me like his own dreams have taken him back a couple of decades and he's gripping his favorite monster-fighting toy.

Sunlight slants sideways through the bedroom's shutters, leading me to believe it's midmorning or midafternoon, but my sense of direction has been turned off since we got here, so I'm unsure which. But more pressing than that is the glare from *inside* my head. The thoughts that clank each other like bricks turned to dominoes.

I'm not just a demon.

I'm a witch.

Somehow, that means something. Well, something beyond the basics.

Something that requires *enlightenment.*

So what does *that* mean?

And why does contemplating it feel so scary? My heartbeat is pounding in my ears and throbbing in my throat.

"Checkered flag for those racing thoughts, speedy?" His sleepy husk has me blushing before I can help it.

"Sorry." I turn my head and press a kiss to the base of his neck. "Didn't know the Kara Grand Prix was roaring that loud."

He strokes a big hand along the back of my head. "I can hear you in my dreams. Remember?"

I burrow tighter against him. "Of course I do."

Though our time in hell did give me one of the best dreams of my life, the blissful escape ended as a nightmare. I'll never forget how Hades basked in his victory over us, taking advantage of our dropped defenses to barge into Maximus's head once again—and, to an extent, mine.

"But you weren't thinking about that just now," he ventures quietly.

I trace a finger into the shallow valley between his pectorals. "You know me well."

"And don't you forget it." He scrapes his fingertips through my hair. It's better than any luxury spa treatment I've ever had. "So what's up, little demon? Talk to me."

I draw air, mentally stripped by the truth in his words and the intensity of his love. I gulp hard while pushing up to one elbow.

"I guess I just have no idea what I'm doing here."

His hand, now at my nape, tightens by a few degrees.

"That makes two of us."

"I meant figuratively."

"That still makes two of us."

"I feel like I should *know*, though." I twist a little piece of the sheet around my pinky. I'm very aware that we're both naked beneath this mochi-soft cotton, but it doesn't feel right to dole more thoughts about the subject. Not when everything else is still so lopsided and confusing.

"Why?" Maximus asks, which has me wondering if he's a secret spellcaster too. His adoring baritone has me helpless about denying him an answer.

"Hecate makes it seem like I deserve a place here. Even the special treatment too."

"But?"

I expect this question from him and am even thankful for it, but it doesn't make my new confession any easier. "But I'm not like any of…them."

He blinks. The outer edges of his gaze cloud over. "I'm not following."

A beat passes, in which I almost expect him to add a commanding *Miss Valari*. I almost beg for it. A return to the way we used to be, just a professor and the student instacrushing on him, trying to hide an overwhelming attraction. But not just from everyone on campus. Even back then, we faced complications. Lots of them. So why did everything still seem simpler?

"I don't think that's completely true," I finally chide back. "You knew every single one of those women from the moment Hecate introduced us to them. Morgana le Fay?

Marie Laveau? Circe herself? They're *real*, which means all or some of their feats must be as well."

"Neither of us knew Kiama or Liseli," he counters.

"Which doesn't mean they don't have the credentials. Only that their stories haven't become legends yet." I raise my free hand and curl my fingertips into his beard. "Stories I can't begin to compete with."

Maximus folds his long fingers around my loose fist. "Maybe not *yet*. But first of all, who said this was a competition? And secondly, I'd say that freeing three people from the center of hell is an incredible way to prove your magical credibility."

"Credibility as good as shape-shifting and teleportation? Healing the sick? Channeling the dead?"

"Powers that led all of them into some dark mental places, if I'm recalling the histories correctly. If so, that means maybe Hecate is right. *Enlightenment* might be the best way to describe what you need right now."

He draws a breath as if to say more, but I watch as he refrains. Doesn't matter. It's the same subject on my mind. *What I need right now ... for what?* There's no denying the underlying urgency to all Hecate's actions since last night. Even when she exhorted us to rest, she referenced the process like we had to get our cuticles cleared or our passports updated. A necessary evil in order to move on with the important stuff.

Stuff I can't begin to comprehend. And not sure I want to.

I know—well, hope—those feelings will change. But for now ...

"I get all of that. And I hear it, Maximus…"

"But?"

His repetition, tinged with a gentle tease, doesn't get him another smile. I try, but it's simply not there now. "I don't understand why I'm so scared about it."

"Oh, sweetheart." He slides his firm touch up to my elbow. "I'd be scared if you weren't. This is crazy stuff. Not that growing up as part demon in the Tinseltown limelight hasn't been, but most of that was woven into your existence since you learned to walk and talk. You've had a lot of years to adjust. Hecate handed you this revelation less than twenty-four hours ago—*after* Hades tried to send LA sliding into the ocean. You've had a lot on your mental plate."

I chuckle now, but still without mirth. "A giant trip to the emotional buffet."

"No wonder you don't know where to bite next."

At last, a smile kicks up one end of my mouth as I lift my gaze—across every inch of his magnificent chest. Those broad and glorious planes are never a sight for sore eyes, but mine are outright achy as his broad, muscled beauty takes over a few of my exhausted thoughts. I actually try to fight the pull, but it's a losing quest.

As I hope, the man's expression gains some new meaning of its own. His eyelids lower over the lagoon blue in his gaze. His jaw tightens. His lips part.

And there's more.

The very best parts of this moment.

The instant that I watch his nipples harden and his biceps curl…as his fingers dig into the flesh at the back of my elbow.

I release a long, husky sigh. And I was fighting this … why?

"Who am I to let the love of my life go hungry?"

His raspy growl excites my every pore. His commanding grip compels me forward. I follow without thinking, filling my breaths with his leathery library essence, though there's still enough smoke in his hair to remind me how far we've come in just a few weeks.

So much life between us already. So much *after*life. Who else in this world, or any other, can assert it and mean it? But our journey to hell and back has only made me recognize the depth of my love for this extraordinary man. This devastating demigod. The love I'll fight for in this existence and all others.

But right now, his eyes aren't beseeching me to fight. Not anymore.

And I'm past the point of grateful.

I'm starving.

"You offering anything I'm craving, Professor Kane?"

I gloat a little, watching how my purposeful formality causes tantalizing shivers down his massive form. In so many ways, including his take-charge affection now, he's been my rock. But for once, for just these few moments before the world forces us out of this shelter again, I want to make *his* knees weak. I want *him* to be fortified, strengthened, renewed.

He starts to get the meaning as soon as I move over him, rolling his broad frame back into the pillows.

"I...guess that depends on the essence of your avidity, Miss Valari."

I dip my face in, lowering a tongue-heavy kiss to his sleek lips. "You trying to turn me on with big words?"

His chuckle is low and lovely. "Hmmm. Perhaps."

I spear him with a narrowed glare. My hand forms a V against his jaw. "Well, it's working."

His eyebrows dance. "In that case ... *Obfuscate. Imbroglio. Susurrant.*"

"Ohhh. You had me at *imbroglio.*"

He laughs again, though I chop off the last of it with another kiss. One that's again full of my demanding tongue, yet so much more. My thanks to him. My desire for him. My connection to him. The fusion that I need now more than ever. The same urgency I feel in his touch, at first skating along my flesh but growing into more adamant presses and gropes. Touches that brand fresh fire into my skin and new lust through my veins.

It's here.

Stronger than ever before.

The power of our bond. The burst in my senses, unlike anything I've known with anyone else, except when I'm this bare and raw with him.

This exposed to him.

This empowered by him.

It's the strength that pulled me through every moment of my ordeal in hell—and to so many extents, the resilience that's kept me sane since the wild ride of last night's events.

Now, all I want to do is lose my mind in a different way.

But first, to make Maximus lose his.

The intent consumes my mind as I fill my mouth with more of his skin, acknowledging my addiction to his heady taste before my lips clear his collarbone. But no way am I stopping there. Not even close. I want more.

And I start taking it.

Traveling my mouth into the shallow plane over his heart. Pausing there to give silent thanks for the life and strength it gives to him, before continuing my journey even farther down...

Down...

"Kara." His rasp, beginning from the depths that I kiss over now, sizzles through the air. Crackles through my senses. And then descends across my skin and down to the space between my legs.

It's my perfect guide, leading me to the corresponding part of him. Closer and closer...already feeling the hot throb of him against my neck...and then my lips...

And then...

"*Kara*." He tangles his fingers in my hair. Unlike his earlier brush through those strands, his digits are taut and trembling. I love it. I love *him*. In so many ways, I think I always have. I know I always will.

He swells against my tongue. I increase my pressure, attentively tracing his veins. He groans, bucking his hips. He doesn't hitch hard or far, but it's enough to keep me going. Rejoicing in my power over this sinewed male. Savoring the gift I'm able to give him after everything he's done for me.

Reveling in what it's all doing to my body in return.

My skin, so hot. My nerves, so alive. My lust, so ignited.

It builds and builds until I have to express it somehow. I work faster, pumping him harder, until—oh, thank God—Maximus clamps his free hand over one of my shoulders and yanks with unmistakable force.

"Come here. I need to feel the rest of you."

That's all the time he spends explaining himself. But I don't even need that. I crave our union just as strongly. It's like a living thing inside me, a creature possessed by passions I never knew existed, taking over and pushing my body atop of his. And then around his.

And then...we're straight to heaven.

Sighing and kissing until we're sharing air.

Rocking and thrusting until we're sharing shudders.

Climbing and reaching...until we're sharing explosions.

My scream fills his mouth as his heat floods my body. And then we're beyond heaven.

We're in the place, so perfect and precious, that no one can reach us or harm us. A world of our hearts, of our spirits. It's indelible and eternal...and untouchable.

And because of that, I can now embrace one truth as utterly sacred.

No matter what's going to happen now—or whatever is coming at us because of it—we're ready.

As long as Maximus and I are together...we'll always be ready.

CHAPTER 4

MAXIMUS

THE WIND CUTS ITS way through the canyon with little mercy, cold one minute and hot the next, turning my truck's cab into the world's first refrigerator-sauna combo. But I brave the strange switch-ups because this is the only spot in Iremia that'll provide a clear cell signal.

I dial back the missed call from early this morning, when Kara had me distracted in all the best ways. Then, after that, when we gifted ourselves with an hour that was blessedly clear of the dreaded *h's*—*Hades, hell, and high emergency.*

I'm much fonder of thinking about the ABCs we explored instead. I learned that *avocados* are the one food she can't live without. And that she's the best person in her twice-weekly *boxing* class.

Best of all, kissing the outer edge of her *collarbone* is as good as sucking her in other places…

The ringtone ends abruptly, bringing me back to the present. Not a bad thing since I'm calling my boss. It wasn't difficult to recognize the number, originating at Elizabeth McCarthy's home in a swanky section of Pasadena. It also wasn't surprising, considering that I imagine Alameda's president has turned the place into her operational headquarters for now.

"Professor Kane," she croons.

"President McCarthy." I answer with a polite smile out of habit. Though she can't see it, I'd offer the exact same brand if we were rubbing shoulders at a university event.

Our relationship has always been like that. Pleasantly polite. Warm enough to foster a friendly connection but never casual enough to blur the line between her professional status and mine. Which is why I finally forced myself away from Kara's arms and our warm sheets to follow up as quickly as I could.

"Sorry I missed your call," I say.

"I've been reaching out to as many of the faculty as I can. I was worried when you didn't answer. The campus is … well …"

"What? I was there yesterday, and nothing seemed to be damaged. Has something happened since?"

"Structurally, no. But logistically, things are a tad … tousled," she explains. "The national guard needed to commandeer our offices as a temporary command center. We're not sure how long they'll need to be here or when everything will return to normal."

"I understand. My mother is a trauma nurse. She was one of the first to be called when they were staffing the emergency response center."

"Special people are called to that profession." Her tone is genial but genuine. "And now I know where you get your considerate spirit from."

I respond with a subtle laugh. "Not sure my students would agree with you."

"Which is exactly what I pay you for," she quips. "On that note, the board and I met for an emergency session this morning and unanimously decided to cancel classes for the next two weeks." Her measured breath is audible. "I know this isn't preferred, but the needs of the students must come first. Many of them have more to worry about than their studies right now. Big pockets of the city are still without power, if not under rubble."

I exhale quietly in relief. I haven't had the chance to press Hecate on a syllabus for Kara's enlightenment—not that such a timeline would be forthcoming—but my instincts have already picked up an underlying *something* in the goddess's energy. Urgency? Impatience? A mental hourglass with a wider throat than most?

All three of them make sense, which I acknowledge with a grimace. Maybe they're the reason for Hecate's strange energy, a force that pushes against her earth-mother serenity with nearly visible force.

Or maybe it is that obvious. If so, does Kara sense and see it all too? If so, she hasn't said anything. Maybe it's just a thing between Olympians, but my instincts are hazy because of my mixed blood.

And maybe it's a little thing called sleep deprivation.

Because even demigods have limits to their gas tanks. And lately, mine's been running way below the comfort line.

That being said, I refuse to get compliant about our current situation. The streamside Perugian villa, with its spa tub and enchanted forest garden and five-star Michelin kitchen, is everything alluring to Kara and me, but it's not home.

Because as real as it is…it isn't.

It's only a placeholder for the reality we do have. The one we'd started to build with each other. That reality is more tangible than any force I've ever known, including my long-suppressed powers. But continuing to grow our love in a land of fantasy—one that's more surreal than Los Angeles—already feels like piling shoddy bricks atop a risky foundation.

"I think that's the right call," I continue, re-grounding myself in the conversation with McCarthy. "Students aren't going to retain anything if they're constantly looking outside, wondering what the elements are going to do next."

"I appreciate that, Professor Kane."

"I appreciate you taking the time to call and check in personally."

"Well, I've had a lot of help," she says good-naturedly. "Professor Levin lives nearby and has been here to help with organizing the recovery effort on this end."

My mouth flatlines. I'm sure my pulse does the same thing. "Professor Levin. You mean…*Erin* Levin?"

The next few seconds stretch too long.

"The very one. Did you meet her at Saturday night's fundraiser?"

"You've got to be kidding me."

"Pardon me?"

Her insertion is well-timed, arresting me from vocalizing the profanities streaking through my brain. "Sorry," I finally mutter. "I thought she'd left town."

"Hmm. No. Why would she have?"

"I thought she mentioned it the other night, that's all," I supply with astonishing calm, considering my thoughts have done nothing but stomp on the instinctual gas pedal. But what the hell was I thinking? That Erin simply *poofed* herself to nonexistence?

She was so much more than she pretended to be on the earthly realm. The redhead with the gleaming eyes that missed nothing was actually Megaera from Olympus. A Fury. Worst of all, a messenger for Hera. But after she disappeared last night, I assumed she'd simply turned to dust before our eyes. End of story.

Idiot.

I'm a tenured *literature* professor and didn't consider that the Furies are famously strongest in dust form. If myth proves true, as it repeatedly has since the moment Kara walked into my world, it would be completely reasonable for Erin to jump on that spiritual fast train between Olympus and the underworld. She'd be unbound to any physical form. Free from all mortal boundaries.

Which means she'd be able to come back whenever or wherever she pleases.

Like showing up at McCarthy's front door during moments in which the woman needed her the most. Which is exactly what McCarthy starts relaying, gushing about Erin's dedication and tirelessness. Somehow, I'm able to keep listening. I maintain my charade of normalcy—whatever that means anymore—inserting all the right sounds of active listening until a long tone breaks in on the line.

"I'm so sorry, Professor Kane. That's another call for me, and I have to take it."

"Of course. Go ahead. I'll be in touch again soon."

Maybe sooner than I was anticipating.

Air erupts from my nostrils with the force of blast jets. Instead of fire and rocket fuel, I'm spewing with confusion and apprehension. But I'm sure as hell not going to sit around and wallow in it. Not when there's something I can do about it.

But my emotions have jumped ahead of me.

Before I'm done lurching out of the truck, clouds collide with the canyon's converging winds. There's a sky-wide swirl of purple and green, so pretty it might be worthy of a snapshot—in other circumstances. But these are inspired by something more ominous. A few things, to be exact. One after the other, I send new thunderclaps into the clouds. The booms strengthen like approaching bombs, louder and louder, but I refuse to feel guilty about the celestial stomping. Zeus was never there to help Mom deal with my childhood temper tantrums. But these have purpose. Maybe now is the big guy's chance to make up for lost time.

A furious crackle splits the air. It fissures my truck's front windshield before whipping the hair back from my face, but I don't relent my stance. If the god of all gods thinks his fireworks will wilt me, he's never been a ten-year-old on the receiving end of Nancy Kane's *I'm not mad, I'm disappointed* speech.

"This had better be important." Dark-orange smoke slowly dies from the edges of his hair.

I still don't bend, confronting his more-than-annoyed countenance with a determined one of my own.

"Oh yeah? What'd I interrupt? Cocktail hour at the Labyrinth again?"

He hauls in air through his nostrils. "Even the gods don't have time for debauchery right now. I'm still cleaning up my brother's mess, same as almost everyone in Los Angeles. Thankfully I can do so in peace now that he's busy preparing for Persephone's return. Hopefully he's ceased this ridiculous fixation on losing Kara."

While I'm glad to hear his finishing sentence, the rest of the statement has me arching a brow. "If the city is safe from his wrath, isn't your work here done?"

"Setting everything back to normal just isn't possible in a day or two. Or sometimes, two *thousand*," he mutters, dragging a hand through his hair. At the end of the motion, he yanks free the leather tie that's replaced his boater hat. "If humans could learn generosity and humility from playtime and parties instead of hardships, it would be easier for all the gods to advocate for them. Because they don't, generally, it falls on me to address the other important damage your uncle has dealt."

The reminder that Hades is my blood has me cringing. "What important damage?"

"The spiritual damage is perhaps the worst of all," he explains. "Helping mankind rebuild itself is about more than the wreckage they clear and the structures they repair. There are shattered souls and broken hearts across the city."

I frown. "You can't undo that, even with two thousand days."

"You're right." He jogs up his head while rolling and squaring his shoulders. "But I can mobilize the gods who can—a task you've pulled me from. If you don't mind, I'll be thankful for the chance to dive back in, unless I should keep expecting your atmospheric ding-dongs every ten seconds."

I move forward, copying his motions with an ease that's jarring. But getting to my point is more vital than stressing over that.

"Megaera isn't gone."

His features widen. "Oh?"

"After she vanished last night…she didn't go back to Olympus."

He pauses. "Hera didn't call her right back?"

"Apparently not."

He sobers by notable degrees.

"Figured you might want to know that a Fury had posted up at the Alameda University's president's house, out in Pasadena. And that she definitely wasn't there to sell solar energy panels." I turn my head into the wind, welcoming the strong gusts from the direction of the ocean. Essential mind-clearing stuff. "She's obviously trying to involve herself in matters here for a reason."

"Why?"

The grooves are so deep in Z's forehead, I already know he isn't feigning confusion.

"She's still probably acting on Hera's orders, right? So

the end goal could be to stay in the thick of things with the mortals and report back on their reactions and plans. Two, sticking close to McCarthy means she might grab a new pin on Kara and me."

"Or door number three," he mutters. "That she wants both."

I scrape the light sea salt out of my beard. "You must have some clue as to what Hera is up to. She's your wife." I wait through the better part of a minute, enduring a first-row view of the deepening brackets at the corners of his terse lips, before I can't take it any longer. "Z? You know something. Don't you think it's the right time to say something?"

His head shakes as if another force has given it a strong jolt. But he's the top of the Olympian food chain. What could be more formidable than that?

"I have no more of a clue than you, son. I wish I did. But *if* I did—"

"Don't you dare feed me some fancy line about having to protect me from all this garbage." I drop my hand. Ball my fingers up. "You weren't concerned about my safety when dragging me to an extradimensional bar for our first pop-and-son outing. And you *really* weren't after Kara was abducted and I had to—"

"Stop." He jabs out a finger. "Do *not* go there. None of that stupidity is on me. *You* took that idiotic dive without my knowledge or—"

"What? *Consent?* Are you really going to pull insulted and incensed with me? Kara got kidnapped to hell because you wouldn't go toe-to-toe with Hades. If you'd even tried halfway—"

"Then I'd have arrived with a million hell-bound souls in tow too!" he bellows. "Is that what you had in mind? Think about your mortal world nightmare of an internet scandal gone viral, only a lot worse. I'd be obligated to hear out every single one of those pleas, from all Hades's souls who feel they were wrongly doomed, since the beginning of time. That includes swindlers, abusers, murderers, rapists ... You want me to go on?"

I let him gloat about his point for a few seconds longer. The silence between us is marred only by the cruel slices of wind still dueling for control of the canyon. I murmur into the conflicting air with deliberate calm.

"What I *want* is for you to level with me," I bite out. "For once, for me to regard you as a father instead of an untouchable myth. That kind of connection starts with honesty, and right now I need it in the form of you telling me what's going on with my ... stepmother." I release a harsh breath, fully processing that tidbit of surreal information. I square up my stance and confront his unwavering stare. "What's Hera up to? You've got to know something. Why hasn't she called Megaera back to Olympus?"

Z pushes out his lower lip.

A seethe begins in my belly and presses at my rib cage. Though I can count our face-to-face meetings on one hand, I already know his haughty obstinance—and the uselessness of butting up to it. It makes me furious.

"Damn it, son. Do you honestly think she's told me?

That she's revealed her plan of sending secret operatives to the mortal plane for some kind of...advanced reconnaissance?"

I jerk my brows. "Is that what you think it is?"

He shakes his head again, clearly frazzled. "I have no idea. But I promise you, I'm going to try my hardest to find out. When I do, I promise that you'll be briefed too."

I rear back by an inch, more than happy to expose my onset of astonishment.

"What? Isn't that the promise you're after?"

"Yes. But—"

"*What?*"

"What about your golden rule? About not getting involved?"

A new blast of wind cuts across his face, seeming to carve new lines into it. It takes me a second to realize it's not the offshore and onshore flows battling each other. The gusts are all him.

"Don't the humans have some quote about listening to the lessons of your children?"

I park a hip against the front bumper while a small smirk breaks free. "Probably. I mean, that sounds like a good one."

He's thoughtful, turning his face into the intense air. "I can no longer keep you behind villa walls, Maximus. If Hera intended you and Kara harm—and if she's still planning on it, in any way—I'll find out. You have my word."

He swoops up a hand, and the gale intensifies. When it reaches top knots again, he vanishes with it.

I step over, kicking at the circle of cleared sand where

he just stood. As I ram a toe at the dry dirt, a cloud of it collects along my boot and pant leg. But the film is thin, ready to be easily whooshed away again.

Totally matching my level of trust for my father and his *word*.

Perhaps Kara and I have lucked into one of the best hiding places we could've hoped for. For all its *kumbaya* kitsch, Iremia comes complete with a small army of experienced witches who are likely to take strong exception to an unannounced visit from Hera or her minions.

For now, I've got to accept that as enough.

CHAPTER 5

I GET NOW WHY, last night, Hecate labeled this space as *overwhelming.*

During breakfast, conversation buzzes around the crackling fire in the sala's hearth, warding off the canyon's early morning chill. Aradia and Liseli braid each other's hair. Morgana brings out some freshly baked scones. Even our leader seems mellower, petting a sweet cat in her lap while residing over the scene with a maternal air.

An hour later, the day is warmer. The fire fades to a smolder. But weirdly, even as everyone starts to disperse for their duties of the day, I continue to feel like someone's closed the doors in the flue and shut every window in the building.

The feeling doesn't improve when I turn from the hearth to see Circe and Hecate on purposeful approach. Though their faces are open and smiling, I have flashbacks to my first red carpet appearance. Expectations of what to do and no idea how to fulfill them.

"Hey." Maximus tucks me a little closer and squeezes my shoulder. "Don't stress. They're here to enlighten you."

"Says the guy who chargrilled Hecate about it last night?"

He doesn't get a chance for a comeback.

Hecate steps forward, extending both hands. "*Kara*. You must *breathe* for me. We promise this will be fun."

"Yeah," I stammer. "Okay."

But even after a sweet peck from Maximus and a sisterly smile from Circe, it feels impossible to get enough air. My lungs keep up the valiant effort as the goddess and the enchantress lead me to a circular alcove near the back of the sala. The area has been purposely created like this, with polished stone boundaries that are encrusted at the top with different-colored crystals. A diamond-shaped stained-glass window lets in enough light to coat the area in a rainbow glow.

"Come." Hecate tugs me toward the middle of the floor, where three woven rugs are arranged in a balanced triangle. "Sit."

"And *breathe*," Circe repeats, nearly imploring about it. She plops herself down with crossed legs. "Dead is a great status only for serial killers and vampires with perfect hair."

"I'm aware."

I struggle to summon at least half a laugh for her, but Jaden's the only actor in the family. Luckily, Circe's okay with that. She extends a friendly hand as I sit next to her. The firm wrap of her fingers is exactly what I need, filled with welcoming warmth and affirming vibrance. I don't even care if she's using a spell to boost it. My lungs are able to function again, and it's nice.

"Ah. That's it," Hecate croons as soon as her own hand is linked with mine. As she adjusts her position, all our knees come into contact too. It's like a circuit being completed between the three of us. "Yes. Deeper breaths now, Kara. *Deeper.*"

The circuit flickers. Then even more. But how do I say it's because of her semidramatic overkill? If I wanted a repeat of Master Mohan's Conscious Breathing class, I'd have stayed at home for a private session. Mother would likely join in and cover the yogi's tab.

In hopes of gaining an ally in Circe, I dare a glance in her direction. One side of my mouth kicks up once I see she's mired in equal frustration—until realizing she's getting impatient with *me*. Not a lot, but enough to notice. Yet if I've learned anything about Circe so far, it's that her supreme confidence isn't just the stuff of classic poems, paintings, and stories. She knows how to shred a person's perceptions with the ultimate of sensual styles.

"Let go and listen to her, diva." She reaches to squeeze my fingers with an enigmatic smile. "You'll be glad you did."

I open my mouth, wanting to call her out for the nickname that belongs more to Mother and Kell than it ever will to me, until my empathy tingles to life. The message there is clear. The croon is actually a compliment.

"I'm trying," I mumble.

"I know," she says sweetly. "So much on your mind.

The stresses you've been through, all you're still trying to control...it's all still here, isn't it?"

I yank my hand back, only to notice she's already let me go. "You can read all that...in my mind?"

Her smile widens. "I can read all that in your *eyes*."

"Which means we should all concentrate on *closing* our eyes again," Hecate interjects. "Give it another go, Kara. Shoulders back and down. Hands on your knees. Chest full and vibrant. And now...air all the way in. All the way out. Once more. Be present for every molecule of atmosphere that fills you. The atmosphere that speaks to you and your power."

To coin my own paltry phrase, I try again. This time, I glue my thoughts to everything they've both said. To make friends with the air instead of blaming it. Getting permission to let everything go... It's like the days when Mother threatened to cancel my horseback riding lesson if I didn't clean my room. Suddenly, I wasn't thinking about the stable, or even my beloved pony, anymore. The freedom I craved from the rides across the foothills...it came from the work instead.

Now, I'm even more free.

I gasp from it, no longer caring about the knowing hums from the women beside me. To be honest, I'm barely aware of them. The forces that flow around me, taking over me, are more demanding. Overwhelming.

So daunting...

"Keep breathing, Kara."

I almost bite back a retort—isn't that what I *am*

doing?—until realizing that I'm nearly choking to reclaim oxygen. But can I be blamed? The swirls across my vision, joined with the energy buzzing through my senses... If I had socks on, they'd be knocked across the room.

For once I'm glad about the chill in my toes, though now it's not so much frost as fusion. The same vibrant, electric thrill that invades the rest of my body. The energy that has me shivering and fidgeting at the same time. Excited but conflicted. Ready to burst but tempted to cower. But fortunately, still capable of speaking.

"Wh-What's going on?" I battle to keep the connection to my teachers by relocking my mind on the basics.

Breathe. Breathe. Breathe.

"What do you see, Kara?"

That's not an answer.

Somehow I control myself from whipping the retort at Circe. Not that I'm rewarded for the restraint, even after opening my eyes. What happened to the room I was just in? The *world* I was just in?

"What do you *feel*, Kara?"

For reasons I can't pull apart, Hecate's question makes more sense. I turn, fully expecting not to see her on this new plane of bright-gold reality—or whatever it is—but there she is, appearing a lot like the first time I ever beheld her. Swirling and shimmering. Her skin aglow, a true match for the gemstones that sparkle around her neck. The hem of her gown is encased in similar colors, though the shards there are still like colored ice. Evolving, iridescent. An aura that leaves me no question about how to answer.

With my truth.

"Like I did when I first found the grimoire."

"In the library in Hades's palace?"

She sounds so fervent about it. Too much so.

But wouldn't I sound the same way in a circumstance like this? Don't I probably sound like it already? "Don't you see all this too?"

The tiny indents between her brows are a clear enough reply. The same puzzlement is stamped across Circe's face.

Until I try once more, releasing them both from my hold.

At once, my hands rise higher. I let them go, extending outward at the same time.

It's not a protest. I tell them so with a soft smile. Inside, it feels more like an expression of...surrender. I hope they understand, but already jettison the stress if they don't. If the goddess of sorcery and her most powerful emissary don't intuitively get this, I can't stop and write a term paper for it.

"*Oh!*"

I'm able to quell a grimace at Circe's outcry for one reason alone. Joy that matches the warm wind that now lifts our hair, bringing a white-gold light that surrounds our bodies.

They do get it.

I know it as truth as soon as Circe lifts her head to return my stare. Her jaw is dropped and her eyes are wide. I almost emulate the look, but a soft chuckle tumbles from me instead.

"Well," she rasps. "This is..."

"What?"

I say that in place of caving to the urge to sing the famous song from the cartoon about taking a magic carpet ride. It'd be appropriate, since I've managed to levitate all three of our rugs—and us along with them. They undulate on the air as if they really are flying, making the three of us bob gently in our original spots.

"Well...*original*," Circe finally blurts. "I mean, if we ignore the huge space between our backsides and the floor."

"Kara." Hecate's voice is rich with its same resonance from last night. Something like an autotune, only more harmonic. "Was this what also happened to you...when you opened the book in Hades's library? During the first time you summoned me?"

"Oh no," I say quickly. "I mean...not right away."

Her head tips to the side. "Not right away...in *what* way?"

"All of them. The light, the energy, the flying—"

"Levitation," Circe supplies.

"Right. Sorry."

"It's all right," Hecate assures. "You're not being tested or graded. No stresses, okay?"

"*Please* no stresses."

Circe's sardonicism is lighthearted this time, despite her pointed glance toward the stone floor below. It makes me giggle for a second, which elevates all three of us by another few feet. My apologetic shrug gets a new interruption from Hecate.

"We only want to help you understand it," she says.

"Can you tell me anything more about those moments?"

"Other than the fact that Gramps, Maximus, and I were surrounded by Hades's henchmen and they were getting ready to toss us into the blackest pit they could find?"

She straightens her head into a defined nod. Despite the solace about this not being a test, I feel like I've contributed a worthy answer. "So your adrenaline spiked, and you fought back with the incantations."

"I think so," I admit. "That makes the most sense."

She examines me with renewed intensity. "But you're not as anxious now."

"Not about henchmen and eternal black pits."

As Circe joins her to pepper the air with melodic laughs, my face returns to normal temperature. Gradually, the three of us descend toward the sala's floor. I'm drenched by more relief than I want to admit. Somehow I've managed to accomplish this without any bumps, breaks, or scratches. Unless the two of them helped without my realizing it. Which wouldn't be so awful to accept. I'm a little more than a day into this journey. A grad student doesn't write a thesis before learning their ABCs.

Circe gives me no clue about that answer while rising to her feet. After rolling through some stretches, she steps into the rainbowed rays cast down from the window.

I don't join her, despite really yearning to. But I still feel … heavy. Significantly weighted by my new wonderment. Figuring out these new abilities is so much more than the ABCs. I have to be okay with that. To recognize—and accept—that there's so much I don't know. Can't see. Can't *measure*.

That's it. I'm overwhelmed again.

I slump over to pick at stray fibers in my mat. Though not for long.

Hecate leans forward to fold my hand between both of hers. "All right. You're not anxious. Let's say that much. But you're not at peace either."

I wish the hitch of my breath wasn't so telling. I wish the truth of the assertion doesn't grab at Circe, making her pause and turn.

"No. Not at peace," I confess. "I mean, not yet. But I'll get there. Training wheels, right? The ABCs and one-two-threes. I'll get there, I promise."

Hecate tightens her grip. "You don't owe promises to me."

"Or to any of us," Circe adds with too much tenderness. *Droll femme fatale* fits her so much better. "You're safe here, Kara. You know that, right?"

"You are a diamond of Iremia now," Hecate continues. "Rare and revered by all of us. And we will fight to protect you and Maximus if things between the gods escalate once more."

My new frown borders on painful. "Escalate?" She really did say that, right? *Escalate?* "To ... what? What *things*, exactly?"

Circe smirks. "They'd have to make it past the perimeter first."

Hecate's smile is nearly feline in its smugness. "Hmmm. That they would."

I shake my head, giving up on hiding the confusion.

"What protects the perimeter?"

"To a mortal's naked eye?" Hecate replies. "Nothing. But to any creature or god from the otherworldly realms, it's a multilayered security boundary."

Circe settles onto a chair while twirling her finger, directing her mat to roll itself up. "Not just side-by-side stratums either. Each of us also cast horizontal spells. It's like a chain link fence, only engineered from—and solely breached by—magic."

"Magical chain link," I mutter, slightly stunned but instantly wondering why. It makes oddly comforting sense. "So that's why this place isn't on any mortal maps?"

Hecate's lips pull up. "The humans who need to know...know."

"And here's where we cue the eerie tunes, right?"

The quip is too confident to be mine and too rumbly to be Circe's. But I don't need half a second to connect it. My bloodstream already recognizes the person who's reentered the building. The male I'll always know—and crave—in an instant.

"Ah!" Hecate calls out. "There you are, Professor. I trust your morning walk was pleasant?"

"You can probably tell me that, Goddess." Maximus's tone is tinged with that same strange edge as his first comment. "Yes?"

He comes over with measured steps, taking hold of my upturned hand. His grasp is firm, but so is the stare he keeps riveted on Hecate. And just like that, my nerves are tossing *comfortable* behind.

"If you're keeping tabs on the guest list around here, you must have been okay with clearing Zeus's little stopover with me."

My serenity evaporates. "Z? He was here? You saw him?"

"Just outside," he says. "Not far from here."

Circe snaps her fingers. "That *was* thunder I heard a while ago."

The usual All-father weather stir-up doesn't explain how Z got past the magical chain link fence. But that's not the most important point here. I drill Maximus with an extended stare, letting him see how my mind already drills to it.

Why did he feel the need to summon his father again?

Not a confession I'm going to get out of him this second. Not with Hecate gliding forward, the hem of her skirt rasping the floor as placid power flows from her demeanor.

"As for Zeus," she says, "we allow him to come and go freely. We have an understanding."

"An understanding?" I query.

"We probably don't want to know more than that," Maximus mumbles.

Hecate exhales, clearly happy to pivot the conversation. "How then, Professor, *can* we assist you right now? You have but to ask."

Her hypnotic tone communicates so much more than words. In strange but awesome ways, it humbles me. Even inspires me.

"You mean that, don't you?" I already feel the rhetoric of the question. The uselessness of the words in the shadows of the brilliance I'm so sure of. "You'd really grant us anything we desire or need."

"Anything within our powers, my sweet diamond." She enfolds me in a hug that feels like so much of what I crave. Have yearned so long for. The fullness of a flannel blanket. The warmth of hot cocoa. The acceptance of family. "But even those aren't infinite, so no mounting a unicorn for a ride across a rainbow."

I pull back with a teary laugh. "How'd you know?"

"I promise we'll take the standard route back to the cottage," Maximus offers while sneaking his hand back into mine.

His not-so-subtle squeeze has me swinging my stare up and around to his once again. There's a perturbing gleam in his arresting blues. If the concern emanating from him weren't enough to sober me from Hecate's embrace, his next statement does.

"We need to talk. Alone."

CHAPTER 6

MAXIMUS

WE START BACK TOWARD our cottage but only get as far as the grove when Kara stops in her tracks and wheels toward me. I fight the urge to pick her up, worried about what the pathway's splintered planks are doing to her bare feet, but her expression brims with purpose.

"Enough," she orders, yanking me beneath the willows. "I can't wait any longer. What's going on?"

I cast a careful glance around. Why it feels vital to check the shrubbery for prying eyes and ears, I have no idea. I'm not bearing state secrets. Just an update that's going to hit her like one.

A couple of butterflies flit between purple and orange wild flowers, but other than that, we're alone. Good thing, since Kara's losing the fight to hide her impatience. Her fidgeting worsens, one hand twisting at the fingertips of the other, as she lifts her head and stabs me with an expectant stare.

"Maximus? Come on. Why do you look like someone burned down a library?"

That earns her my double take, but my gut's already sounding off with orders to cut to the chase.

"It's about Megaera."

She absorbs it with more aplomb than I expect, only flaring her nostrils. At least until she speaks again.

"What about her?" she bites out. "Other than the fact that I'd be thrilled to see her stay in melted-sand-dune mode for another century or two?"

I return a tense frown. "I went for a walk to find a cell signal. McCarthy called me last night, and I figured it was a smart idea to touch back in with her."

"And?"

"And I was lucky and got through to her. During the conversation, she dropped Erin Levin's name. Apparently our harpy friend showed up offering to help out with Alameda logistics, which McCarthy is running from home while the national guard uses the campus offices as a temporary command center."

Kara crosses her arms and rubs nervous hands along her opposing shoulders. "Just showed up, huh? Out of the blue? Out of the *kindness of her heart*?"

"If that's code for ordered by her queen, then very likely, yes."

"Hera." She looks faintly ill at having to declare the goddess mother's name. "You're right. Megaera's too much of a dutiful pawn to think of reaching out to McCarthy on her own."

"Especially when the endgame will land her closer to us. Or, at the very least, learning where Hecate is hiding us."

Her eyes fire with stunned flares. "You think that's what she's after?"

"That's the big bonus question," I return. "But it all seems like elaborate measures if Hera's only wanting to mess with me a little."

She steps in and whacks a flat palm to the middle of my chest. "Do neither of them have anything better to do? Seriously?"

"I don't know, beautiful. Maybe it's been a slow decade up on Olympus. Boredom does weird things to people. If necessity is the mother of invention, then boredom is its sly little sibling."

"Well, if it's anything like either of my—" She cuts in on herself with a sharp wince. "Oh, damn it. I hope Kell and Jaden are okay."

"Ssshhh now." I tug her closer. "I'm sure your mom is helping them … or trying to."

"And you're *totally* positive about that?" Even my embrace isn't helping now. She steps free and paces to the other side of the clearing. Her feet pound the damp earth and dry leaves with decisive *thwunk*s and crunches, until she reaches a pair of Adirondack chairs that face a secluded part of the stream. "Back to the other queen bee. I really don't think Hera is bored. I also don't think she's simply messing around with you."

I settle into another low-lying chair. "Possible."

"But why?" She lifts her head. Her browns are angry

but bleak. "That was why you called out to Z, wasn't it? And he didn't know anything either? Oh, wait." Her posture sags, even in a chair that's already done most of the job for her. "Let me guess. He went for the easy out. Told you he couldn't get involved but then invited you to head to Malibu for some surfing."

"Unbelievably, no. On both accounts. Though some board time might've been cool."

She scoots to the lip of her chair and reaches for the top of my hand. "So what did he say?"

I circle a finger up and around, stroking along her delicate knuckles. "He looked just as punched about the news as you were. And, surprisingly, added a lot of determined to it. He promised that if he learns anything, he'll be forthcoming about letting us know."

She falls into a thick silence. And then, "Do you believe him?"

"Depends on what he discovers. If it really is just Hera up to some hijinks, he'll play it off as nothing and order me to forget about it."

She nods, her expression tightening with bitter lines. "Because why go tempting one's husband into a frothing rage for no good reason?"

"Sometimes a shitty status quo is better than a raging war."

Her fingertips tremble. Her inhalation is just as wobbly. "And what if he learns it's more than basic spousal shenanigans?"

"Then I'll listen to what the situation entails and weigh stuff out."

"Stuff like what?" She surges back to her feet with a nervous breath. "And why?"

"Like what kind of scope Hera's thinking on." I get up too. "Is her scheme just some elaborate jab at Z, or does she want to rope you and me into the mix too? If that's the case, then how far is she tossing that rope? Has she reached out to Hades to unwind what he and Hecate agreed to?"

"Oh my God."

"Kara? Hey, wait! *Whoa...*"

I shout it as she gives flight into deeper recesses of the trees. As in, *flight.* Words clutch to silence in my throat as my gaze travels to the swirling twigs and leaves around her bare calves and feet—only to realize the foliage isn't *around* her.

It's...under her.

My gorgeous demon soul mate is also an incredible witch of Iremia...*who can fly.*

But three seconds is all the time I have to process that. I know it as soon as Kara slows, stops, and glances back to the path I've cleared through the tall grass. Though she's still hovering by a few inches, the new fire in her eyes gives me enough to translate her truth—and the vulnerability beneath it.

And the agony. And the uncertainty.

She's still expecting Hades to materialize any moment. And I don't blame her.

I let her have the moment, even with the wilder whorl of debris between her feet and the ground. My own shock and guilt, no matter how abject, are secondary to the pain that consumes the rest of her features.

"I thought it was over." The words practically trample

each other to be free from her lips. "I thought...I'd never have to worry about that place ever again."

"And you won't."

My own syllables fight each other for dominance, grating from my dry throat as I reach again for her hands. Though our contact brings her an inch lower, it sparks a lot of other results. The instant ignition between our bloodstreams. The flares of awareness, blinding my senses to everything around us. I see nothing but her. The universes in her round brown eyes. The spell of her rich cinnamon scent. But most of all, the wallop of her mounting dread.

"You won't." I repeat it with twice my conviction. "*Kara*. Listen to me. I'm not going to let it happen again. I swear to you, with every breath in my body and corner of my soul...I'll give up both before Hades lays so much as another fingertip on you."

"*No.*" She seizes my elbows. "Don't say that." Her features gain new creases. "Just don't, okay?"

I pull her in close, brushing my lips into her hair. I'm fervent but compassionate, communicating that I understand.

"Doesn't matter if I do or don't. If he ever comes for you again, I won't hesitate to kill him."

She laughs. The sound makes me aware of the world again. It's like the spell of the wind in the trees and as musical as the countless chimes around the complex, blending in an airy symphony, as she sinks the last few inches to stand before me again.

"You'll kill him, huh? The king of hell?"

I narrow my gaze, studying the dancing lights in her

own. "You don't think I can?"

"That's not it. But he's the ruler of an entire *realm*." She grips me a little harder. "You don't yank out a cosmic keystone like that without consequences."

"You mean like a parade in my honor? A promotion from hell invader to underworld hero?"

A new topography overtakes her forehead. I should be focusing on the hundred reasons behind her stress but am consumed by the fantasy of erasing those furrows with my lips while my body does other tension-tamping things to hers.

Damn it. I'm done for. I can't forget the fantasy now. I've tasted a drop of Kara's kerosene and am close enough to feel what the sparks of our attraction will do to it.

"Well, we can always drive to Pasadena and march up to McCarthy's front door to ask if Erin can come out to play—"

"No." She seals a hand over my mouth. "Are you hell-bent on giving trouble another open invite?"

"Not fond of considering anything with the word *hell* in it right now," I mutter against her palm. "But I could be talked into trouble if you have ideas."

The edges of her cherry-colored lips kick up. A wider smile tiptoes across them as I reposition my head, making it possible to nibble toward her wrist.

"Ermmm...Professor Kane..."

"Yes, Miss Valari?" I'm already headed toward her elbow.

"Are you...flirting with me?"

I chuckle. It's hard to believe that I said the same thing

to her less than a month ago. Between then and now, we've been through so much with each other. Learned so much about each other. But in so many ways, we've barely just begun our journey together. At least not like this. Not as a simple guy and his beautiful girl, making moony eyes at each other on a bright autumn afternoon. Even being a little nervous about it, but in all the good ways.

"Flirting?" I'm able to drawl it with a little style. Doesn't hurt to have the silky skin of her inner arm beneath my smirking lips. "I guess that all depends."

She pulls in a quivering breath. "On what?"

"On whether it's working."

Her laugh brings more music to the air. "I guess that depends on your ultimate intentions."

A chuckle tumbles out of me. But it's strangled halfway up my throat when the little minx reveals *her* objective. Just before I dip low to show her my intentions with a lusty kiss, she's backed up and lowered herself away. Gotten herself very cozy…in the sexiest pile of leaves I've ever seen.

Especially because the mound has gotten so thick due to being caught between some sizable rocks.

I watch, gulping hard and grinning harder, as Kara leans back to take advantage of the boulders' unique positions. With her knees pressed against two of the stones, she rests her head against a third. Her hands reach above for purchase.

It's a perfect halo, formed from my little demon's own flesh and muscle. Best of all, it's so close to the pretty fan of her skirt made by the splay of her legs. Does she think I need the fire of redemption or a cool breeze of relief? What about both?

I'll take both.

"My intentions?" I drop to my knees in the leaves with her. "Does taking advantage of you right here and now count?"

Her seductive grin is dappled in golden sunlight. The sight is sheer perfection. I lean over, grabbing the curves of her knees to scoot her closer by another inch. Another. I don't give her a chance to approve or veto the plan. I'm too busy plunging forward until my tongue is in her mouth, her thighs are in my hands, and my cock is straining at my zipper, aimed toward one goal alone.

CHAPTER 7

Kara

JUST WHEN I THINK Maximus can't take me to higher planes of pleasure, my body tightens its hold around his. Our sighs turn into moans, mixing with the whirl of the wind and the chatter of the leaves in a symphony I vow to remember until the end of my existence. No. Beyond that.

It's perfect. A cavalcade of awareness. A torrent of emotions. A mesh of entanglement. These chains, I never want to be free of.

Ever...

Maximus rolls his hips with quiet but firm intent. I reply with a needy whimper. *More*, I beg him from deep inside. Or is that *him* pleading from *me*? Does it matter?

More...

"Oh *fuck*. Kara..."

It trails away as my hands emulate my desire, rising up. They seek and then find the broad purchase of his shoulders.

He leans down and sears every inch of my mouth with

a decadent kiss. He's giving but greedy. Honest but erotic. Soft and tender but thorough and deep. I give it all back in equal measure, moving a hand around his neck to keep him locked to me. Craving him here. Reveling in the untamed heat of him. The damp sweat beneath his hair. The slick exertion that helps me trace his muscles. But most of all, the pure force of his passion, tumbling into me. Reawakening me. Binding him to me like no other connection we've shared.

It's urgent and wild. It's fast and frenetic and free.

It's magic.

Nothing that makes me drop my shoulders, funnel my mind, or hone my energy. Nothing I have to think about or learn about or focus on. It's none of those things because it just *is*. Everything that's true and right about me. Everything that's clear and bright about him. Everything that's simply *us*, without expectation or anticipation.

Except maybe one.

The zing of fire he sends through my core and then up my spine. The spark in my mind, igniting to the point that it's blinding, that he's really going to do this again. He's seriously going to send me over the edge, into a cosmos where there's no light at all.

There's nothing but the wild flight...

The soaring sensations...

And then the carnal collision.

"Maximus!" I cry out, unable to help myself.

This is good. Really, really good. So perfect that even the shout is ripped off my lips and thrown into deep silence. We're in a place beyond sound. Past every comprehension I ever fathomed about desire and pleasure. Because officially, these moments are pushing my libido to Mach Twenty.

Thirty?

A hundred?

Again, it doesn't really matter. That there's very little I care about right now, beyond every circuit he keeps zapping between the secret spot inside my sex to the grateful receptors in my brain. If Maximus Kane has become my drug of choice, then I'm shamelessly addicted and rejecting all the rehab. I only want more. So much more.

But despite my pouty moan, Maximus slows. But not all the way to stillness. All over his massive form, there's still a lot of interesting movement. Twitches down his spine and through his ass cheeks. Silent flexings along his limbs. And most awesomely, the tender strokes of his hands, over my hair and down my neck, that quickly have me matching his tremors.

"If you're going for Professor of the Year, you've got one very ecstatic vote."

He chuckles and gives me a soft peck on the lips. "Well, your check mark might be lonely. There's only one woman who gets anything like that out of me."

"Really, now? Tell me more. Who is this wondrous woman?"

He rolls a little to the side, far enough to settle his head atop one hand. "Wondrous is a great word. I've been lucky enough to figure that part out already."

I copy his smirk, even turning to my side a little more. His breathtaking blues deepen, reflecting the sky and trees.

His powerful muscles still gleam with his sweat—and mine. His hair, thick and tousled, catches the sunlight in gold and copper striations.

He's powerful. Regal. Gorgeous. *A god.*

The god who belongs...to me.

"Already?" I echo his last word so glibly, even I'm impressed by the save. "But it sounds like you've learned all the important stuff about her."

"Like all the ways she's wondrous?"

There's no more teasing in his tone. It surrenders to a silky grate that matches his soft touch into the valley between my breasts. I shiver for him, even beneath the light T-shirt that I've kept on during our unexpected tryst.

"Like how she's also my tether to sanity and sorcery at the same time? And how she speeds my heart just from feeling the thrum of hers?" He pushes in at the exact spot from his reference. "And how she's made it possible for me to accept the darkest secret about myself?"

I grab at his hand, crunching his big fingers as hard as I can. "Your truth *isn't* dark, Maximus. It's not shameful or horrible either." I lean over, forcing him to meet my relentless stare. "You're a *prince of Olympus.* Why aren't you accepting that with the pride that is your birthright instead of the disgusting brainwashings of Hera and her harridans?"

His stare on me is more determined. "I never told you about all that."

"You didn't." I let go of his hand to brush some windblown strands from his eyes. "But when memories are especially strong or impactful, especially if they're newly dredged, they're going to bleed into your current consciousness and feelings. Think of it like hearing a drumbeat in a song. If the kit is bigger or the drummer more motivated, the beat is more discernible. After a remix, maybe that track isn't so loud anymore. But through a new sound system, the drums are loud again."

He grimaces. "That makes more sense than I want it to. And ..." Then drags a hand through his hair. "Well, fuck. I'm so sorry if—"

"Why? About what?" I playfully nudge his jaw. "It's not like you can control it. And I know how to tune it out when I want to, which is the case with most people." I chuckle. "Okay, with all people. But I love all of *you*, Maximus Kane. That includes all that you survived and everything that has molded you into the incredible human you are today."

He pushes in and takes my lips beneath his again. "The same way I adore all of you, sorceress."

I regard him for a long, careful moment. "But if it weirds you out, I can always—"

"No." His gaze intensifies. "It's not weird." He curls a hand in, tenderly plucking stray leaves off my cheek. "Everything I am is yours, Kara Valari. All the yesterdays, todays, and tomorrows. In your hands, I know they'll always be safe."

Oh ... this man.

I long to hum and sigh and roll over, and then invite him to get back on top of me. But we've been out here nearly an hour, and I can practically feel Hecate's curiosity drifting along the stream.

"So, mister… I wish we could talk about extended mixes of other kinds, but something tells me we'll be known as the Iremia flashers if we don't button up here."

He's begun to brush my collarbone with his lips but stops the caresses for an enticingly agitated glance. "The Iremia flashers. That has a nice ring, don't you think?"

I laugh. "Not nice enough."

"We could get it printed on bowling shirts."

"On what? No. I don't bowl."

"Have you ever *been* bowling?"

"Once." I scramble to my feet to retrieve his shirt, cast off in the nearby leaves. "For a charity thing that Kell and I did. Correction, that Kell roped me into with a promise of puppies to pet."

"Filing that as a pro tip." A chuckle replaces his frown. "So were there? Puppies?"

"It was an animal rescue promotion, so yes. Thank God, because gutter-balling on every other turn wasn't fun."

He sits up. "Well, that won't do. Next time you go bowling, you're learning from me."

"Next time? What makes you think there'll be one of those?"

I can practically see the gears churning in his mind while he hikes his jeans back up. But before he can crank up the charm for a comeback, a series of ethereal chimes drifts over the water.

"Saved by the sala bells. Sounds like we're expected at lunch."

"Agreed," Maximus says with resignation. "Guess I'll

have to store my bowling date fantasies for another time."

"Like for another century? And another girl?"

For a second, he looks irked. But even after I tug him in for another sweet kiss, the look persists. "No other girls," he growls. "Not in this century or the next dozen." This time he initiates the kiss. It's longer and wetter. Exquisite and perfect. "None of them will be right. Not as right as you."

I swoon inwardly, drinking in his energy again. It tumbles into my psyche with warmth, protection, and devotion. I feel like taking it all and forwarding it, spigot-like, into the stream. That way I could take a bath in it too.

I do my best to hold on to the fantasy as Maximus takes my hand for our walk back to Iremia's center. In the sala, a feast is laid out to rival last night's spread in the grove. The dishes range from a plate of old-fashioned fried chicken and a colorful fruit display to more exotic-looking salads—and of course, an array of desserts that looks like a high-end magazine spread.

"Ah! Here they are." Hecate walks out to greet us on the veranda. "Have you been busy refreshing our girl for the afternoon illuminations, Maximus?"

The others smile knowingly, though my clothes are tidy and my hair is free of leaves. The man next to me has a replying smile, but it's just his surface version. The expression he saves for people like flaky students, paparazzi, and my mother.

"Interesting. They're *illuminations* now?" He drops his head and adds a remark for my ears only. "Still sounds a lot like tests and training."

In the meantime, Hecate has lifted her head up and away. Weirdly, I almost expect her gauzy skirt, bright tank, and knitted headscarf to transform into a nun's raiment and wimple. "And you, Professor, still sound rather untrusting of the process."

I'm not surprised she heard him. But I'm also not sure Maximus was going for full secrecy.

"Oh, I'm all for processes," he replies without a flinch. "Even this one. If it's going to actually help Kara."

And now I get my own turn with the spiked apprehension. I already don't like it, but the knot in my gut won't be ignored.

"She's safe." The insertion is from Circe.

"I'm just concerned, on a lot of different levels," Maximus asserts.

"Understood," the enchantress says. "But the hornet's nest in your brain is only going to give you pointless stings. We've all been through the enlightenment and illumination coursework, and you can see that we're all still here. Whole and healthy."

"Even though there are actual gravesites with some of your names on them," he counters.

"Documented death comes with many attractive advantages," Marie adds.

"Let's not let lunch get cold." Hecate gestures toward the food that's been set up on a round table near the kitchen. The grace of her movement is a fluid presence in her steps. I admire her for making it all look so easy, when I have to concentrate to look that polished any time the media jabs a camera at me.

I keep watching her innate aplomb even during lunch. I admire the way she eats her food with thought, as if she can see every stage that went into its creation. The love that went into raising the chickens. The seeds that were placed into the ground and then cultivated into fruits and vegetables. She expresses as much to everyone who had a part in those different phases—in short, every person seated at the table except Maximus and me.

But at no time do I feel left out. It's a pleasant sensation to acknowledge. Throughout it all, I'm equally as grateful for all these amazing beings who inserted as much care into our meal as they would into a potion or spell. It's a jarring difference from Hollywood, where just about everyone is too occupied with the jostle up the fame and fortune ladder. Or if they've climbed high enough, how and when they'll fall off.

It feels really good to be off that ladder for a while. Maybe forever.

That wouldn't be such a bad thing. Not at all.

CHAPTER 8

MAXIMUS

KIAMA AND LISELI, THOUGH likely a pair of talented witches, would make lousy poker players. Not only do they wear their pity for me like fresh tattoos, I can practically smell the emotions as they cross the library on their way to me.

"Greetings, ladies," I remark as they settle on the love seat that I've pulled closer to my easy chair. The worn velvet piece has become a leaning post for my second stack of reading material.

"And hello to you, Professor," Kiama says. "Lovely afternoon to enjoy a book in a comfortable chair."

I hitch up a brow. "Is there ever not a good time for it?"

"Ah. My suppositions are confirmed," she says with her pretty inflections. "You're an insightful man."

"You mean demigod." Liseli's addition lacks the bite Aradia and Circe fling at each other. It's incentive enough for my own gentle grin.

"I'm flesh and blood too. And more comfortable with that label, to be honest."

"The same way you're comfortable with these to-be-reads?" Kiama pulls a couple of tomes off my stacks. She brandishes a well-reviewed military thriller in one hand and *The Alice in Wonderland Omnibus* in the other. "Am I also right in theorizing you're a creature of broad tastes, Mr. Kane?"

Liseli's eyes pop wide. "The Grand Canyon is broad. Those selections are ..."

"Interesting," I concede with a shrug. "I know. But I'm a fast reader, and it's fun to sprinkle in classics from time to time."

They both add smiles to their impressed nods, meaning I've woven my confession close enough to the truth to pass. I grabbed Carroll's work off the shelf on what I thought was an impulse but now recognize it as my subliminal side having a little fun. Three days ago, I followed Gio through a looking glass disguised as a cemetery pond and ended up in an afterworld only missing a disappearing cat and a hookah-huffing caterpillar. Though my new surroundings are different, some themes remain the same. *Curiouser and curiouser ...*

Or maybe another expression is better. Like *we're all mad here.*

Kiama smiles a little wider. "Why decide on just one?" she says amiably. "If they apply equally, I mean."

"I didn't mean anything by—"

"Of course you didn't." She sweeps up a hand, and I

swear there's an opaline aura between her fingers. "Just as I didn't mean to intrude on your thoughts again. I apologize."

"Why?" I frown. "If that's your power... It's not like you have an off switch, right?"

"*Everyone* has the shutdown lever." Liseli's the one offering the information this time. "A major aspect of the enlightenment exercises is about exactly that. Power that cannot be controlled is tyranny."

"Or terrorism," Kiama murmurs.

"Perhaps both at once," I add.

"*Most* of the time, both at once," Liseli says. There's too much sadness in her words and darkness in her gaze—the kind that can only come from firsthand experience, according to my deeper instincts—to warrant a verbal response that'll have any meaning. "Which is why we pay so much attention to control," she finally goes on. "And everything that has to stand behind it."

I dig deep to find my voice again. "Everything like what?"

Kiama folds her hands in her lap and straightens her posture. "We all have the capacity for self-control. It's part of our bridge from toddler to greater puerility, then again to puberty, young adulthood, and so on. But willpower with anger only acts as a stopper. It isn't lasting management. And eventually, it explodes in ugly ways."

"And then tries to level cities," I supply in a low growl.

"Or worse, if it isn't stopped in time."

Again, Liseli's overtone is painted in dark hues of *been there, done that, seen too much.* Once more, I give her a fast nod of understanding.

"Perhaps this helps a little with discerning why Hecate had to show up last night and then whisk you two away so quickly?" Kiama adds another careful smile. "Her intention wasn't to interfere."

"I don't think that," I state, leaning forward. "Honestly, we're both just here to learn. Well, Kara is. I'm not exactly sure about—"

"What?" Kiama prompts before I can catch myself and zip my trap. "It's all right to ask questions, Professor Kane. Enlightenment isn't an exclusive experience, nor does it have an expiration date. We both still inquire, and challenge, things every day."

"And *definitely* did when we first arrived," Liseli adds.

"Which was when, exactly?" They did say curiosity was okay …

"Nineteen ten for me," Kiama supplies. "And nineteen thirteen for Liseli."

I study their faces with interest. "Which makes you officially how old now?"

Liseli grins. "I'll be celebrating my 147th birthday this year. Kiama's a year younger than me."

Her friend matches the smile. "We were both a little over twenty-five in our corporeal state when our powers manifested. Marie was even younger, though Morgana was a few years older. We know that's hard to believe, but the manifestation does different things to different witches' aging processes. For both of us, it halted everything."

I nod. "But Kara's grandfather kept maturing like a mortal guy."

"One of the lucky ones," Liseli comments. "We were able to get away with our younger looks for a few years, but once we got deep into our thirties, artificial pigments were necessary to appear older."

Kiama scowls. "When we could even find them."

"Damn," I mutter. "So, what happened?" I hate asking the question, though I can't avoid it. What if Kara's situation is the same? How long will she be able to get away with it if her beauty is that permanent, even in youth-obsessed LA?

"Neither of us kept up the ruse for long," she relays. "I was thrown out of my town, accused by the elders of brokering deals with evil spirits to entice the younger men away from prospective brides. And Liseli was married to a gambling addict who started offering *her* as his ante at the card tables."

The other woman clutches her hands in her lap. "I avoided the worst possible outcome by mastering sleeping spells. But eventually, Gaspard would've caught on."

Kiama rises to her feet. "But Hecate got us both out. Without her, we would've been doomed to fates worse than death—and fully permitted by the 'civilized society' of the day. You can't imagine the fear in which we were existing."

My brows slam toward each other. "You're right. Even a not-so-touristy jaunt through hell compares, I'd wager."

My point is backed up by the fresh shadows that creep across their gazes. Which leads, for the first time ever, to my gratitude about being half human. If mortality led everyone to their nobler sides, Hades would be ruling an empty kingdom. An eternity in those circles suddenly doesn't seem like enough time for some of the sinners there.

"But don't discount our input just because we're the youngsters around here." Liseli steers toward a lighter mood. "There's a million things we haven't done, but just you wait."

The three of us laugh aloud at the popular musical reference.

"Well played," I say. "But officially, you're not the junior stateswomen anymore."

"Which is why we're reaching out now," Liseli says.

"Just as we wish someone had done with us."

The last remark is strange to receive from Kiama, who maintains the smile that should be her trademark. But this time, she doesn't share the disposition with her eyes. I don't hide the observation from my own demeanor.

"Well, I'm thankful to you both for doing so," I offer. "As you're already aware, Kara was *my* diamond first. But while we're here and she's busy getting enlightened, I'd be happy to help wherever the rest of you may need it."

Kiama's back to her charismatic smirk. "Now don't you see?" she murmurs to her friend. "I *knew* we'd like him."

Liseli giggles. "You definitely said that." And then nods my direction. "But I'll like you even better if that offer extends to helping with animal feedings."

"Absolutely." I surge to my feet, newly energized. *Make me useful, please.*

The farmhouse next to the animal enclosures is homier than I expected. "Do you live here?" I ask Liseli after we cross the wide porch and enter what looks like a main sitting room. The couches are overstuffed leather, the rugs are intricately braided, and colorful baskets and bowls are tucked into alcoves between the stucco walls and exposed beam ceilings.

"Sometimes," the witch answers. "There's a small bedroom past the kitchen. If one of the animals is having a rough go, either Kiama or I will sleep in there to keep watch."

"Does that happen often?"

"Not with most of the regular beasties in the yard and paddock. But the familiars are, for obvious reasons, different. Even if one of them has been out to the realms with us and anything intense has ensued, the shift in their energy carries an impact on the others."

"Another reason why we are all schooled in proper control of our powers," Kiama says. "But sometimes we're called to do unexpected things, and—"

"Sometimes?" Liseli murmurs.

"*Most* times," Kiama amends. "Nobody wants to watch their familiar suffer. But we can't always help that consequence."

"And they probably know that." My comfort sounds shallow, an intention I wasn't going for. "I mean that. Animals sense more than we think they do."

Liseli huffs. "You know that sounds odd from a downtown LA native, right?"

"Of course." I jam my hands into my back pockets. "But growing up, only my jungle was concrete. My imagination wasn't. If anything, I was even more fascinated by animals—especially after *The Wind in the Willows*, *The Mouse and the*

Motorcycle, and that series about the feral cats who were always at war."

Liseli pumps a fist but wiggles it like a cat paw. "I devoured that series. The ones about the dogs and the bears too."

Kiama doesn't join our commiseration. I step over upon observing the new tension across her slender face.

"What's wrong?" I prompt. "Is *your* familiar all right?"

She nods but tugs at the side of her neck. Once again, I observe a faint outline of iridescent energy brimming between her fingers. "For the time being, yes. But Cally isn't a young tiger anymore, and the constant spellcasting this week has worn us both." As her hand slips down, the unique glow persists in tiny threads across her palm. As soon as she wiggles her fingers, the light attempts to shoot up into them. The effect is alarmingly fleeting. "Right now, I couldn't even use these to heal a fly."

Still, I jack up my eyebrows. "You have the power of healing, along with your other abilities?"

She smiles and nods. "Think of magic making like music or food making. Or even teaching. Are you an instructor for only one kind of literature?"

"Hmm. For being tired, you two are on intellectual fire," I return.

After Liseli bows to acknowledge my praise, she steps over and pulls Kiama into a hug. "Your big boy is going to be just fine, dear. I promise. And it *was* an intense week, but worth it. Consider what we accomplished! A brand-new home for our two new friends."

"Who are both really grateful for your hard work," I add.

Kiama casts a stare at me from over her friend's shoulder. "You truly like it?"

"Did you think we wouldn't?" I use verbal bold type on the words only because she's so unsure. "Seriously, as my buddy Jesse would say, it's the cat's meow."

At once I'm wincing. Kiama reacts with a light laugh.

"I'm sure Cally would give your humor two paws up."

Liseli tugs at one of Kiama's elbows. "Why don't we go ask her for ourselves?"

I grin. "Lead the way."

The house and barn are directly connected through a short breezeway. Once we're traversing it, I'm hit by the smells of fresh grass and hay. A few less pleasant things too, but I focus on the former.

Kiama motions me toward a large open-air enclosure behind the building, where a huge striped wildcat eagerly lopes toward the rail as soon as the witch approaches. Kiama's joy is just as tangible, and she buries her face into the tiger's fur with affectionate croons.

"Told you she was going to be okay." Liseli's voice is also drenched with happiness. I look back to her in time to catch a brief sheen across her gaze. I won't deny how that affects me, with a clutch in what Jesse would call *my feels*, centered somewhere between my middle ribs. It inspires my wider smile at her, along with a new question.

"So now I'm curious. Where's *your* familiar?"

"Sleeping," the woman replies while quickly pulling

her hair into a ponytail. "He's a fennec fox who, like me, prefers the moon instead of the sun."

I toss around a curious glance in the early afternoon rays. "I get it. Sometimes I'm most productive at night too."

"Ah. Then I look forward to introducing you to Koko soon. Though there's certainly no rush."

The woman is just as easygoing while guiding me toward the barn's interior, allowing Kiama some private time with Cally. On the outside, I continue to be an interested tour taker, nodding and humming at the right junctures. But on the inside, Liseli's casual remark sticks to me with glaringly opposite results.

There's certainly no rush.

It's a broad statement. Words that can be translated in a lot of different ways. I only wish one of them was a relief valve for my sudden tension.

The loose interpretation is that Kara and I are going to be here for a while. Maybe a *long* while. Or worse.

Is Hecate expecting us to move in permanently?

Technically, that prospect shouldn't be tempting my pores to sprout a thousand hives. This is Topanga Canyon, not Iceland. If I throw a rock hard enough, it'd likely shatter a panoramic window in a movie mogul's mansion. Malibu is half an hour west, and Burbank is a doable drive the other direction, if taken at certain hours of the day. We're close enough to LA to make it all work.

But maybe that's the core of my issue.

Maybe we're too close.

LA is home—in many ways, it always will be—but for

Kara and me, is it safe anymore? Is Iremia and everyone in it?

For now, I have to believe as much. I have no reason to doubt Hecate's promises to the same thing. She's formidable—I watched her bring Hades to a respectful heel in less than ten minutes—and she obviously cares for Kara to the core of her heart. To the depths of my own, I suspect that my woman needed that maternal touch even before Hades swooped her into the pit of hell.

But hell isn't always a literal realm. And home isn't always a physical address. Especially when the queen of all the gods has decided to keep her operatives sniffing in Kara's and my shadows.

Which means that for now, this has to be home. I'm not comfortable with the thought, even with its qualifier. *For now.*

This isn't going to be for good. I know that much as fact. But what or where *will* be for Kara and me?

My mind replies with a pitiful blank. Even before Hades's not-so-fun little ordeal, I'd started to consider backup living plans for Kara and me. Not *plans* so much as a whole new start, created by the two of us alone. It wouldn't need to be far, but I've saved enough to afford a place close by. Something similar to what she shares now with Kell, only it'd be ours. No prying paparazzi or mothers with front door keys. Best of all, someplace Hera couldn't locate us.

But is that even possible?

If she lets the world think she's still back in the Hollywood Hills, would it be enough to fool the *mortal* world, let alone the otherworldly powers who all continue to have such strange compulsions about us?

Too many questions. Not enough answers. And none of them are going to come right away.

The threat of Hades's obsession is still too fresh to forget. Why was he so incensed about giving up Kara? Is he that huge of a megalomaniac, or are there other, scarier, reasons? And why is Hera continuing to sic her minions on our trail, using Elizabeth McCarthy as an unknowing accomplice?

I can't let go of the suspicion that Z is troubled about all this but won't let on why. Only one fact seems rock solid right now. I'm not going to learn any of those details by brooding here in the dust.

But maybe *here* is exactly where I need to be.

In a bizarre but brilliant manner of speaking.

Maybe here, basically beneath Hecate's nose, is the most ideal launching pad for rocketing to those answers. The route doesn't get any more direct than this. Besides, I'm here with Kara, who's being nurtured and cherished by some women I'm truly beginning to like.

Right now, that's more than good enough.

CHAPTER 9

"**S**HOULD I GO BACK in and get some meditation mats?"

I'm already chastising myself for not thinking about the offer sooner. When Hecate suggested we take our afternoon session outside, I was too pleased about the novelty of it—sunshine, flowers, and a warm breeze—to think of practical details.

"You have such an observant and generous heart," the goddess replies. She links her elbow through one of mine. "Thank you, sweet one, but I thought we'd take a walk instead."

"Oh. Great." I glance back to the sala anyhow. "Should we wait for Circe, or will she know where to go and catch up?"

"We don't need Circe this time." She folds her other hand across the place where mine rests along her forearm. "I want a chance to talk to you by myself."

At once my senses are slammed with the earnestness of her proposal. It's swiftly followed by the warmth of her affection. Still, my guard shoots up. Not by a lot, but by enough. I can't help the instinct, nearly woven into my DNA as a Valari by this point.

"Talk?" I lift a sketchy smile. "Ermmm... About what?"

Maybe this is the moment where she gives me the full tea steep about things. The actual things she was referring to before sweeping Maximus and me out here. *We have so much to do.* She surely meant more than enjoying bleu cheese flowers and honing my levitation game.

That must be what's pressing so notably on her mind—and what I tell myself to listen for now. Nothing in life comes without a cost. Some are higher than others. Some are more of a joy to pay. I wonder what the goddess's will be, but a fast probe of her energy reveals nothing beyond the constant chamomile she sips. Not exactly a telling conclusion. Hers is an ancient, almost timeless power. If she wants to shield herself from me, she's likely got a dozen variations for the task.

"Do you need an agenda?" Hecate says with a laugh that's also oddly comforting. "Haven't you ever just walked and talked with a friend before? Chatted? Chin-wagged? Perhaps there's some new idiom I haven't yet heard for it."

I enjoy the chance to chuckle. "I just..." I shrug. "The truth is...I *haven't* ever done this before."

Not without it being staged for some media thing, with a reporter by my side and two cameras in my face. Certainly not with someone who ever just wanted to *chin-wag*.

"My goodness. Well, that's a shame."

I want to halt in my tracks but don't. I also refrain—barely—from blurting that out.

I'm not ashamed.

Right now, I'm just a little uncomfortable. But I mentally shake it off while letting Hecate lead the way over a simple footbridge, onto a packed dirt path that bisects a meadow of dry grass and wild flowers.

"So where are we headed?"

Sunlight hits some bronze lowlights in her curls as she flicks a fast look over. "Come now. Most certainly you and Kell decided to play hooky from time to time and just jumped in the car with nowhere specific to go?"

My chest pangs. *Kell.* Though my sister and I have exchanged a few messages since everything that happened at the mansion, it's not the same as getting to see her every day. Or having the certainty of her smirk and snark during all the *un*certainty I've been calling my life lately.

Despite all that, I'm able to level an answering look that's backed by complete conviction. "If Kell ever did that, it definitely wasn't with me."

Hecate's brow furrows. "I thought you two were close."

"Of course. But we're also different." In a lot of key ways. But I don't say that part aloud. "Being our own selves, and having lives outside of each other as well as the family, is probably a factor that keeps us close."

"Lives outside the family," she echoes, almost like an incantation. "I imagine that's not easy for either of you."

"It takes some doing," I admit. "But it's not impossible

with the right logistics. And, in the case of college courses, some basic humility. Once we have the chance to show others that we're just like them—I mean, aside from Kell's obsession with fried pickles dipped in peanut butter—people start to relax once they see that we're no more special than—"

"But you *are* special."

"There are parts of me that are *unique*," I argue gently. "But there are other parts that are normal, and I like them too. It feels good to let them out from time to time."

"Why?"

As easy as it was to detect her curiosity, it's simple to sense her puzzlement. "You're … serious?" I say with matching surprise.

"Absolutely." Her scrutiny deepens. "Kara … *normal* is for the unchosen. The masses who are content with … settling."

"Being at peace with yourself isn't the same as—"

"It's such a nice day. Let's not squabble over labels, sweet one."

I pull in air, battling the onset of a fume. She only means well with the endearment, as my intuitive side confirms. I just wish the other side, still grinding like I'm a dismissed servant, would settle down.

She is right about one thing. The day is truly perfect, weatherwise. I lift my face to appreciate its clarity and warmth.

"Hmmm," I croon. "Sometimes a girl just needs the wind in her hair and the sun on her face."

"Built-in stress relievers," Hecate remarks. "Athena and Califia certainly knew what they were doing when sculpting this canyon."

"Califia. The great spirit of California." I lower my gaze with a quizzical frown. "But Athena too? Isn't she busy with stuff like war?"

"Yes. But wisdom as well. Remember that she was born as an adult, similar to how California graduated to statehood without being a territory first." An impish grin teases her lips. "That, and she was in the neighborhood a great deal."

"The…neighborhood?"

"A generality. Someone had to ensure that the wild wild west stayed true to its nickname."

As we ascend a small knoll, I look over the miles toward the sapphire haze over the ocean.

"And speaking of wilder things…" At the crest of the hill, she disengages our hold with a diffident laugh and clasps her hands at the front of her waist. The pose brings her a Mother Superior vibe. "Tell me how you and Maximus met."

My senses tell me she's still just genuinely intrigued, though I'm bursting with a question of my own in reply. "You really don't know?"

"Only what's been printed in the tabloids. Which, as you know, are as reliable as a disappearance spell. Trusting the acropolis gossip chains is going out on a similarly sketchy limb."

A tighter frown takes over my face. "What are they saying? In both places?"

Once more, her gaze darkens, but her features barely fluctuate. "The mortals think you're a student who paid your way into Alameda. The new library bears your mother's name, after all."

"Only one wing," I bite back. "And not a single one of those reporters thought to hack into my transcript and learn I *earned* my place at college, grade by grade?"

She hauls in a steady breath.

I want to scream, anticipating what the rest of her account will reveal.

"At least the humans agree on their specifics. In Olympus, the theories vary. Some say you're a demon unwilling to accept your destiny, who seduced your teacher to escape your incubus. Others think you're already a succubus and used your wiles on both Maximus and Hades. But neither of those are my favorite."

"Oh God." I moan. "There are more?"

"Just the theory that you've always been merely mortal and Veronica has covered for you since birth. That your incubus was convinced to capitulate so fast because your mother disclosed that secret to him."

I press a hand to my forehead. "So there's nobody who wants to accept the basic truth? Maximus and I are in love. Neither of us forced it. Neither of us *needed* it."

"But now you cannot imagine needing anything more."

I drop my hand, pressing it over the new detonation that threatens my composure. The cacophony takes over my heartbeat.

"It's obvious to anyone who gets within ten feet of you

two." Her tone teases, but her demeanor is open, accepting. As if she knows it's the perfect medicine for my soul in this moment.

My exhalation is a jittery rasp. "He's everything to me."

"I know that too," she assures me. "As we all do."

Though this beautiful witch has admitted that her powers don't extend to omniscience, it's once again like they do. She seems to know exactly what I need to hear—but more than that, how I yearn to hear it.

Like it's true.

Like Maximus and I really do have a chance to find our forever happiness, in spite of everything that's happened—and everything that might still happen.

I can't ignore that possibility. But for now, maybe it's okay to just accept the happiness and completion of this moment. This peaceful and perfect now.

It's not a feat I'm familiar with. And I'm definitely not good at it. I ache for the moments when Gramps struggled to make me practice it, but those never lasted long before a text or call from Mother beckoned me back to chasing our Hollywood dreams.

Her Hollywood dreams.

Or were they?

Have I ever been able to exist in a world without a dozen places to be, a hundred things to do, a thousand fires that need to be doused?

Maybe that's part of my lesson here too. My real enlightenment.

If so … I'm ready.

CHAPTER 10

MAXIMUS

BEFORE THE NEXT MORNING'S dawn, there's a freak thunderstorm in the canyon. Technically, any storm is a freakish thing south of Santa Barbara, but this is an unexpected gale that even I can't take responsibility for.

Anticipating Kiama's and Liseli's need for some help with the undoubtedly skittish animals, I should probably make my way over to the farmhouse. After rousing Kara long enough to let her know where I'm going, I quickly change into jeans, boots, and a T-shirt—sending silent thanks to the Iremia diamonds for accurately nailing my fashion needs—before hurrying through the soggy light toward the buildings that must be chaotic with animal anxiety by now.

Sure enough, the barn and farmhouse floodlights make the place look like a rock festival in the making, but that's where my expectations hit a brick wall.

Definitely not a rock concert.

Not even a smooth-jazz-by-the-bay thing.

There's no sound in here at all. Literally, not a creature is scurrying. Or bleating or squawking or growling.

I scuff to a halt, expecting the crunch beneath my boots as an assurance I haven't gone deaf. But the newly wet earth only gives up only soft *ploofs*.

I frown twice as hard. "What the ...?"

A sharp gust rattles raindrops out of the trees. I shake off the wet, tie back my hair, and close in on the animal habitat structures. Still not a single scratch in the air.

It's unnerving.

I don't like it, this suspicion that's become my instant default, but hiking several circles of hell will make a guy look at every blind corner in a new way. Better a neck full of spiked hairs than a surprise tackle from a hellhound. Oh, yeah. Even here. Until I'm shown otherwise, the witches' enchanted perimeter is as good as cheesecloth to me.

I skirt around the farmhouse, thankful for the damp soil cushioning my steps and calming my pulse. But not enough. I glance down at my spread fingers, hoping they aren't really sizzling from the light socket into which my bloodstream feels jammed.

No sooner do I confirm I'm still presenting as flesh and blood than Kiama appears from the stables, her wide grin coinciding with the sunbeams fingering through the clouds. "Good morning, Professor. I was just wondering if you'd come around so I could properly thank you."

I already feel my eyes tighten. "For what?"

An instant cant of her head, making her long braid fall over her shoulder. "The storm. Isn't it your doing?"

"Not a single drop. But if it was, why would you be thanking me?" I nod back toward the animal enclosures. "Isn't thunder and lightning as good as stirring up the asylum?"

"Absolutely. But sometimes that's a good thing."

"Poking the beasts?" I dot that with an arched brow.

"More like ... inciting the libidos." She quirks half a grin. "Over the years, some of our beloved brutes have landed on the endangered species list. Under controlled circumstances, bringing in a thunder buddy for them can be a good thing."

"Thunder buddy." My mutter is infused with a laugh. "I guess that's a thing?"

"Look it up." She hitches a teasing shrug. "Or perhaps ... you don't have to."

Interpreting her intimation isn't a mental hardship this time. I drop my head as wild memories of the first time with Kara wash over me. That night, not even two weeks past, feels like forever ago—yet I wish it were only last night. I'm already breathing down the telltale hardness in my jeans as if it were.

I mask the deeper feelings with a casual smirk and its matching one-liner. "So is this the so-called calm before *their* storm?"

She chuckles. "Let's just say everyone has their dance cards in place, and I've got the situation under control. Liseli's already inside, lending some additional support."

"Cool." I nod. "Well, if anybody gets out of line and wanders a paw where they shouldn't ..."

"We know exactly where to go for the backup."

"For the next few minutes, I think that'll be the sala. Time for me to find some sorcery called caffeine."

During the walk to the main building, the canyon gusts on my face are once more an alternation of warm and cool. The currents turn the sunrise into a mesmerizing mix of golden light and lingering asperitas clouds. The cosmic light show gets so brilliant, pewter and blue swirling with amber and pink, that I stop for long seconds to absorb the colorful glory.

"Next time the squall *is* my fault..." I conclude it by pointing a determined finger to the sky, a weird promise that my next storm will be more of a creative endeavor. When and how I'll accomplish that is my own desperate guess, but I've been officially inspired now.

As I approach the sala, I start to think my hour of solitude is becoming a good thing. I'll make some coffee and then take it into the library with me. The idea of dedicated reading time is enough to spread a smirk to my face.

Until...

"No. I can't agree to this. It's too fast. *Much* too fast."

"We have no choice."

"We *always* have a choice!"

"Not now. Not when our hand has been forced like this."

I go totally still. And am instantly thankful that Circe and Hecate are so embroiled in their confrontation, they haven't noticed the whispered *whoosh* of the closing door behind me.

I scoot behind a group of hanging plants. I'm just in

time, able to cloak my startle as one of the witches smacks a kitchen counter. I take a guess on Circe. Hecate would opt for a more dramatic demonstration, if at all. The harsh breath that follows is also Circe's.

"That isn't the girl's fault, Goddess."

"No?" Hecate counters. "Defying her underworld edict? Going to Maximus and lying with him when she did?"

"Events that were foretold! A destiny that was—"

"Accelerated by them both. Unnecessarily."

"Which is now *their* mistake?" Another whack on the counter. "I told you all that we should have arranged the coordinates differently. Had they met at the start of next spring, it would've been more than enough time. This isn't on them. We're responsible. We lost sight of the true magic. The power of the connection and passion we were unleashing. That *we* created."

"All right," Hecate bites out. "Fine. Do you want to hear that you're right?"

"I want to hear that you're still listening." Circe shifts, giving me a chance to peek from behind the hanging tapestry. She's in profile, though her slumped shoulders serve to hide her thick red curls. As soon as she jerks her face back up, I duck back into my hiding place. "In the space of just three mortal weeks, the girl has given away her virginity, defied her family, and been absconded to the underworld. When she finally thought her world was returning to normal, she had to face Magaera and uproot her life again. You can't keep pushing her out of her comfort zone if it doesn't exist anymore!"

There's a new sound from Hecate. I can't figure out if the huff is one of exasperation, authority, or both.

"I cannot care if she is comfortable or not," the goddess issues. "For better or for worse, we've had to rewrite the coordinates and rush the timeline. The time for us to act is now. Unless you wish to wait another millennia for the next chance to do this?"

"Of course not," Circe says. "She's just…special. So rare. And watching her with him…" She pushes out a wistful sigh. "Their union is the best thing I've ever accomplished with my powers. That *all* of us have. But the idea of breaking her… I can't stand it."

A fresh rustle has me spying again. I peer out in time to see Hecate gripping the other witch's shoulders. There's an intense gold glow around her fingers. Though Circe seems to grimace, she also doesn't make a move to fight the brutal hold.

"We're about to declare war, my little lustre. You and I both know what that means."

Even from twenty feet across the sala, I can feel the weight of Circe's gulp. It thuds through my own senses. The pain only worsens as the poor witch raises her head and answers her goddess in a sparse croak.

"Yes, Goddess."

Hecate sags a little. Leans in to rest her forehead against Circe's. But the intensity of her vise grip only gets brighter and thicker.

"Good," she murmurs. "So tell me. Out loud."

Circe swallows hard again. "Sacrifices," she finally whispers. "It means sacrifices, my goddess. From everyone."

"Thank you, lustre," the willowy goddess whispers back. "A most perfect answer."

Shit.

That's *not* a perfect answer. And I'm not in need of caffeine anymore. My frontal lobe burns as if Hecate's already gotten her ruthless fingers on it as well, searing a new priority into me. A prominence that pounds through me, over and over again, to the cadence of my sprinting feet on the muddy ground, all the way back through the village of cottages.

When I crest the knoll in front of the house that Kara and I share, there's a din of rain in the river beneath the chaotic sky.

This time, the storm is all me.

But I don't care about the art of it anymore.

I don't care about anything except getting inside and calling out her name—terrified I'm already too late.

CHAPTER 11

"MAXIMUS?"

I call it out while lurching up in bed. One second I was having a great dream about being with him in a convertible, road-tripping along the coast somewhere between San Clemente and the Mexican border. The next, his yelling voice is jolting my heart and all the walls around here.

Here?

For a second, I'm too disoriented to pull up any answer. But I look out across the narrow river, to where the lights of the sala glow, and cherish a matching warmth inside.

Iremia. Of course. *Home.* For a little while, at least.

Maximus doesn't look like he agrees. At all.

"What is it?" I prompt. The atmosphere shakes with simultaneous lightning and thunder. "What's happening?" My throat is tight and dry. "Has Hades—"

"No," he growls. "But it might have something to do with him."

I twist fists into the sheet I've clutched to the base of my neck. "*What?* How? Maximus, you're scaring me."

He sits on the bed and ardently reaches for me. I'm too freaked by the stress on his face to care about the water he's getting everywhere. I only hope I can infuse his clammy skin with some degree of warmth.

"Hey. Come on, talk to me." I grab his other hand and squeeze tighter. The effort makes the sheet descend to my waist, but modesty isn't going to help a thing at the moment. He's not noticing anyhow. But why do I sense that he's also aware of everything? I mean *all* of it. The spectrum of sounds and smells through the canyon. Every sensation that sweeps across his skin. Things he can and can't see. And it's all hurting him. Cutting him. "Oh my God. What's going on?"

Finally, he takes a deep, hard breath. "Kiama and Liseli had things under control at the barn, so I went to the sala. To make coffee."

As he exhales, so do I—indulging a rush of relief. His explanation is so simple and normal. Maybe I'm jumping to a lot of unnecessary conclusions. "You brought me some, right? Name your price for the java, mister."

"Kara." But my playfulness doesn't rub off on him. The gravity tenaciously sticks, making me wonder if someone's been messing with the planet's magnets. I'm weighted into the mattress. Dragged into his dark energy like nothing I've felt from him before. "I didn't make coffee. I didn't make it all the way into the kitchen."

"Okay." I shore up my posture. He still looks like he's

seen a ghost. "What happened?"

"Hecate and Circe were already in there."

"Okay." I scowl, confused. "And anyone else?"

Not Hades. Please don't say Hades. You can say anyone but Hades.

"No. It was just them," he says. "But ... Kara ..." He moves a few inches closer. I'm beyond being chilled, especially as he drags a hand free and scrapes it along my neck. The contact of his damp hand and the warm skin beneath my hair ... I'm electrified by him. Beautifully connected once more.

But hopelessly held by his open concern, even as it escalates into a weird despondence.

"They didn't know I was there."

"Wait. So you eavesdropped on their conversation?"

"Not their conversation. Their *confrontation.*"

I don't even have to turn on the empathy to get his point. I startle back by an inch.

"They were arguing about you."

"About me?" I hate sounding like a stuck video loop, but what he's saying right now is worse. "I'm sorry. I can't wrap my mind around this. Are you sure they were referring to me?"

He's not happy about my skepticism. "Unless there's another person around here that they'd refer to as *the girl*. One who's also taken a new lover recently and been kidnapped to hell because of it."

"Oh dear." My turn for pulling in a labored breath. "Okay. What were they saying?"

"Hecate is insisting on rushing your lessons. Circe feels

you need some recharge time."

I crunch a new frown. "That's all? Why can't I do both?"

Maximus shakes his head. "That wasn't all. They also discussed how things have progressed between you and me."

For some reason, that section of his account feels like a steel file on a hangnail. I'm grateful he finishes by sliding his hand down and around mine again. "Hecate was asking questions about that yesterday too," I confess. "But there was nothing insincere about her energy. She was genuinely interested."

"Oh, I absolutely believe that."

"But?"

"The one thing they agreed on is the fact that you and I are destined to be. They even talked about their role in it all. About aligning coordinates for us."

"Sweet but a little weird. Coordinates? To what?"

"They weren't doling out details."

"Because they were busy fighting." I use my free hand to gather the sheet close again, needing a purpose for my fidgeting tendencies. "About stuff *other* than that."

Once more, my stab at levity is quelled by his tension. He's as still as a human thunderhead, in his wet dark clothes and droplets glistening in his yanked-back hair. The hairstyle means I can gaze my fill of his high, strong cheekbones, as well as the bold line of his Olympian jaw. I know it's not right to be fixating on his magnificence when he's clearly rushed here with an urgent message, but I can't help my human side sometimes. And right now, despite his continuing gloom, I'm glad about it.

"Maximus," I prod. "Come on. You've got to tell me the rest. We're still partners in all this craziness, right?"

His head jerks up at last. "Of course." He's soothing about it now, likely speaking to the wobble at the end of my query. There's so much flowing from him. Unease. Uncertainty. A larger dread that hits as soon as our gazes lock again.

"Then you need to trust me here. I'm not going to break."

Another jolt hits him. Not as huge this time, but there's no mistaking the unease that flows from him along with it. "Circe…she used those same words," he explains. "She said…she couldn't stand the thought of breaking you." His eyes darken, intense to the point of indigo now. "And I don't think she was being figurative."

I make sure he sees the tender intent in my gaze. "And *I* think that we probably don't have the whole story about this."

His lips compress. "I know what I heard, Kara."

"And I'm not doubting that." I resecure our hands together. "But in the sala yesterday, there was a moment when I could've broken Circe, and she trusted that I wouldn't. I think she probably deserves the benefit of the doubt here."

That doesn't lighten the load on his composure. Nor do I expect it to. "What happened in the sala?"

"It was productive. I mean, if you consider levitating myself and two other certified witches by twelve feet as *productivity*."

His eyebrows jump. "Oh. I thought your floating fairy

thing in the grove was a first."

My cheeks get warm. "I'm sorry I didn't explain more. At least back then. To be honest, I'm hoping I can get that under control."

"Wait. You mean your ability to fly? And to invite others to do it too?"

"*Levitate*," I correct. "And it may only be a temporary thing."

He replies with a somber look. "I know you have a lot of respect for them. But you need to know one more thing. Hecate ended their little chat by reminding Circe that they were going to war."

"*War?*" I rear back, though continue to return his stare. "With whom? About what?"

Oddly, Maximus's mien is calmer. "If I knew, I'm not sure we'd still be sitting here."

Agitation pushes in, feverish and frantic, until I'm shoving aside the blankets and bounding to my feet. It's easy to pull out a long cotton dress from the closet and then tuck my feet into a pair of ballet flats. I don't bother brushing my hair before twisting it into a hasty ponytail.

"But sitting here isn't doing us any good either."

My tone brings another surge of surprise. Why do I sound like a steely spy heroine when I feel more like a frazzled female in peril? Somewhere between the two extremes is where I actually need to be. I work toward that composure goal while quickly washing my face.

"What are you thinking, little demon?"

I don't miss the undertone in his voice either. That

overcompensation of confidence in place of his stress.

"That there's a truth here we're not seeing or understanding. And the only way to get it is by asking Hecate herself."

"All right, then. I'm going with you."

In silent thanks, I frame his face between my hands and kiss him with meaning. "Along the way, maybe we'll figure out how to tell her you were...ermmm..."

"Lurking? Or, as the good girls say, *eavesdropping?*"

I chuckle. "I'm a good girl about as much as you are a serial snoop, Professor Kane."

He nods again, giving it twice as much conviction. "Which officially validates my concept about how we're going to handle this thing. The truth, all the way up front. I really was only going for coffee. I couldn't help it if the two of them decided to use the kitchen as their wicked plotting den at the exact same—"

I smack his chest. "And now it's time to grab your verbal editing pen, please."

He presses an earnest kiss on my forehead. "I'll keep it respectful."

Now I raise both my hands to the firm valley between his pectorals. "Promise?"

"Cross my heart, hope to—"

"Don't you dare finish that."

Because even in this cozy cottage, in this hidden valley, specters lurk too close in my mind. The writhing wraiths below my window in a dismal castle. The vengeful death in the eyes of the king who imprisoned me there.

The god who would've let his henchmen kill Maximus and then toss him into that eternal doom.

Will I ever be free of those haunting visions? That cold terror? Or was this Hades's plan all along, to make me fear every moment and every*one* in my life—even the goddess who freed me from his captivity?

No.

I refuse to accept that, the same way I send a silent promise to Maximus that I won't keep censoring all his dark-humored one-liners. Only for a little while longer. At least until we get to the sala—and determine what turned my commanding demigod into such a spooked, if unintentional, spy.

Once we uncover the misinterpreted messages, I'll let him hit me with every moody joke in his book. Perhaps a few about his own demise.

Because maybe, just for a few minutes, I won't keep dreading that Hades will rematerialize and make it a reality.

CHAPTER 12

MAXIMUS

MY RELIEF IS SIGNIFICANT when Hecate looks up like it's the first time she's seen me today.

"Look who's early for breaking their fasts." The goddess's gazillion bangles clink as she rises from her chair at a small table near the sala's back window. On the deck outside, a pair of hummingbirds taunt a trio of squirrels. Hecate seems oblivious to the wildlife turf battle, folding Kara and then me into affectionate embraces. "*Kalimera* to you both."

"Good morning to you too," I say.

The goddess flares her gaze and flashes a smile. "Ah! A man who knows his Greek. I hope you two were able to get some rest through the storm?"

"We did, thank you," Kara replies with a strangely mild smile. "And *philia mera* to you, Goddess."

I toss an awkward smile to them both. "That's nice too. I'm not sure I've ever heard those two words together."

Hecate gives a disconcerting little wave, as if

acknowledging but dismissing me at the same time. "But I'm sure you agree they're a perfect match, hmmm? *Philia*, meaning deep love that is shared by friends, and *mera* for the morning. It's the Iremia way of inviting energy and productivity into our days from the beginning."

Kara dips a compliant nod. "Mindfulness is the gateway to mind*full*ness."

"Oh, *yes*!" The goddess flows to her feet and cups Kara's shoulders. "My amazing learner!"

Thankfully, she's too enraptured to notice my discreet grunt. Less than a month ago, she was *my* remarkable student...

"All right, now. Pop quiz," Hecate teases. "Do you remember the rest?"

Kara has the grace to let a blush stain her cheeks. "I'm afraid I'm usually only good for the big sound bites."

"And that's fine too," Hecate soothes. "But it's good to be reminded. When we stay mindful beyond the usual pleasantries, which are often like gloss on the rock, we won't hide the essence of what and who we truly are."

"Okay." I say it slowly but amiably to make my interjection clear. "All of that does sound really good..."

"He means it," Kara rushes to say. "You do...right, Maximus? Daily rituals set our intentions for the day. The greeting is a lot like you getting out to the gym in the morning."

Hecate gasps. Not loudly, but with more than enough drama for her point. "Ohhh, sweet one. It's nothing like wasting time in one of those caveman pits."

As the goddess adds a subtle nostril wrinkle, I hide the angry flare of my own. Barely. Those *caveman pits* have been like therapy to Jesse and others like him. They're not for everyone, but some people choose deadlifts as therapy—and one thing I've learned from being a spot guy is that if someone thinks they're ready for more weight, it's useless to argue with them.

If Hecate's got her sights set on more weight than she can handle, what if Kara gets crushed during the inevitable drop?

I can't shake what the goddess and her first lieutenant said to each other, nearly in this spot, a half hour ago.

I cannot care if she is comfortable or not.

The idea of breaking her... I can't stand it...

Hecate, finally seeming to read the tense pause, clasps her hands and freshens her smile. "On to more interesting subjects!" she ventures. "Such as you two and this early morning surprise. Morgana's barely begun preparing breakfast. You have at least another hour to enjoy your pretty bedroom view."

Kara's still close enough that I feel her small squirms beneath her sketchy laugh.

"The bed is definitely comfortable," she concedes in a diplomatic murmur. "And we're grateful..."

"Excellent. That makes me so happy."

"It's been an...interesting...morning already," I say, firming my hand against Kara's.

Hecate's gaze is still dipped toward her tea, almost as if she's fixated on the curling steam over the china's Greek key pattern. "Has it, now?" She lifts an equally quixotic smile. "And we've barely completed the ...interesting ...repairs on your cottage from yesterday."

Her riff on my words isn't missed—by myself nor Kara. Though my woman manages a bashful giggle, I focus on making our handclasp into a stronghold. Demonstrating a deeper truth to her. *We're doing this together.*

"The cottage is fine," I state. "And if it weren't, I'd be capable of making the fixes myself. But we're not here to collect hardware supplies." I pivot, moving closer to the table. "We need to talk, Hecate. And this isn't light mealtime chatter."

That earns me a glance up from the tea steam. The goddess's light laughter is, I hope, the highest volume of sound this conversation will warrant.

Until Circe runs in like she's got fire on her heels.

"We have a breach!" she yells. "Northeast perimeter."

Hecate is drained by three skin tones in just as many seconds. "Morgana," she calls. "You are needed now."

But the summons is unnecessary. The tall enchantress, already shedding her kitchen apron, is already sprinting across the room. "What's happened?"

"The perimeter. We're breached."

"Are you sure?"

"Northeast perimeter," Hecate intones. "Investigate immediately. And thoroughly."

"Yes, Goddess."

With one downward sweep of an arm, Morgana leaves only a dusty silhouette to represent the spot in which she just stood.

The moment doesn't earn a second of my admiration—or even Kara's notice.

"What is it?" she demands, twisting her fingers against mine with hot anxiety. Sure enough, I turn to see twin bonfires rising in her wide eyes. "What's going on?"

"Not sure, sweet one." Hecate is a little less earth mother and much more mama tiger. She reaches and clutches Kara by the shoulders. "But keep your energies at one with your light. We will find out. Soon."

That might as well go down as prophecy. A few seconds later, the sala's main door flies open. In the doorway, a pair of figures are outlined by the sunlight that's now broken past the clouds outside.

All too swiftly, they gain form and features.

Faces that I've readily shoved to the back of my mind—and have had no intention of dredging back up for a long while.

Certainly not here. Certainly not like this.

"Kara." I jerk her close. "Get behind me."

Without hesitation, she obeys.

"We intend no harm," the man utters.

"You have to know how rich that is from your lousy mouth, Arden Prieto," I snarl.

The coal-eyed woman beside him speaks next. "We truly haven't come to stir up trouble."

Hecate moves up with a pair of gliding steps. "Words that are equally as nebulous from you, Veronica Valari."

"And I care more about a fabricated headline in the *Daily Spill*." Veronica hitches her hip with a sleek extension of a stilettoed boot. "Which provides great piddle paper for my dogs' crates and little else."

It would be stupid to assume that the demon mother of Hollywood would be close friends with the mage mama of Olympus. With so many veils lifted, I see that glaring truth.

Kara steps around from behind me. "Funny. That's not what you say to the *Spill*'s editor in chief when he visits every month."

The faintest blush creeps across the woman's cheekbones. "I do what I must to keep you kids in their good graces."

"Is that what this is? Getting some exclusive shots for tomorrow's splash page?"

Veronica's fresh expression is a strange combination of sad eyes and pursed lips. "Why are you going there, Kara? Is that any way to talk to me, after not checking in for nearly a week?"

"Because our last check-in ended so well?" Kara folds her arms. "With you ordering me to get lost so you could tear a new one into Gramps?"

"He was fine," she defends. "You've always looked at that man with rose-colored glasses."

"Better than refusing to look at him at all."

Veronica rocks back on a heel, though her mien isn't from verbal bruising. It's a semicasual move, as if she's heard the line a hundred times before. But her expression is a stark contrast. Her seriousness has surpassed stealth and arrived at full gravity.

"I didn't come here to argue either, okay?"

Kara nods, accepting that much—but nothing beyond.

"So what do you want, Mother?"

Veronica swivels with the precision of a trained dancer. It's impossible not to assume the move is planned, seeing how perfectly it flares the tails of her tailored brocade jacket. "To see you, of course."

"Well, here I am." Kara flicks up an impatient arm. "Satisfied?"

Veronica balls up her hands as if physically forcing herself back. Her tension is obvious. "Are you okay?"

Circe scoffs. "We're not forcing her to scrub the hearth and pluck the chickens, if that's what you're implying."

Veronica goes on as if nothing but a silent beat has fleeted by. "I left for an afternoon at the spa, and then the whole city went Mad Hatter without the good tea. When I got home, it was no better. At first I thought Jaden had thrown one of his afternoon fiestas for the boys, but the tequila wasn't touched. And the pool looked like lava. And Dalton was nowhere to be found!"

Kara shakes her head. Only once, but that's enough. "Don't light any candles for Dalton, Mother. And if he comes back, kill him."

A hard pair of blinks from Veronica. "You cannot be—"

There's a sound like breaking glass in the air. A glittering silhouette is again filled in by Morgana, her stance braced for battle. She grimaces as her focus lands on Veronica and Arden. At the same time, she resheaths her sword with a brutal *shink.* "Oh, bloody *hell.*"

"Mistress le Fay." Arden eyes her up and down with an inscrutable expression. His silken croon is easier to figure out. "What a not-so-surprising turn of the cosmos. How have you been?"

"Bugger off."

Veronica rushes forward. "We have to talk, Kara. This just can't wait. Can we go somewhere more…private? Please?"

I'm about to suggest that might be a good idea, when Kara speaks again. "Whatever you have to say to me is all right to voice with my sisters."

Now Veronica clenches back a grimace. I almost join her. *Sisters?* Two minutes ago, they were all just *deep friends*. I'm not fond of the closed-off look that my woman wields in return, even if it's lasered solely on her mother.

"You have an actual sister," Mama Valari says. "You remember *her*, right? And right now   "

Hecate flows both hands in the air as if preparing to conduct the LA Philharmonic through a gentle concerto. "As you've eloquently stated, Veronica, these are not times to stir negative vibrations. Surely we can get to the point without italicized accusations."

"Exactly," Kara says. "Do you seriously think I haven't thought about Kell a thousand times since we left?"

"How would I know that when you've been hiding away here?"

"For a higher purpose," Kara insists. "Hecate is helping to enlighten my abilities. Circe too. And they're doing it without secrets or flowcharts or half a thought about likes, engagement, and followers. On the other hand, I'm sure you already know how many bars your phone *isn't* getting out here."

Veronica gives up a heavy huff. "Circe. Hecate." She carves nods to both. "I see you and *all* your magnificent powers, all right? Is a minute with my daughter too much to ask on top of that?"

Kara clears her throat. Steps clear of me by another half step. Circe already moves to back her up.

"You've already been here for five, Ms. Valari."

If there's a supernatural version of a red-level smog alert, Veronica's ire just took us there. But her daughter's deliberate decorum has stirred other things into that mix and then painted it across the woman's face. Pain. Disappointment. And, surprisingly ... despair.

"Kara." Arden surges forward as Mama Valari's weird but adamant wingman. "Listen to me, damn it. You haven't exactly been on a pleasure cruise lately, which is why I've given you a pause of patience here."

I spread my fingers and splay them hard against the scarf tucked into his shirt. "You'd be best served to take a breath and find that rare gem called your manners."

"Do *not* interfere, Kane. Not now."

"Already have. And always will."

"Stop," Kara pleads. "What's so urgent?" she demands to Arden. "Have you heard something? From the underworld?"

Before he can utter a word, Hecate steps forward and swooshes out both hands.

"Enough," the goddess intones. "Can't you see that she's already worn out? The trauma she's been through—"

"Which could have been easily prevented," Arden snaps before a force whips him up and away from me like a hurricane gale. Five feet up. Twenty feet back. A *whack* on the wall and a shudder of the windows.

Kara and Circe gasp. I tilt a thankful grin toward Hecate, but she doesn't acknowledge me. The full brunt of her stare, as violent as a thousand daggers in the sun, cuts into Arden.

"I. Said. Enough."

"And *I* say put him down." The venom in Veronica's reprisal is unmistakable.

With a *whunk* that makes us all grimace, Arden drops to the sala's wood floor. To his credit, he springs back to his feet and into a fighting stance. But not for long. He's pulled backward as soon as Veronica stalks forward and hooks an elbow through one of his.

"Arden," she murmurs. "Let's go."

Arden's face mottles to a crazy shade of dark red. "We can't just—"

"We must and we will. There's still a little more time. We'll simply have to use it wisely."

Her words prompt new stress across Kara's features. "Still more time? For what?"

Veronica snaps back with such severity, I yank Kara in again. But the violence of her voice has turned into something else across her face. From her dark eyes to her corded neck, there's nothing but sorrow. A desperation she pummels into Kara now.

"All I ever wanted, and fought for, was for you, Jaden, and Kell." Air skitters in and out of her trembling lips. "I don't expect you to believe that. Not without the chance to fully explain. But if I have to do it this time without your approval, I will."

In any other time and place, I'd be stomping forward after a heavy eye roll. The theater is classic Veronica, accusation and evasion in a tidy trio of sentences. But I'm witnessing her despair in living colors and textures, from the stiff battlements of her shoulders down the coiled length of her form.

And now, in how her energy takes over Kara too. My little demon is a solid ball of empathetic anxiety and fear. So much fear.

"Mother. Just tell me what on earth you're talk—"

But while she struggles to stammer out the words, Veronica grabs Arden and sprints from the room, almost as if they've been given a cosmic triple-speed button.

Hecate's command for pursuit is also too late. We all rush outside, but neither of them is to be seen. Seemingly turned to mist and then carried off by the wind.

The only proof of their disruption is the disgustingly long list of questions at the forefront of my mind. And, judging by her nonstop shivers, in Kara's.

On the sala's porch, I pull her close. Tenderly, I tuck her head against my shoulder and her small body into my larger shelter. But she refuses to release her tension. I feel it in the balls of her fists in my chest and in every clenched vertebra down her back.

"What did she mean?" she grates. "And why did she even do this? And say all those things? But then withhold so much more? What's she getting at—and what the *hell* does she want from *me*?"

"Because it's her MO." Hecate paces over to us, cloaked

in more of her don't-bump-the-chakras solemnity. But right now, I welcome every thread of it. "You know this, Kara. And *I've* known it since the day I first met your mother, many years ago."

Kara swings her head around. "You...already know her?"

"Define *knowing*," the goddess returns. "We have definitely met, if that's what you want to know. Giovani reached out to me once the girl reached her unruly years, hoping I could help with recentering her wild thoughts and ways."

I nod, hoping to convey commiseration. At the same time, Circe cocks a hip and glowers.

"There's a really good reason why I opted not to teach middle school."

Hecate scrunches her nose too. "Middle school? The girl was five."

Kara responds with a tired laugh. "Of course she was."

"Kara needs rest," Circe says gently. "Take her back to your cottage, Maximus. I'll have Morgana make up a breakfast tray for you two." She pauses and looks pointedly to Hecate for her conclusion. "Morning enlightenment will have to wait."

After mumbling a fast thanks, I take Kara's hand and lead her out of the sala before the goddess and the enchantress end their truce in front of us.

More worrisome, though, is whatever Veronica was alluding to while rebuking Arden.

There's still time.

I don't admit it to Kara, but my curiosity presses as direly as hers. Still time for what? And why did Veronica feel so skittish about revealing it in front of Hecate and Circe? Not that either was ready to roll out the welcome mat and tea tray.

I harbor another concern too. One that feels more critical.

For all Hecate's promises of our safety, Arden and Veronica were able to breach her perimeter with seemingly few issues. What's keeping anyone else from doing the same?

For the immediate moment, I have to focus on the stuff I *can* control. My ability to get Kara back in bed and healing. There I can sprawl next to her and hold her as close as I physically can, though nothing will take the place of her nearness in my spirit.

Because she's every better part of both.

CHAPTER 13

Kara

"OH, NO. *SERIOUSLY?*"

I'm not so much irritated as embarrassed when Maximus decides to carry me up the boardwalk toward the cottages. The swoony applause parade begins with Kiama and Liseli at the barn and then continues when we near Aradia's porch. The cheering Italian even rouses her three snoozing cats to witness her enthusiasm for Maximus's chivalry.

"Hey." I kick my legs, hoping to look playful instead of spiteful. "I'm tired, not incapacitated. I can make it the rest of the way on my own."

"And make me a liar to Circe?" As he glances down, one of his eyebrows shoots up. "I promised her I'd take care of you to the fullest, remember?"

I narrow my eyes. "Those weren't the exact words."

"Same theme." He cocks his head. "Come now, Miss Valari. You've been my student long enough to understand the importance of themes."

I dig fingers into his beard while tossing a deliberately feisty look. "How about the one where the professor uses fancy literary talk to evade the subject?"

He chuckles while picking up his pace. "Oh, I remember every syllable of the subject. Just like you're going to get every second of the rest you need."

I want to banter back again—even a few seconds of feeling like a normal couple, having a normal tease of a disagreement, is so nice—but we're already back at the cottage, where I have to remember that the eaves are still dripping from a storm that he could've created. And that I could've flown us into a nearby tree to watch the weather unfold.

Maybe I should've done just that. This morning's ordeal continues to bully my nerves, even as Maximus marches me into the bedroom and lowers me into the luxurious linens. Mother and Arden's sudden arrival was no doubt as unsettling to everyone else as it was to me.

I replay every second of their visit in my head.

"All right. So what was all that?" I twist my lips and shake my head. "Clearly, canyon spring water isn't the only thing that's passed under the bridges around here."

An alluring curl takes over Maximus's mouth too. "Something way past the plot of Circe's little story."

"She's a Titan, right? That's a life span nearly as long as a goddess. So in all that time, she never once had to deal with a bratty little kid?" I shake my head. "Mother doesn't even have any powers, unless you count the ability to play the press like a fiddle, so that should have made things even easier."

"There are definitely puzzle pieces that haven't come out of this box yet. From both sides of the battlefield."

He treads carefully over that last part, as if wondering how I'll accept it, but a revelation moves me to surprise both of us.

"Battlefield indeed..." Suddenly, my chest pumps hard. I douse his deeper frown with my jolt of comprehension. "And battlefields...belong in *wars*. And sometimes, wars pit even close friends against each other."

Thoughtful furrows press over his eyebrows. "You think Hecate had some kind of premonition about your mom being on approach?"

"I wouldn't write it off." I've only known the goddess for two days, but her perceptive abilities are nearly an enchantment of their own. "Maybe not a full-blown vision, but she probably sensed it. Maybe she wasn't sure about the timing and didn't want to scare everyone prematurely. But grabbing Circe for an early augury would make complete sense."

"And they locked horns about what the game plan would be?"

I study the faraway glint in his gaze. "It doesn't look like you're buying that theory."

"Probably because I don't."

"Why?"

"No idea. But I'll work on getting over it while you sleep. Sometimes you have to stand back from a puzzle to stop obsessing the minor grooves."

I scoot down and nestle deeper beneath the cloud of covers. I know he's going to attempt just that. He's not letting go of something here—some strange perception of what he saw earlier in the sala or the mystery beneath Iremia's own War of the Roses.

All the things we still can't see…

I want to tell myself that the same thoughts don't hammer at me. Whatever history exists between my mother and the witches should probably stay shrouded by the past. Poking the veil will only lead to things I don't want to know, about people I want to keep on trusting.

People who don't try to tie me back down. Who tell me I'm a diamond.

"A…diamond…"

Why does it sound so different out loud? Like I haven't had a sip of water in days? Worse, that my brain is crash-landing back to reality.

Or maybe just consciousness.

Oh, wow. How long have I been asleep?

"Good afternoon, beautiful."

I look across the room, to the big easy chair in which Maximus has camped himself with a book. Sure enough, beams of September sun slant in through the panes, giving away the midday time frame. There's a mild breeze that flickers the rays across his head, turning his hair into a gemlike collision of tawny colors.

I prop my cheek on a pillow and hitch my shoulder into the sultry move. "Well, *now* it's good."

He closes his book with a frown, and again my stomach flips in all the good ways. The look reminds me of simpler days in his lecture hall, when a random student's question would inspire him to deeper levels of contemplation. Usually that random student was me, which made those moments even sweeter to savor.

It all feels like so long ago. And I want it back so badly.

"You sure?" he finally murmurs. "You were talking in your sleep."

"Oh?" Somehow I avoid blushing to my roots. "Ermmm...what was I babbling about?"

"I think you're more worried about Kell than you're willing to admit."

That takes care of stressing about a blush. Instead, I push against the pillows until I'm upright. "Oh, I'm fully willing to admit it."

He cants his head, still thoughtful. "Your mom said she was okay."

"Yes, she did. With Arden by her side." I roll to my feet and cross toward him. "When he's around, *okay* turns relative."

"Solid point. But I don't want you wearing yourself out again. And you'll do that by worrying about it."

I don't resist as he leans forward, hooking an arm around my waist to pull me from my stressed pace. After another little pull, I land gently in his lap. The chair is roomy enough for both of us, so it's not a hardship to settle in.

"Okay." I sigh as he combs those addictingly long fingers through my sleep-mussed hair. "But I also think you're trying to distract me."

His chuckle rolls across his chest, sending warm vibrations into the cheek I rest there. And that's it. Whatever lies beyond addiction, I'm there. I'd sign away my rights to every vice on the planet just to keep this one. The refuge of his body. The strength in his touch. The connection to his heart, and even deeper places.

"You know I don't need to resort to that," he murmurs into my forehead. "Exhaustion is just going to dull our blades. If we're going to unravel this knot, rest will be our best sharpening stone."

I drum light fingers across his chest. "Says the guy who's done nothing but catnap since we got here?"

He taps at his book while tucking me closer. "Rejuvenation comes in many forms."

He feeds my soul without trying. And gets even sexier when lowering his finger to stroke the book's spine as gently as he would an open rose. I glance over, trying to discern the title, but that part is blocked to perfection by the angle of his arm.

"What's been your literary recharge today?" I grin, basking in the adoring look he's already sending back.

I get it from his spirit before I see it across his face. He scoops up his book and pokes in a finger at his bookmarked place. Smooth move, but not near the enthralling grace once he shifts his hand to easily brace the tome, exposing one of my favorite sights in the whole world. Words on pages. Perfect gateways to a different world.

Maximus gets it. I knew it before, but the new sparks in his energy are impossible to ignore. My spirit is drawn to them like a child to fireflies, only with deeper wonder. Expanded awe.

Feelings that only get better after he clears his throat and begins to read.

" 'It was much pleasanter at home,' thought poor Alice, 'when one wasn't always growing larger and smaller, and being ordered about by mice and rabbits. I almost wish I hadn't gone down that rabbit-hole—and yet—and yet—it's rather curious, you know, this sort of life!'"

"Well. Curious indeed," I murmur into his next respite. "Just like me, wondering how you possibly picked Alice Liddell's adventures as the afternoon read."

"And just like me, marveling again at your ocean of literary trivia."

My laugh is brief. "Not an ocean. More like a big pond, especially when the book is one I'm passionate about."

His hum is thick with contemplation. "This one? About Alice's crazy tumble into Wonderland? So how many times have you castigated your younger self for *that* pick of a prophecy?"

I answer with a fast shrug. "The story itself is relevant for a lot, if not most, young women. The symbols themselves are filled with pastel romanticism, yet express greater meanings with safe prose."

Maximus beams a broad smile. "Don't tell me you were developing all these insights at the age of ten or eleven."

"No. Those were developed for a sophomore-year paper—for which I got an A, thank you very much. But when I first read the books as a girl, I was less captivated by the story than the real-life Alice who inspired them."

"The reason her name rolled out of you so easily."

I get more comfortable in his hold. It exposes my form

to newer parts of his, and the fresh warmth spreads into my very marrow. He's the cocoon I always need. My embrace of spirit as well as body.

"Alice Liddell was an interesting person before being channeled into the famous Wonderland girl by Charles Dodgson."

"Who published as Lewis Carroll by translating his first and middle name into Latin and then back into English and then reversing them."

I pat his chest playfully. "Now look who's making waves in the trivia ocean."

"Not my first ride down the rabbit hole either. If I remember right, Liddell grew up in … Oxford. That's where her father was the dean at Christ Church, right?"

"And her mother was the prototype of type A overplanners," I supply as dryly as I can.

"Something you can't relate to at all," he deadpans.

"Even more so when I was little. Reading Alice's biography was more captivating than the story she inspired. To escape her mother's obsession about social skills and refined arts, she and her sisters would elude their governess by hiding in the garden."

"A lot like you did with going to Gio's place."

"You catch on fast."

"So was Alice also promised to a pretentious incubus?"

I allow a smile to underline my ready answer. "Not directly, though she grew up to be a beautiful and refined woman and was expected to marry well. Consequently, she almost became a princess."

"Almost?"

I tilt my head back and my gaze up. He's just as responsive, ready with his encouraging eyes and full smile.

"She had a close friendship with Prince Leopold, one of Victoria and Albert's sons," I murmur. "Many think they were passionately in love, but the queen forbade a lasting union. Leopold was ordered to marry a princess instead."

His face gains new tension. A rough rumble rolls in his throat. "Harsh."

I nod, which works my chin into the soft cotton of his shirt. "It astounded me, reading that part. I was stunned to be so moved by the story of a woman I never knew, who was long dead. Looking back, that was probably my gateway drug to the power of great stories, fictional or not." I bite my lip and glance down. "After that, I paid one of our maids to smuggle any kind of romance to me."

There's another low vibration from his chest as he lightly strokes my nape. "That's my girl."

I reach up and squeeze his neck too. "Ohhh no. Hold up there, teacher. I'm not talking Austen, Brontë, Tolstoy, and Gabaldon. I held out for the good stuff, like Jackie Collins and Danielle Steel."

His brows scrunch low. "How old were you?"

I shrug. "Their characters were my versions of Cinderella and Rapunzel. They fought the odds in situations I could relate to. And just like them, I grew up and found my perfectly modern prince."

Nothing about his reaction is a surprise. But I'm ready for his sheepish tension and push in closer to emphasize my point. Fighting to fit as much of my body along his as I can.

"It's true, Maximus. Beyond true. You're my templar and my troubadour…my savior. You believed in our love even when I mourned that we'd never have it again." I slide my other hand up, spreading my fingers into the rugged landscape of his jaw. "You believed and you fought…and you loved deeply enough for us both. For that, and so many other amazing reasons, I'll never stop loving you."

There's only one way to seal the point into him, and I'm beyond willing to offer it. With a kiss that's as boundless as everything I feel for him and know about us. As our lips mash, I enforce it with my devoted moan. As our mouths part, I expose it with the matching doors of my heart. As our tongues collide, I imagine every drop of my passion as indelible ink, writing my truth across the beautiful sheafs in his soul.

I see the pages now in the depths of his stare as we break apart to catch our breath. And for him to arrest me with the fresh message that he readies, wrapped in the waves of feeling that flow from him. Devotion. Passion. Need.

Love.

"Show me," he grates out at last. "Show it to me now, little demon. All your love…in all our favorite ways."

CHAPTER 14

MAXIMUS

IT'S ALL THE GO-AHEAD Kara needs.

And every cell of my being is so grateful.

She's eager and invigorated, as if offering her guilty reading secrets has granted a passport to other parts of her too. Parts she's been hesitant to reveal...or perhaps hasn't looked at herself yet. Passionate parts. *Audacious* parts...

My pulse rate hardly recovers from her brazen grabs at my groin before she's unzipped me down there. She reaches in and pulls me out.

And strokes until I'm fully swollen.

Strained sounds spill out of me, low but high, needy but seductive. The whole world quickens but slows. I'm caught between consciousness and oblivion. It's complete heaven.

"*Kara.*" I drop Alice and her adventures—I have no choice—as my body slips in the big chair until I'm nearly prone. "Christ. Oh, Kara."

And then I'm as wordless as I am motionless, my arms locked around her torso and my legs braced beneath the thighs she straddles over mine. But she's still maneuvering in a way to keep rubbing me. Pumping me. And then squeezing me.

Right…where…it…matters.

"Good?" she whispers, her fervency another caress of its own.

I can do nothing but nod, but even that's like telling myself to hold back the tide.

"I love you so much, Maximus."

My head rocks back and my eyes slide shut as my mind absorbs the aural alchemy of her words. I feel them in other places too, like a wave pulled toward its destined shore. It moves me to depths just as deep and inexorable, an ocean tied to the cosmos itself. The most natural and incredible progression of all. Our primal needs. Our perfect connection.

"Then show me more," I finally manage to rasp. "All of it, Kara. In the best way possible."

Her happy hum betrays her blissful compliance. The sound intensifies, flowing from her lips to my ear, as she strips away her panties and then repositions herself.

In one gorgeously graceful move, she guides her slick heat around my demanding cock.

"Fuck." It escapes me again, riding the crest of a desperate husk. But my vocal cords aren't any good for forming anything better, especially as her body clamps mine tighter.

Tighter…

My breath stammers out of me. My lungs pump hard, struggling for sustenance. An impossible ask. Already I understand...this is more than a simple exchange of pleasure. This is about worshipping her spirit. Exalting her body. Seeing every inch of her heart and treasuring it as the gift it is.

Kara. My breathtaking demon angel. She's around me but inside me, her physical grip only half of what she's done to my mind and heart. The places inside, light and dark, that beg to be seen in full by her. Accepted by her.

Released by her...

As soon as the thought gongs my brain, my whole body jerks. I almost withdraw all the way from her. This wild temptation...it's part of a beast I've barely seen, let alone accepted. It comes with shadows I've ignored most of my life. That I've forced myself to mask from everyone, including myself, to the point that they terrify me.

"Maximus. My love."

At first her voice is another aroused sigh. But my trepidation takes care of that fast enough. She acknowledges it by hitching back an inch.

"Hey. Are you all right?"

I answer her with another extended moan. But it's not without conflict. The complete contrary. "My God," I mutter, before pushing volume into a command. "Say it again." I delve a hand into her hair. So undone and untamed, just how I love it.

The corners of her mouth curl out, an alluring start to her full smile. "Maximus...my love."

Her breath caresses the syllables across my bottom lip. I let my head fall back. "You do things to me," I confess in a croak. "Things that aren't always sane. Or safe."

A small, tight sound reverberates up her throat. And then, hesitating as if she's trying another language … "Safe."

I dip my head and reopen my gaze. She's waiting for me with a huge, seeking stare—and I already know it's because she's feeling me too. All my conflict. The vacillation between staying proper but being primitive. Between feeling so exposed by her—and recognizing every zap of the arousal it brings to me.

"Who says you have to be safe?" She tilts her head, twitching her lips again. "Or even sane?"

It's not the sexy gist of her challenge. It's not even the raspy threads that take over her voice as she does.

She undoes me with the new expression on her stunning face.

The look even she doesn't look ready for, like a novice lion tamer with her little stick and chair, facing her unpredictable beast for the first time.

The beast who now tremors beneath her. Clenching and growling…and wondering how long he'll last until he shatters.

And then digs his teeth into her.

It's another thought I should be shoving away. Another impulse I should be ordering into submission. But the smile she continues to wield—holy hell, that tremulous but marvelous smile—pulls on me hard.

Nearly as ruthless as the matching yank I give to her hair.

"*Unnnnhhh*," she groans out, her head jerking back from the force of my clamp. I've caused her pain, which should be causing me a thousand stabs of shame, but the ecstasy on her face is too riveting. Too addicting.

I want more.

And I demand it at once.

Pulling harder. Growling deeper.

"Oh!" Kara gasps out. "Maximus. *Yesss*."

I reach up and splay my other hand along her hip. But also *into* it, securing my hold with ruthless authority before pushing her back down onto my arousal. Then again. Once more. Each time, our flesh smacks louder. Air bursts off her lips with greater force.

When those explosions are accompanied by high-pitched whines, I compel myself to ease the pace. Except my nervous system is lit up like the 110 during Friday rush hour. But I do it for her. "Am I hurting you?"

And here she comes again, with those gorgeous little gasps. With that alluring little smile. And, more bewitching than both, the perfect clenches of her core. As if she's gripping me with more than her physical walls.

As if she's pinning my soul to the center of hers.

A surety that sinks in as soon as her big, sultry browns lock on to me again.

"My beautiful man..." she murmurs. "Isn't that the idea?"

Her soft challenge brings a rush of comprehension—along with the heat that replaces the stings where she yanks my beard. They're the same sensation in different forms.

Blasts of heat and awareness. A flaring matchstick to my heartbeat, turning the area into a carnal burn zone.

Could this be what she wants me to give her? To show her?

And to show me in return...

That to her eyes, I'm not a beast. Even when my claws are out and my teeth are bared.

I still don't believe it, not in full—but I'm willing to test it. And I do, by yanking at her hair again. By sucking in the vibrations of her answering moan by leaning up and actually biting her. By savoring the warmth along her carotid and her pulse beneath my tongue. By letting her feel what it all does to my own body, quickening and throbbing along with hers.

The instincts rise higher as she ropes her arms around my neck. But as soon as she bites me in return, they're something more.

So primitive, as she nibbles at the flesh of my ear.

So heated, as she scores her way down my neck.

But then, as she makes her way to the center of my chest, something beyond definition. Beyond comprehension.

As her mouth settles in the space over my heart, I give into it in full. By using all the places we're anchored to swiftly flip us over. I topple us both to the floor but hardly care, especially when I see that Kara doesn't. Her hands and mouth explore me with more ravenous intent. She's gouging my shoulders and champing my chest, even through my cotton shirt—until, after a frustrated moan, she moves her hands down and tears the thing down the middle.

At once, an appreciative rumble moves through my chest. The sight of her flexing muscles has my erection doing the same. Such blissful demand. Swollen authority. Pounding insistence.

Until that imperial march makes its way into my brain. And takes over.

"Do it again," I order in a commanding grate. "Only with *your* shirt."

She bites her lip and obeys the order, allowing my gaze to absorb the perfection of her exposed chest. Her creamy flesh and erect nipples ...

Holy shit.

I'm no normal animal anymore. I'm a ravenous one.

I drop my head, teeth and tongue at the ready. I dig in, sucking hard and licking long. My groan is wet and hot against her skin. Her cry is high and lusty against my neck. At once, my blood is recalibrated to the rhythm of her pantings.

Yes. *Yes.*

It's so damn fierce. It's so fucking good.

Through the smoke of my senses, I hear my lips slurring out similar words. Everything below my neck is a taut, torrid wire of tension. A coil of blinding light, climbing a spire of cruel need. A beast that's given in. An animal that needs to conquer.

Except *she's* already vanquished *me*. Everything I am and every move I make is hers to claim. Every brutal thrust. Every lunge that scoots us farther across the floor. Every drive that eventually takes us to the foot of the bed, where my sweat-drenched demon throws her arms up and grabs a support foot before throwing her head back in a joyous scream.

A bellow moves through me as her shivers surround me. It's electric thunder in my throat and pure lightning on my lips. It bursts into the air as my body empties into hers ... and a bridge of pure energy joins my soul to hers.

And I feel all of her. I *see* all of her in the fires that are crackling to so many depths of her incredible eyes.

Incredible. Incandescent. A brilliant culmination of all her yesterdays, leading into a bright path of all her tomorrows.

Our tomorrows.

I know it as fact, as thoroughly as I acknowledge the force that's still spilling from my center. The heart of my beast, hers to tame forever. The essence of my life, hers to hold for all time.

I'm lost in the magic of the admissions, hoping that this layered maze has no findable exit door.

But all too soon, someone's hauling that hatch wide open.

This time, it's an actual door. Somebody's opening the big wood thing that leads in from the cottage's front porch, with its discernible weight and Zen chime door decoration.

"Hello inside? Anyone up and about?" The cheery call is followed by puzzled mutterings.

"It's Morgana," Kara whispers. "Oh, no. She must've brought breakfast earlier too."

"All right now?" the witch calls again.

"Uh ...yeah!" I croak-shout in return. "Just a minute!"

Kara breaks into a fresh giggle as I stand to stuff myself

back into my jeans. After one more moment for a couple of calming breaths, I'm relieved to learn my legs still function. Though I'm only capable of Frankenstein steps, I manage my way to the main room. On the way, I take care of yanking my hair into a sloppy half bun.

My hands drop fast as soon as I open the door and behold the huge tray the woman on the porch is hoisting.

"Morgana. Hello. Wow, look at all this. You really didn't need to walk up here with—"

"Nonsense." The woman rolls her shoulders and waves a dismissive hand. "When you two didn't come 'round at lunch, I thought it best to save a new platter and bring up the victuals."

"Only to walk in and see we didn't touch the breakfast platter either," Kara returns while entering behind me. "That's on me, Morgana. I'm so sorry. I was more tired than I assumed. So once we got back here—"

"Hush," Morgana injects with firm force. "Everything is right as rain, got it? You've been dragged through one trial after the next. It's astounding you're up and about at all. Honestly, if Hecate wasn't insisting so much that—"

"What? Morgana? *What* is she insisting?"

I'm the one punching it out first, though it's a relief to see I've probably beat Kara by only a few seconds. Her features sharpen with the same demand underlining my voice. Is she hearing and seeing what I do now? That some edges of the Iremia fabric aren't stitching together?

The witch fiddles with a long brown curl that's broken free from her kitchen kerchief. "Oh, *bugger*. I . . . uh . . . I think

I've already said too much."

I stalk forward, not ready to let her back off, but Kara hooks an unnaturally strong grip around my elbow. The shake of her head is just as adamant. For a second, past all the ferocity, I glimpse something else in her reaction.

Is she ... afraid?

Why?

"So, if either of you need anything else, just head to the sala. One of us will be happy to assist."

Morgana doesn't let a second pass after her offer. While she leaves with dedicated speed, loaded breakfast tray and all, Kara and I remain in place.

Once the tall sorceress is gone, my little demon releases my elbow. But her stance remains tense. I don't tell her about the relief beneath my observation. She probably already knows. Though clearly the machinations of her brain have taken precedence for the time being.

She nibbles at a nail while pacing across the living room. After crisscrossing in front of the hearth, she settles onto a couch arm with a frustrated frown.

"Okay, maybe something *isn't* adding up around here."

I stay where I'm at. My growling stomach wants to see what's on the lunch spread, but my mind overwrites it, too obsessed with the unsettled glints in her gaze. "I wish I was glad you finally said it."

She looks ready to chew her thumb again but instead pushes tight knuckles against her chin. "Still, not adding up doesn't mean that the numbers are bad. I'm sticking with my first point. I really don't think we have the full story yet."

There's fresh tautness across my forehead. "And you still want that? Even after the little pop-by from your mom and Arden?"

"Especially after that."

Her reply isn't a breezy one. My mention of Arden is as crappy for her as it is me. We both hate that he remains entangled with her family, but there's no changing that. There won't ever be.

"So what's our plan?" My nonstop attention pays off when I see one brewing behind her beautiful eyes. "A second try with Hecate?"

She shakes her head. "Now that everything you said is connecting more dots, I think Circe is our wiser choice."

"You don't think she'll try to walk us around it, like Morgana?"

"She might. But we don't know until we try." She rises and starts a direct path back to the bedroom. "They've all probably dispersed from lunch. Let's go now. Maybe if we catch her alone, she'll tell us the truth."

I nod but keep more ruminations to myself—along with the deep hope that the truth doesn't send us too far off course.

*✳

Fifteen minutes later, we're both dressed decently for semipublic view and heading out of the cottage toward the sala. Or so I originally think. A few steps clear of the front porch, Kara veers off to the left. Though I let her lead, it's with a confused grunt.

"Circe might be in her cottage right now," she explains. "After meals, Hecate likes to take a walk by herself. Additionally, a couple of little birdies told me that Circe's addicted to *Hathaway Harbor*." She halts for half a second. "Sorry. I shouldn't assume you know what that is."

I toss back a smirk. "I teach college, beautiful. I know every daytime drama there is, including the important plot points and broadcast times."

"Oh really?" Kara rolls her eyes.

"But by now, I might be a little behind plotwise. I wonder if Ilsa finally told Chase how she feels. Or has he dragged her off to the yacht and gotten it out of her in other ways?"

"Oh my God. I don't know whether to be impressed or scared."

"Well, if Circe's on as many pins and needles about Ilsa and Chase as all the freshmen who use them for comparison papers, there's a good chance we'll find her glued to a monitor of some sort."

But best of all, we'll find the enchantress away from Hecate.

The conclusion is far from vilification. It's obvious that Hecate cares for every one of her diamonds, especially Kara. Her maternal affection is what Kara's needed for years. But I can't ignore everything I've seen and heard since this morning's weirdness, given the deeper layers yet to be revealed by Veronica and Arden's intrusion.

I can't help recalling the event as we walk through the dry leaves and grasses beneath stately oaks and eucalyptuses.

It's not the first time I've gotten the mental knock, and I'm certain it won't be the last. Still, I push it far enough aside for some appreciation of our surroundings. Sunlight peeks through the branches in golden intervals, and there's plenty of aviary chatter over our heads. The air is clean and camphorous. It's hardly a spooky scene at all, so I blame my skittering nerves on the memories refusing to stick to the sidelines.

That has to be it...

So why do I continue to feel worse than weird?

"Hey." I add some deep stares beneath low-hanging branches. "You positive this is the shortcut to Circe's?"

Kara turns a matching scrutiny at me. "She showed it to me herself last night after dinner. Everyone uses it to skirt around to each other's place. There's even a small path here. They just decided not to put boards over it so the wilderness remained pristine. But look. You see it, right? Hey... Maximus? What's wrong?"

"Stay close," I order on top of her last query.

As I wrap her close, she startles against my chest. I'd feel vindicated about the moment, an affirmation that I'm not losing my mind, but the jump of her nerves just shoves my own higher. "You're right. What's happ—"

I yank her in tighter, wishing I could become her flesh and blood silo as soon as an oaky shadow starts to shimmer. The changing light reminds me of Morgana's teleportation display from this morning, only it's not the sorceress taking form on the air this time.

Our new guest is taller. It possesses two long, regal arms

and braced masculine legs. A torso that's proud but not broad. A confidence so palpable, it borders on intimidating...

Until it paces fully into the clearing.

"What are you doing here, Prieto?" I call out.

The incubus rolls his head with measured arrogance. I lurch forward, positioning as much of myself between Kara and him as possible. All the better for him to note that I'm not going to surrender my scrutiny anytime soon.

"If you think I jumped through the hoops of sneaking away from Veronica and then returned to Camp Witchy-Woo in my good Ferragamos just to roast marshmallows and bead bracelets, I'm terribly sorry to disappoint."

I expel heavy air. "Get to your point."

Kara cups my forearm, inserting calmer energy into our fray. "To be clear, we're not breaking out the marshmallows, Arden. So why are you here again? Is it that dire?"

I steel myself for more pompous posturing from her once-betrothed. But I'm more tense when he's got nothing for Kara but a somber stare.

"*Dire* is an outstanding way to say it." He finishes by drawing a measured breath. Along with the slow release, he fixes his eyes on Kara. His features, as patrician as his cashmere sweater and pleated khakis, have completed their steady turn into somberness. "It's Kell..."

Before he finishes, Kara's knees buckle. I keep her upright until the wave of anxiety passes. "I knew it," she says. "I *felt* it when Mother wouldn't let herself finish any of those sentences."

"But Hecate cut her off too."

I don't like that I'm the one to mention it. Even more, I hate that Arden's supporting it with an emphatic nod.

"Hecate was so set on derailing the subject, I've started to wonder if she had something to do with the whole thing."

"The whole thing?" Kara demands. "As in what?"

Arden's expression only changes in one way. His frown is tighter. His posture is stiffer. His nod is more defined.

Troublingly so.

"Kell's in trouble. And Jaden too."

"Wh-What do you mean?" Kara blurts.

"I mean that your sweet siblings are *not* in a sweet situation—and at this point, you might be the only one who can help them."

CHAPTER 15

MAXIMUS TIGHTENS HIS BIG hands at my waist, but I don't sag into him this time. Sagging isn't an option now. Peace, solitude, even enlightenment...all no longer on the activities calendar. That truth is evident in every corner of Arden's gaze. In the zero-bullshit timbre of his voice.

In the warning that he's gone through a lot of effort to relay. Yes, behind Mother's back.

But why?

I don't waste time on the pretense that he's in it for noble concerns. So what else? What's he gaining from this?

Arden's eyes narrow as if the skeptic in my soul has escaped into the air. If it has, in some arcane way, I don't care.

"Arden, please. If you came here to do the obtuse and obscure dance again, then cut the record short and go back to Mother now."

My attempt at dark wit sounds more like it rolled in the

prickly eucalyptus bark at our feet, but I still don't care. My system can't handle this apprehension.

"You're suspicious," he finally says. "Understandable, but unproductive. Because like it or not, I'm nearly a member of the family now. And believe it or not, that's something I take seriously. Family gets protected—at all costs."

After a long pause, I relinquish my answer. "All right. I believe you."

But believing his words doesn't mean trusting his intentions. *Family gets protected.* Okay. Sneaking behind Mother's back is one thing. Betraying the demonic bureaucracy is another. How far is he willing to take that grand rally cry?

I can't afford the time to push for that statistic. Not right now. I've committed to believing him, and the urgency in his expression makes me commit anew to the effort.

"Physically, Kell is fine. But geographically, there have been some unforeseen challenges."

"Challenges … geographically?" Maximus's tone is thick, conveying how deeply he shares my bafflement.

Arden braces his hands behind his back. It lends him more of the arrogant air I'm used to, despite his diplomatic nod. "The powers that be … well, at least enough of them to count as a quorum for a vote … ordered that she be transferred."

"What?" I snap. "You mean, out of the family villa?"

"Yes."

"Why?"

Maximus has hardly stopped shaking his head. "So,

these *powers*... They're who, exactly? Is this, like, the judicial branch of your government?"

Arden raises a smooth eyebrow. "That would be implying the underworld is a democracy."

"Where did they take her?" I'm so agitated, I'm shocked my skin's still intact. "And again, why? She's not a criminal."

"Nobody agrees with you more than me, little sister."

The tacks in his tone aren't lost on me. But if he added the new nickname as some kind of bonding tactic, he failed. Badly.

"That's not an answer," I bite out.

He tilts his head, seeming to concede. "Not a criminal," he repeats. "I'd say she's more like...a prize awarded for good behavior."

My throat constricts. Tears push at my voice, but I battle to gulp them down. "A...prize?" I stammer, too late to block awful assumptions of Kell in that dismal castle bedroom, gazing out at Dis's dismal hellscape. "For what? To whom?"

There's a thoughtful—and unreadable—flicker across Arden's face. I yearn to close my eyes, battling supreme frustration. If he's contemplating lying to me, even by one syllable, violence will be an easy afterthought for me.

Thankfully, he firms his stance and meets my gaze. He doesn't even blink.

He's going to give over the truth.

"Rerek."

"*Rerek?*" Falling apart helps nobody right now, especially Kell. "That's...nonsensical."

He jogs his chin up, smooth and haughty. "It is also the truth."

"What was Jaden's lockdown, then? Just a down payment? Was Kell always part of this deal too?"

As swiftly as it came, his attitude subsides. A minor tic starts at the corner of his right eye. I don't want to watch. Not a thing inside me wants to acknowledge that my stress has bloomed enough to agitate him too. He can't convince me that he actually cares for my sister. Not ever. But especially not right now.

"My best guess?" he finally ventures aloud. "Rerek probably jumped in, more than willingly, to help Hades with the chaos across the city during the earthquake swarm. In addition to the favor it obviously courted—"

"You mean imprisoning my brother."

I'm unable to control my furious injection, earning me conflicting scowls in return.

Arden's is solemn and sympathetic. "With a hex, sadly, powerful enough to hold more than just Jaden."

Maximus is drenched in a slew of new questions. "Kell too? But he cast it right on Jaden. I know that much for certain. I was able to leave the place without any issue, but Jaden looked like a bird ramming a plate-glass window."

Arden rolls his eyes with a lot of purpose. Strangely, the look gives me leave to breathe again. His arrogance might be aggravating from a dozen angles, but it's also familiar to the point of reassuring.

"It's a basic holding hex. Its parameters can be stretched easier than plastic wrap," he states. "Certainly even you know that, oh learned one?"

"Stop." Flames climb to the forefront of my gaze. I don't

attempt to hide them in the glare I fling across the clearing. "Just get to the point as if you're not impressing a room full of swanks at a Van Gogh appraisal."

He purses his lips but settles his figurative feathers by adjusting his sweater cuffs. "It was probably all of five minutes' work for Rerek to expand the curse, wrapping Kell as well as Jaden in the boundary. While it's a troubling situation to contemplate, there's a chance of turning it around in our favor. It's why I was able to talk Veronica into coming here in the first place."

My gut knots. "A vibe I didn't help with at all. If I'd known..."

"Or perhaps if your mother had put aside her pride for a moment," he adds coolly. "But yes, the outcome indeed could have been different. But it's water under the bridge now, which means there's no time to be tossing in our wishing pennies."

Maximus clears his throat. "So, this *chance* you're talking about... Can you elaborate?"

Arden glances at his expensive watch before looking up again. "Every hex lasts for only a certain amount of time. It's a necessary limitation for obvious reasons. The timer is proportional to what the curse is asking the cosmos to do for it. Weather and fortune hexes can last up to months at a time. But those involving biological creatures, like animals and human beings, are shorter out of necessity."

"How much shorter?"

"Well, not just a few minutes," Arden states. "If demons could trap someone anytime they wanted but undo the curse after just a few snaps... You can likely imagine the chaos that would overtake the realms."

Maximus nods. "Every conflict from bar fights to border wars would be bedlam."

"That's only in one realm," Arden says. "But I don't have time to show-and-tell you the colorful glory of a Fifth Circle barge battle."

Maximus folds his arms and tilts his head. "Yet what does any of this have to do with what's happened? And why Kell as the target?"

"It's my fault." I start kicking up leaves, unable to stop myself from pacing. If ever there's been a valid reason for it, it's now. "However you split the details—how it happened, where it happened, why it happened—all of it circles back to what I did."

"You couldn't have predicted an iota of this." Maximus moves fast, suddenly blocking my beeline between the trees. He's so adamant, I barely have a moment to process his hands raising to my face. Then his palms pressing tenderly at my cheeks. "*Kara*. In no logical reality, even the one that Hades is so fond of twisting for his whims, could you have known this would happen."

Arden laughs haughtily. "A little respect? His Godship Hades does not have *whims*."

Maximus retaliates with an expression that's far from genteel. "You don't want me to go there with you, Prieto. Especially not now, but really not ever."

I surrender to half a breath of relief when Arden seems to back down, going for the arrogant sweater-cuff-adjustment thing again.

"Let's move on. I've come with some actionable items."

There's a rough sound from the base of Maximus's throat. "You couldn't have led with that?"

"Admittedly, the whole matter has been…kilometers past bizarre." It's as close as he'll likely swoop toward vulnerability, which he counters by straightening his spine. "So I've been trying to piece it together. I've been owed a large number of favors between here and Dis. They've come in handy."

"You can get Kell and Jaden free?"

It's breathy and tearful, perfectly matching my rush forward—until I run into the brick wall of his ongoing scowl.

"A million favors couldn't work that special magic, little sister."

The zap of mental revelation is all my own doing, as facts stack on each other like perfect ice cubes.

That special magic…

Geographically…some challenges…

Your sweet siblings…

My breath catches. I release it on a strangled choke. "Oh my God. They actually took her to Rerek's, didn't they? Is she with Jaden?"

Arden already confirms that with his heightened tension. "Hades took advantage of Rerek's weakness for all it was worth. Forcing Kell's proximity meant a new and extended hex, ensuring that Jaden would go nowhere. Unsurprisingly, Rerek's plans for wooing and winning over Jaden probably didn't go as planned. Especially if he was off cracking open freeways and toppling the *Hollywood* sign."

I frown. "Or if he was figuring out the meaning of *wooing* at all."

He winces, as if hating to agree with me so fast. "Point is, the plan went through. Seems like everyone just went along for the ride in approving Hades's call, no matter how they feel about Rerek's brown-nosing."

I shake my head. My brain is still struggling to assemble his bombshell. "This is outrageous. Jaden and Kell...they didn't ask for any of this. Why punish my family for *my* actions?"

Arden jogs a brow. "Are you sincerely asking that about a god who sanctioned the Romanov execution? The Three-Generation Rule in old Asia? *Any* ethnic cleansing throughout history?"

"And there's the existential hole we don't need right now." Maximus moves forward. "Back to facts. When did all of this even go down? We left the mansion only two nights ago. At that time, Kell was upstairs in her bedroom. We saw no sign of any trouble."

"Of course not. That would've been too soon, despite how fast Rerek got this favor granted," Arden says. "We think the decree was issued early yesterday morning. Your mother checked on Kell around noon and found her gone."

Maximus's jaw hardens so completely, it's battling the trees for stubborn texture. "So what's the full deal about the expiration on a holding hex? How long do we have to wait Rerek out?"

Arden's face becomes a second study in harsh tension. "We don't. We *can't.*"

Too swiftly and too clearly, my logic fills in the follow-up. "Because once the time limit is up, Rerek's under no obligation to any more underworld laws."

"At least until his antics create more messes than they're worth." With the return, Arden's again gotten stiffer than an undertaker. Inwardly, I beg for the return of his arrogance. This somberness is awful, unpredictable, and scary. That fear makes me jumpy. And mad.

"Antics?" I blurt out. "Do you really believe that? Because I don't. I grew up with the pathological bastard. He doesn't know the meaning of merciful or sweet. Believe me, some of the things he's done to creatures, mortal and mythological, have haunted my worst nightmares. They're not just *antics*." Nausea hits me in a dizzying wave. "As soon as that hex expires, he'll be unhinged and able to play with Jaden and Kell in any depraved way he desires. And take my word on this... Rerek doesn't *play* like the rest of us. We have to stop him before he's granted free rein over them."

"For once, we're in full agreement. Why do you think I was so adamant to double back here?"

Maximus mutters some choice profanities beneath his breath before throwing his head up and his shoulders back. "All right. So what's our time frame?"

Arden pulls in some new confidence. It's not his whole hauteur yet, but it's enough. "A holding hex on a human only lasts thirty-six hours. We have to assume that the same rule applies for any creature with human blood."

My throat clutches. "So Jaden's time is already up."

Arden shakes his head. "When Rerek stretched the

curse to include Kell, it would've also reset Jaden's timer. Now, assuming that the *Hysminai*—the underworld's special forces—swept in for Kell during the three hours between Veronica's checks on her—"

"Then the time limit for the stretched hex is up at midnight tonight," Maximus fills in.

My heartbeat runs up one set of ribs and down the other. "Okay. So we have between seven and nine hours to figure out a way of undoing it."

"No." Arden's new stare throws a red light onto my cardiac sprints. "*Undoing* is impossible. Best we can hope for is a disruption. A long enough release on the cage to get your brother and my betrothed out and away."

"And that's where I can help." And now, I actually feel like I can. A few minutes ago, that wouldn't have been the case. Contemplating a full reversal of Rerek's curse was a thought on the same level as blowing up the sun. The demon has existed for centuries, armed with frightening and painful powers. But working with Arden and Maximus to press a pause button on his powers...

Maybe I can do something for the better this time.

"And if Kara's successful..." Maximus shores up his stance. There's a steely glint in his blues. "If we really do this, what's that do to your standing with the underworld brass?"

I don't fault him for the question, just for the timing. The last thing we need right now is Arden glaring like the words are a wedgie. But weirdly, as he pivots, it's as if he's wearing a velvet robe instead.

"Kell is *mine*," he all but seethes. "Rerek may be Hades's

obedient puppy, but many have grown tired of his stunts, even with the thin excuses for approval. And staging that little 'beach party' for Hades wasn't as impressive as it looked. You think His Godship has only one Tinseltown shaker in his back pocket?" His chuff is sharp and bitter. "Those boys are scattered everywhere from Irvine to Ventura. But Hades can't afford to lose a more established voice like mine."

Maximus jogs his head to one side, like he's picking up on something my inner sensors aren't. Good thing. Something tells me I'll need every drop of my mental mojo in the next nine hours.

"Good enough," he declares. "You do the politics. We'll do the logistics." His jawline tenses. "But, Prieto?"

"Hmmm?"

"This doesn't mean we're friends."

Arden wrinkles his nose. "My good professor, I believe in reliable colleagues, interesting dinner companions, and females insatiable about getting fucked. I do *not* believe in friendship."

For a fast moment, Maximus and I trade a glance. I don't need any extra senses to read him. Is rescuing Kell from Rerek only tying her to a worse fate with Arden?

In the depths of my soul, I don't believe that. Arden's a ruthless ass, but he doesn't pull punches. From the time his true purpose was revealed, I've always known where I stand with him. Rerek's as shifty as the sand his villa is built on. I've been on the receiving end of his wicked pranks over the years, including his most elaborate deception of all. The illusion that led me right into Hades's trap and then locked Jaden in his hex.

Now, because of me, J's been imprisoned longer than Kell. And for all his lip and swagger, my little brother hides a more fragile spirit than most assume.

"Come on." I charge forward, grabbing Maximus by a hand. "There's no more time to waste."

"About what?"

There's not enough bass in the interruption to be Maximus, or even Arden. But enough of a rich alto husk that I halt in my tracks, already knowing whose gaze to expect when I lift my head.

Sure enough, even from ten feet away, Circe gives the sunbeams a run for their money. But her rays seem more determined to fry my retinas, despite the hesitant quirks that tempt the corners of her expressive mouth.

She rolls her thumbs along her fingers in nervous little circles. "Did I miss something?" she says slowly, until her gaze refocuses on a spot just past us. "What are *you* doing back here?"

Arden's low hum is more aggravating than the crow that screeches at us from overhead. "Lovely to see you too, Circe."

She sends him a withering look. Then, all too quickly, she swings the glare at me. "What's going on? You're supposed to be resting."

Only now do I detect what her urgent tone is truly about. She's not being a nagging proxy for Hecate. She's being herself, looking at me with a full-blown case of gut-deep fear. There's so much intensity in her eyes…

Does she already *know*?

"Hey. Kara? You're really scaring me. What is going on?"

When she issues that last part at Arden as well, I have my answer. She doesn't know and is now unsure if she wants to. It's embedded in her energy worse than a wad of gum in her hair.

I use my free hand to reach for hers. "My family is in trouble," I explain. "The underworld took my sister. She's trapped in Rerek Horne's holding hex along with my brother."

"The new expiration is at midnight," Arden adds, now blessedly serious.

The irritation fades from Circe's irises. Her skin, milky as it is, blanches by a number of shades.

"And you think you can break the curse?"

"No. Maybe just pause it," I say. "Long enough to get Kell and Jaden out."

But she's already shaking her head. "Impossible. Not even with the incubus's help. You've only had one day of enlightenment, Kara."

Arden steps up and around. "And when you first came into your powers, there was no such thing as that training."

"*Training*." Maximus jabs a fast but celebratory fist. "Right?"

Arden doesn't waver his regard at Circe. "Yet you persisted and learned, did you not? And you were brilliant, were you not?"

The enchantress spears Arden with an unsteady glower but ends it like a lightning bolt to a dry tree. Between blinks, she shoves a good eight feet away from him—before redirecting her punishing stare at me.

"Please, Kara. You can't run off and try this right now. This is not going to end well."

I square my shoulders. "What do you think will happen to Jaden and Kell if we don't try?"

She squirms. "Fine. Then I'm going with you."

My shoulders dip beneath the weight of yet more shock. "I can't ask you to—"

"You're not asking. I'm volunteering. Besides, I can also distract Hecate with a story and cloak our passage past the perimeter." She adopts a regal pose, as if she's just hauled a sword out of its scabbard. "You know...I'd venture to say you need me."

I squeeze her hand, but the gesture isn't enough. Even yanking her into a fervent embrace feels like a small plop in the ocean of my gratitude. "Thank you," I whisper. "I don't know how I'll make this up to you."

"A stress to strike from your mind this instant." She soothes a firm hand up and down my back. "A diamond of Iremia never struggles alone—even if it's for a mission of utter insanity."

CHAPTER 16

MAXIMUS

THE LAST TIME I stood on this spot along the Coast Highway, my heart was somewhere in my throat and my legs had turned into in concrete. It was a dark night, bested only by the dread that threatened to eat me alive.

The situation's only marginally better now. At least Kara's by my side, and the fading purples and peaches of the sunset do amazing things for her classic dark beauty.

But now's not the time for odes and poetry. Though we've still got hours to spare, the hex's ticking time clock isn't far from my mind. Or nervous system.

"So...plan of attack, anyone?" I mutter, not bothering to lock the dinged old ranch service van that Circe rounded up from some obscure corner of Iremia for our transport out of the canyon. But even if it were a stagecoach and some tired Clydesdales, I'd be grateful to her for not defaulting to her powers and zapping us here. Between my field trip to Labyrinth with Z and my zip through the underworld with

Gio, supernatural teleportation isn't high on my bucket list anymore.

"Please don't call it that," Circe responds. "Starting a war isn't our intention. Not here. Not now."

"Make love, not war," Arden croons, earning him an instant snarl from the enchantress.

"Prieto. I swear, if you keep taking credit for lines that your black soul will never comprehend..."

"How about disruption, not detonation?" Kara offers a bit too brightly. But it accomplishes the purpose, defusing them both.

"Ah. There's the golden ticket," Circe commends. "Except that motto might be easier declared than done."

Arden pulls out his phone and wakes up the screen. "Not all the favors I redeemed were in other realms. Courtesy of the Malibu Planners office, here are the up-to-date blueprints for Rerek's place. Wish I could say it possesses anything unique from every other residence along this stretch. The front entrance basically seems like nothing, though it's a heavily monitored fortress in its own right. The majority of the larger entrances face the shore at the other side."

"Viable entrances that are surrounded by clear glass walls," I say with a frown. "So our element of surprise might as well be some hand sparklers and a marching band."

It's a better metaphor for the moment than I think. As Kara steps forward again, she looks like one of those symbolic sparklers, ignited in breathtaking human form. "Unless..." she ventures, eyes agleam and feet rocking, "we enter *another* way."

Circe's the first one to comprehend that declaration, lifting her head to follow the figurative comet trail behind Kara's look. "Another way…as in the *roof*?" Her gaze bugs wide. "And that's deflection over detonation…how?"

"Ah." Arden smirks. "For a dour demon who enjoys card games with Rasputin and Lizzie Borden when summoned down under, Rerek is strangely fond of skylights."

"The villa came that way," Kara explains. "For a bunch of years, Rerek planned to get rid of them. He even talked to some trendy gothic artist out of Rotterdam about doing murals over them."

"What happened to all that?" I ask.

"Jaden mentioned that he liked the skylights."

"Then Jaden might get to thank himself for his rescue," Arden remarks. "If we can figure out how to make this happen."

Circe sweeps us all with a puzzled look. "Why am I suddenly lost here?"

"A breach through the roof." Kara peels away from us, angling herself right and left in a desperate bid to get better glances at the rooflines, only to huff with frustration. I doubt any of us will be much help. It's impossible to observe anything about the villa other than its modernistic front atrium.

"The…roof," Circe echoes, her throat hoarse. "Skylights…" Not as gruff this time, but that's because of the dread replacing it. "Ohhh, no. Ohhh, Kara, you *cannot* be thinking—"

"Circe."

Kara finishes by spinning back around. There's new confidence in her stance. Brighter flecks in her gaze. Even the way her hands and fingers are poised, spread and ready at her sides ...

I'm not just dazzled.

I'm proud. To immeasurable depths.

"Circe," she intones again.

"No." The high sorceress knows the reiteration tactic too. "Hecate and I spent only a few hours with you yesterday! If something happens and you—"

"Nothing's going to happen except what *should*."

"You don't know that."

"Did you tell yourself that before *your* first magical calling?"

"I changed a prince into a frog, Kara. Yes, that's right. Why do you think they turned the story into a fairy tale and not an epic hero's poem? Because it was basic spellcasting. As easy as brushing my teeth. None of it involved ... gravity." She shakes her head. "And getting past whatever mortal security perimeter Rerek has in place. Not to mention the crafty bastard himself ..."

"Negative," I say, unable to tamp a subtle but wicked smile. "Rerek will be the last of your concerns."

Circe looks up, eyes wide and piercing. "Is he not home? How do you know?"

I crack my knuckles. "Oh, I very much look forward to him being home."

The sorceress groans. Her shoulders sag. Desperately, she snaps her stare at Arden. "You understand all this, right?

You're *fully* aware of what we're talking about here? She wants to levitate her brother and sister by a distance we still don't know, out a skylight we're not sure we can open. That's if we can even find the right one."

Kara moves back over without an instant of hesitation. "That's less of a concern than keeping Rerek occupied." A new concentration takes over her form, especially every gorgeous angle of her face. Any second now, I expect my little demon to start glowing from the inside out.

She's become that forceful that fast. That astonishing. That brilliantly beautiful.

But there's still no eerie glow in her veins. The edges of her hair don't burst into flames. There aren't any isotopes blaring in her eyes. At least not before she closes them all the way. Slowly. Purposefully. With intent that matches her gentle murmur into the twilight.

"Jaden. I know you can hear me." She takes a shallow breath. "Okay, so I really hope you can. If so, you need to find a way to let me know."

"Supercharged auditory skills," I explain in response to Circe's frown. "Kara's not the only Valari with interesting abilities."

"I just need them to penetrate whatever's between us," Kara murmurs, raising her head and reopening her gaze. "Come on, brother." The final embers of the day catch and hold in the worried intensity of her big browns. "Give me a sign. Just—"

From inside the house, there's a loud crash—the residual shatters of glass in a million pieces.

The acoustic equivalent of a thumbs-up from Jaden.

"Guess his radar's up," Arden utters.

"And pinging loud and clear," Circe adds with a triumphant smirk.

Adrenaline is my bloodstream's buddy once more. It eclipses most instincts, but that's for the better. It's the main one that keeps me moving. "This has to happen now. If we didn't miss that commotion way out here, bet your ass that Rerek didn't either."

Maybe my anticipation is feeding my decree. This time Rerek won't evade me so easily. It's going to feel so freaking good to show him what a gut punch feels like, though it won't compare to how his actions nearly ruined me last week.

I lead the way, Arden hot on my heels as we head straight for Rerek's Zen-infused atrium. Talk about looks being deceiving.

I stop only once. To swoop an arm around Kara's middle and haul her into my side again. And to mash her lips with mine. And to infuse her senses with my determination—and limitless adoration.

"You've got this. Just be sure nobody gets *you*."

Circe jogs both brows. "That's what I'm here for."

"And me."

I blink very hard, several times, before realizing the declaration isn't mine or Arden's. I'm that visually blasted—and stunned—that Hecate's light show is more brilliant than her fire-and-ice light funnel atop Kara's swimming pool. This time the colors fan out, sizzling with a thousand hues at once.

Just as swiftly, the light show fades. She walks calmly forward, now clothed in a modernized Greek toga. The purple fabric at her shoulder is secured by a jeweled dog that moves like a real version of the animal. The bottom part of her gown is actually billowy pants that are tucked into knee-high gladiator sandals.

"Goddess." Circe sounds a lot like she did in Iremia's kitchen this morning. "Ermmm...hello?"

Kara cants her head as if a fresh angle will clear her confusion. "How did you..."

Hecate pushes forward, her silky purple layers billowing as if she's got a full production team to ensure the perfectly powerful result.

"All we need to worry about right now is how you are going to do this, Kara. About how you *can* do this."

"Perhaps with a few words of wisdom from the goddess on high." I can't help but say it. No matter how deep in the dark I still am about the real situation between Circe and Hecate, I can stand completely in the light about this point. "Unless you want to do the honors yourself."

Hecate is stoic about her expression but firm in her reply. "Kara is a Valari, and two Valaris need saving. This is clearly her quest. Besides, there's no better challenge to use one's powers to the fullest than when lives hang in the balance."

Deaf to Hecate's last words, Arden keeps stalking toward the house. I sprint to catch up, following him down the modern white steps until we skirt the tiered bowl fountain in the vestibule before facing the villa's wide double doors.

Beyond it, fast-paced stomps echo along the marble floors and spacious walls.

Clearly, Rerek doesn't think we're delivering Szechuan.

"We've got to get in there. Now." And not solely because my fantasies have blossomed about permanently wiping the droll smirk off his face.

"Stand back. I think I can singe this off at the hinges." Arden's scowl gains new wrinkles. "Gads, little Rerek. You really can't do any better than a second-level barrier net? No wonder you're still clawing to get into Hades's favor."

I heed his order, backing up by a few steps, but am still bouncing on the balls of my feet. "After I'm done with this little shit, he'll be lucky to have claws left."

Arden side-eyes me. "Not unless you stay back."

"Fine." I push away, letting Arden slide fully center between the panels. "Just do it, all right? Burn it down. And then let me at him."

CHAPTER 17

FROM WHERE WE STAND, there's a direct line of sight to Rerek's front door—or what's going to be left of it once Arden finishes fizzling its hinges off. I can't believe he's doing it. He's standing there more like a handyman than a superhero, giving the hinges some simple brushes of his fingers. But metallic sparks are flying. His power is working.

"Oh my," Circe mutters, stepping up at my side. "I guess incubi *do* have magic hands."

An observation that, in this moment, I should be especially grateful for.

Instead, insecurity just slams me in two dozen new ways. Arden's showing up for the mission with his gear intact and his abilities activated. But can *I*?

I flick all ten fingers like they've been dunked in ice water. The day never really warmed up, meaning the twilight gusts off the ocean only intensify my shivers. Maximus isn't here with his size and strength and warmth either. But are any of them the real reason why I can't stop shaking from head to toe?

No.

I have to take accountability for that.

I already know what this feeling is.

I've bitten off more than I can chew.

Oh shit, oh shit, oh shit.

"Kara." The hail comes at me like the wind has brought mud along with it. It's no better when I watch Hecate repeat it, bracing me by the shoulders. "Listen to me. You are a *diamond*. Shattering is not an option."

Things start to refocus. But my senses are far from fully dethawed—not even from the serenity she guided me to in the sala yesterday.

Yesterday ...

"Repeat it to me, Kara. Now."

"Shattering ... is not an option." I finish it with a nod, hoping that helps my mojo. Not in the least.

"Good," Hecate still says. "Now again."

"Shattering is not an option." Better this time. But still feeling like a hummingbird staring up at Everest.

"Good. *Good*. And now—"

"But what if flying isn't, either?" I blurt. "What if"—I snap my stare to Circe—"*you're* right? How can one day of enlightenment prepare me for ... for ..."

Hecate jostles me, almost rag doll style. "For who you are meant to be?" Her fingers are firm clamps into my upper arms. "For the purpose for which the cosmos has been preparing you your whole life?"

I have words for an answer, but they never form on my tongue. I can feel them in my stare, though. The truths I've got to make her see as clearly as the ones she's just intoned. *Purpose? Until three weeks ago, that consisted of preparing for a lifetime as an incubus's property. The only diamond in my existence would've been the hell rock on my finger.*

None of what she's saying is hard to hear.

I just need some time to get used to it.

Please. Can't I have more time?

Real life answers that one for her. Too loud and too clear.

More crashes from inside the villa. Bigger things are getting toppled now, hopefully under Maximus and Arden's force. There's no more sign of them at the front door or even in the foyer beyond, so my heart squeezes in a silent plea that they're on their way to finding Rerek. Arden, at least, has to know that permanently ending one of Hades's stooges is not a luxury they can indulge right now.

Still, the din continues. So many crashes and clatters. Too many ominous thuds that visibly shake the walls, even from our view out here.

"Oh *my*." Circe doesn't mess around with the reiteration. "They're not wasting any time. Or perhaps ... Rerek isn't."

I startle. "What?"

But my wrenching belly already confirms that I've squandered breath on the word. I already know exactly what she's saying, and I hate it. Rerek is many things, but a lax idiot isn't one of them. His sleek white walls probably hide a hundred booby traps.

For all we know, Jaden or Kell could be taking the brunt of those blows right now.

Or Maximus.

"No. Ohhh no, no, *no*." But as I wrench back and then pivot around, more words tumble out of me. Syllables no longer drenched in dread and protest. They take me to a place of wonderment and power.

Of surrender ...

"*Fax accenditur superiores. Hecate declarat. Ego sum unus cum Hecate.*"

And of flight.

The lightness that comes from the words, pushing through me with their forceful familiarity. Now, as Circe translates, even more so.

"The torch burns higher. Hecate declares it. I am one with Hecate."

"Yes," Hecate exclaims from behind me. And then ... from beneath me. "Yes, you *are*, Kara! I knew you could do it. I knew it!"

"That's ... that's ..." Circe gasps out.

I don't blame her for giving up on the words. I can't find any either. I'm rising beyond the villa's vestibule, up and over the top of the structure, until even the indigo expanse of the Pacific is like an endless painting before me. Astonished air spills off my lips as I extend my arms a little, experimenting with the air currents. I'm not exactly swooping or going prone, but learning some control is good for a needed confidence boost, especially as my speed ticks up.

"Okay, okay, okay," I mutter anxiously. "Get your shit together, Kara."

The crazy throbs inside my head and stomach are on the verge of dizzying. As fun as all this is to consider, I wonder if my lunch is preparing its second appearance for the day. Maybe I should've been more daring during Kell's birthday party at that trapeze place on the Santa Monica pier.

But that doesn't mean I can't handle this. Hecate and Circe are still down there, flowing their energy and faith. Arden and Maximus are still inside, needing me to fulfill my part of the mission. And my siblings...

Are the mission.

I just have to take this chance. Commit and continue.

That also means...asking again.

"Okay, Jaden," I mutter as best I can. The wind is crazier up here, and the sea salt dries my throat. "Now it's your turn. I need another sign, brother."

There it is already.

The light beneath a double set of skylights goes out and then back on again. Once more. A third time.

I giggle in time to my leaping heart rate. "Thank you."

I coast in closer, to the point that I now feel his adrenaline. The sound of my name reaches me firsthand after I pull up on both vented skylights. In a tandem arm motion, I rip the latches free from their mountings.

Logically, that should plaster me with a gape to match those of my siblings, watching from the luxurious den below.

But not now.

Not with enough energy rushing my veins to charge

Alameda's whole computer lab. It's like the force that zapped me in the library at Hades's castle, only more so. So much more.

There, I was surrounded by darkness, damned souls, and the ongoing weight of my spirit's dread.

Now, I've flown through a bright-purple twilight on an endless ocean breeze, lifted by the belief of a goddess and the love of my demigod.

It's worth a moment's celebration since I'm not so certain about measuring up to Rerek's hex.

Though I send out another desperate wish that he's getting pulverized nearby, it's folly to think that the hex is so flimsy as to be tied to the demon's physical force. Rerek's wilier—and stronger—than that.

"Okay, okay," I mutter, shaking out my fingers again. "So what now?"

And again, I'm overloaded with anxiety. Fear. All the atrocious what-ifs.

What if I can't figure this out?

What if the hex is too strong to cut into?

What if Rerek *is* annihilated and Hades finds out—and decides to take his anger out on a pair of trapped Valaris?

"*No.*" I verbally pelt myself with it, at least fifty more times, but the mantra doesn't help. The fear digs in. My mind spirals. My balance teeters. Though my feet are planted for now, this isn't boding well for flying back to safety.

What would Hecate do?

I desperately scramble for the answer. Thankfully, there are a few that come.

Breathe.

Deeper.

Focus.

Slower.

Slow down. Slow down. Slow down.

And remarkably, I feel myself smiling.

The hurrier I go, the behinder I get.

And filling my senses with the words of a rushed rabbit in Wonderland.

I am not crazy. My reality is just different than yours.

Lewis Carroll, in the nick of time again. Just repeating those two lines peels back my anxious veil, letting me see every necessary reality there is about this.

Rerek's hex... It's right here in front of me now, as visible as a bright-red fishing net that's been wrapped around the villa. It vibrates with energy, like see-through power lines filled with chaotic currents. The bedlam is frightening to watch, as if just touching a cable will equal an awful demise. It's a terror attack funneled into a two-inch tube and then woven into a giant trap.

But now I see...

That its most daunting strength is also its most glaring weakness.

Only the insane equate pain with success.

With that affirmation on repeat in my mind, I'm able to flow the energy in my veins toward the centers of my palms. From there, the brilliance spreads out into my fingers, taking over with tingling force...

As I lower them toward the glowing mesh at my feet.

As I wrap them around a couple of the tethers.

As I watch them burn the netting away.

"*Whoa,*" I choke out. It's working!

I believe it, but I don't. The chaos magic is already fighting back, trying to break down my energy. It sets charges along my pores, waiting for just one of them to give in to their insidious tactics.

But I fight back harder. With forces much more powerful.

The awe I absorb from the horizon. The peace I pull from the early stars.

The connection I feel to the two awesome people below.

"Everybody ready?" I call down, already deciding to ignore Kell's visible gulps.

"Huh?" she retorts. "Kara. Are you freaking kidding m—"

Her own long wail is her interruption, starting as soon as her feet leave the floor. But I can't focus on it. The moment has come to tap fully into what's inside. The force of my power. The lift of my love.

"*Fax accenditur superiores. Hecate declarat. Ego sum unus cum Hecate.*"

And the dominating power from those beautiful words. Bringing my brother and sister closer.

Closer . . .

"What the living crap is going on?" Kell demands.

"Not sure, but it beats heli-skiing ten to one."

I can't afford a single second to laugh at their typical exchange. I haven't torn a huge hole in the net here. They'll have to go through one at a time. If we don't do this quickly and right, one or both of them will be imprisoned again by it. No do-over margins. I'm still stunned we've found the one-and-done window.

Though we're still painfully far from the *done* part.

"Jaden! You're first. Tuck in your arms and legs. As soon as you're out, head toward the pergola over the front patio and climb down from there. You remember enough from parkour class, right?"

"Hell yeah."

My brother's enthusiasm is the right ingredient at the right moment for this stress soup. I just wish Kell would take a bigger taste of the new broth.

"So any suggestions for the girl who barely survives twirls in barre class?" she bites out.

"Watch Jaden. Just do the same thing, and make like a mummy," I encourage. "I've got you."

Holy crap, I hope I've got her.

But I have to do more than hope.

I have to *know*.

That means focusing. Remembering those moments yesterday when I had Hecate and Circe too. I had both of them and have to think that some of it wasn't just their powers reflecting in mine. Some of it was me.

Some of it *had* to be me.

It's only a shred of confidence, but I cling to all of it with everything I'm worth. Tighter. *Tighter.*

"I'm out!" Jaden yells.

"Then get going." I force myself not to bask in his fast

hug. "Rerek might burn this place down any second!"

"Thanks," Kell grouses. "So uplifting."

"Shut up and get your cute backside up here."

"Yes, bossy. Oh, holy *shit*. Kara, are we—"

"Can you just be quiet and hold on?"

"But we're flying."

"Levitating. The word is levitating."

"Is there a difference?"

We're only ten feet from the ground now, so I give myself permission to chuckle at last. "Sister, I'd like to know the answer to that too."

CHAPTER 18

Maximus

MOM TAUGHT ME NEVER to solve anything with my fists. But maybe she never anticipated a moment like this—in which I already gave up on solving anything.

When the only purpose is to make everything feel better.

Cutting loose. Going free. And not in the drunk-with-my-dad-at-Labyrinth kind of way.

This is deeper. Darker. Feeding stuff that's been starved too long. The parts that still remember the too-tall sixth grader who steered embarrassingly clear of every conflict. Or later, in high school, the nerd who was approached by every sports coach in school but had to say no. Because so much could go wrong. What if I ever chose a left hook to a kid's face instead of talking things through? What if I decided the same thing about a referee's? I put Jesse in a wheelchair for life, and I wasn't even pissed at him.

But Rerek Horne is different.

Scathingly, deservedly so.

Not the indelible demon part. If anything, that makes the blood on my fists no more than dirty puddle water. Bothersome and meaningless, to him more than me.

He's different because he's not some stupid kid at recess or a well-meaning coach on the playing field.

He's spent centuries in the pursuit of one goal. Weaving destruction and confusion. He's *proud* of it, openly wearing that glee now. It's in the shine across his cruel irises, even after I've blackened both his eyes. It seeps from his blood-stained grin and gurgles in his chuckling throat. The bastard won't surrender a single chink of his urbane arrogance, even as I curl a fist back once more.

But suddenly my arm shakes. Through some insane force of will, I uncurl my fingers. "You're not worth it." And maybe Mom is more right than I want to admit. "Or maybe I just need to kill you."

His glare dims. But the inky shadows that take over his eyes … they're worse. "Easier said than done, even for you."

"He's right," Arden says from his perch on the edge of the living room's sectional. Despite the blood spatter along the cream upholstery, he remains unstained down to his canyon-tromping Ferragamos. "Physically, you could probably do it. But politically …"

"Which is absolutely why you should." Rerek pushes up to his elbows, unashamed as a pop star at an all-night orgy. "Come now, Professor. I won't get a chance for a more deliciously tragic ending. Shakespeare, Hemingway, Sophocles … all our favorites will be welcoming me to eternity." He backhands blood from his lips with deliberate languor. "The hero, having lost the love of his existence, expires by the hand of those who ripped happiness from his fingers. But he smiles through it all, knowing they'll soon join him in the abyss..."

Arden groans. "Fire and fucking brimstone, Rerek. Shut up."

Miraculously, he accomplishes what I couldn't. Silencing Rerek and his distressingly cultured sulk.

For all of three seconds.

Until real emotion bursts across his face.

"I do love him, you know. To the depths of my soul."

"Then show him in the right ways," I bark back. "Support him. Be there for him. *Court* him. You've got centuries of life and experience to draw on. You must know how this works."

He flops back down with a bitter laugh. "Is that what you think my existence has yielded? Ah, well. I suppose love *is* a chaos all its own."

And here's the unnerving silence I didn't expect. Rerek is obviously happy to let me wallow in my discomfort too. Arden jitters a knee even harder, making it clear he wants to get on with this either way. He darts agitated glances toward the other sections of the villa, as if he's after hidden treasures there. Or maybe just one.

His intention isn't erroneous. I should probably be ripping a giant page from the guy's book. I pledged to get in here and prevent Rerek from interfering with what Kara had to do, not follow him down a philosophical rabbit hole about life, love, and purpose. I already have the best of all three, and I'll fight to the death to hold on to them—but no way will I be talking about them for a moment longer with this confused loser. Not after his scheming nearly ripped them all away from me.

"We're leaving," I say, hoisting to my feet. "And as you already know, we're doing it with Jaden and Kell."

Back to his hiked elbows, Rerek laughs without caring about the fresh blood that spurts out. "Oh yes. Of that I'm sure." He jogs his head back a little. Regards me with a resurgence of his lazy rock god stare. "I only hope *you* are."

I swing toward the door, ordering myself to focus on the important stuff now. There are no more rushed footsteps across the roof. And too much desperate tension in *here*.

But as much as I yearn to write off the demon's last-minute clickbait, I stop. Not clicking yet . . . but not navigating away.

No! Don't give him the pleasure of getting a millimeter under your skin.

Move. Now. One foot at a time. Do it.

But after one step, I'm pulling back up short. It's impossible to do otherwise when facing off with the new figure who fills the doorway, tidal waving her empyreal energy through the room. As I take a second to regain my balance, even Arden finally rises to his feet. Only Rerek seems unfazed, rolling his head like it's dangling from a silk ribbon.

"Well, someone strip the beds and make some togas. This party is getting better and better. Goddess Hecate, as

I live and breathe." He frowns while pressing a hand to his breastbone. "At least I *think* that's still happening..."

Hecate rolls her eyes. "Regrettably, yes."

"I must say, it's oddly invigorating. Having to actually face the existential big ones, you know?" he drawls. "The possibility of being...*ended*. After all these years, truly contemplating it. There's an odd exhilaration about it."

Hecate takes a pair of measured breaths. "Your point?"

My discomfort spikes as Rerek slides out a languid grin.

"Hmmm. I suppose I don't have one. I'm babbling, aren't I? And why? You'll have the joy of the experience yourself once Hades gets word of how you've all defied him by crossing me."

So much for discomfort. Raw rage is its replacement, rushed by the arctic wind of fear. I can't stop or even slow it, even with the glaring knowledge that Rerek's driven me here on purpose.

I jerk back around and set murderous eyes on his gangly neck.

Except that an invisible force lassos around mine. It snaps my gaze around, until I'm ensnared by Hecate's glittering glare. I practically hear her intent as real sounds in my head. *If you kill him, Hades* will *demand retribution. And will break our agreement to get it.*

Arden pushes in at my side, grabs my elbow, and nods as if he's heard the same message. "He's not worth it. And you're needed much more elsewhere."

With a gruff grunt, I acquiesce.

This time, I lead the way through the wide spaces of

Rerek's place, which feels bleaker than even a few nights ago when the faux Tinseltown partiers were here. They were all repurposed demons, but at least they warmed up the stark decor.

Now, there's only one kind of heat that matters. The fires that ignite in Kara's eyes as soon as I step free from the vestibule. The fierce blaze of her arms around my neck from the second we rush into each other's arms. The desperate heat of her lips, lifting and mashing against mine.

"You're okay?" she rasps when we drag apart, despite raking her hands along my shoulders to confirm the fact.

"Yeah," I murmur. "Yeah, beautiful. You?"

She dips a bunch of fast nods, working off the remnants of her adrenaline and tension. "I think so..."

"But holy shit. You're also—" Kell cuts short with her adamant charge. "K-demon. What *are* you?"

Kara turns to grab her sister by a hand. She pivots more when Jaden steps over, scooping up one of his too. "We have some catching up to do."

Kell scoffs. "I last saw you *two nights* ago."

"When you were high as a kite and Maximus and I had to practically pour you into bed. Yeah, you were in great shape to process a bombshell like *can ya smell the witchy on me yet, girl?*"

"I knew it." Kell rolls her head and wrinkles her nose. "You *do* smell different. But I was having a devil of a time getting to the core of it..."

"Do you mind?" Jaden sweeps up a hand with furious speed. "All devils, demons, and daimons are hereby banned from this chat thread for an hour. My human half thanks everyone in advance." He visibly tightens his grip on Kara. "But that's not the end of my gratitude. Sister of mine, I owe you a thousand favors and a million free frappes for this."

There's a happy glimmer in her gaze to match the joyous quirk of her lips. "*And* a million frappes? Don't you mean *or*? Whichever comes first?"

"I know what I said and what I meant," he returns. "Which still doesn't scratch the surface of my thanks. For everything."

"Well, in that case ..." Kara tugs harder on him, forcing an embrace despite Jaden's evident dislike of the mushier stuff. "But I didn't do it alone. None of this would've been possible without—"

"Maximus." Jaden flashes a fast wave for me. "Of course. I owe you one, man."

Arden pointedly clears his throat.

Kell and Jaden go still and pale. I see the changes plain as day, even in the dimness out here. Kara fortifying her stance by at least another inch.

"If it weren't for Arden, I never would have known about Rerek's back-channel bullshit and you getting taken because of it," she says to Kell. But Jaden's not spared the point for very long. She brings him back into the exchange with a decisive sweep of her stare. "And I wouldn't have learned what awful game plans Rerek was dreaming up for *you* after midnight."

It's even easier to observe their pallor now. The siblings could successfully audition for roles as brother and sister ghosts.

Still, Jaden nods with scary sagacity. "He gave me a few veiled previews already. I kept hoping he was high or kidding."

Kell rears back with a wince. "And you were going to share all this with me … when?"

"Never," Jaden retorts. "Trust me, you don't want to know."

"Right." She thrusts her left hand up. There's a diamond rock on it, as thoroughly shocking for surviving her ordeal as it is for the carat value. "And I'm still wondering how this got there. But sure, keep me in the dark some more, everyone."

"Oh my God." Kara gasps. "You did *not* have that two nights ago."

"And you weren't a witch two nights ago."

"Not officially."

"Well, this wasn't official either," Kell counters. "But I guess Arden put a ring on it just in time."

Unsurprisingly, the air stills again. Like jarring cymbals in the lull of an opera, a trio of waves crashes against the sand.

But contrasting it all is the sole person here who has a right to new dramatics. Arden Prieto is almost unnerving in his composure, laying calm crunches into the gravel upon approach to his betrothed.

Before Kell can lower her hand, he secures it with a strict thumb into her palm. His fingers fold around her knuckles. She flinches and gasps, but Arden's grip is fiercer. I expect sparks to fly as soon as her sister resorts to verbal retaliation. But it never comes. Kell is barely able to part her lips, and the only sound from them is a ragged exhalation.

Arden hardly moves either.

Except for the rhythmic circles of his thumb against her palm.

And, moments later, the rise of his free hand over her ring finger.

Until he slowly pulls the engagement ring off.

"I didn't come here because of this."

And then hurls the jewelry high, with enough savage force to send it over the villa and into the ocean.

"Arden!" Kell's eyes widen like a stunned cat's.

"Don't." He presses in on her, using the extra force to curl her fingers back down. "Like it or not, you've been chosen for me. Now you're bound to me, and I do *not* take your safety lightly. Nor will I ever."

There's a thing such as words, and then there are words with meaning. I look over to Kara, wondering if she, like me, has just heard a lot of the latter out of Arden.

The only person who doesn't look convinced is the only one who matters. Kell squirms up, back, and then side to side. No movement alleviates her discomfort or the brutal tenacity of the incubus who's causing it.

"I think I just want to go home," she mutters. "Right now. As in, five minutes ago."

Arden frowns. "I'm afraid that's not possible."

Her laugh is high and brief. "That so? Is this about my *safety* again?"

Jaden moves forward, rolling his jaw and rubbing his

neck. His scowl practically mirrors Arden's. "I'm sorry, Kell. But antiques guy has a good point."

"*Antiquities*," Arden clarifies through clenched teeth.

"Whatever. Point is, if the *Hysminai* found you before, they'll be able to do so again—faster and better than before. For that matter, I'm likely on their list now too."

"Until I have a chance to make sure Rerek is clear about where his liberties with this behavior stop, you both have to lie very low," Arden adds. "That means even my place is off-limits."

Jaden's gaze bugs. "Small miracles do exist."

"But so are the Ritz, the Maybourne, the Peninsula, and"—he cocks a brow at the last vestige of hope on Kell's face—"the Marmont."

There hasn't been a word from Hecate since Arden and I reemerged, though her composure has been an even keel of quiet alertness. "The question about your hiding place is already solved. Iremia is for all our diamonds, as well as those they love," she says. "I'll proceed ahead and ensure the others are preparing for your arrival."

She's barely finished before there's nothing left in her place but glitter bits in the air. None of us bat an eye except for Kell and Jaden, who make up for the rest of us. Half demons or not, their last twenty-four hours have featured supernatural interference of unreal proportions.

Kell underlines the point by hinging back toward Kara, already shaking her head like a truckload of glitter just got dumped on her too.

"You are *not* kidding, K-demon. We've got some catching up to do."

CHAPTER 19

AN HOUR LATER, AFTER settling Kell and Jaden into Iremia's two-bedroom guest cottage, Maximus and I head up the little knoll that borders the stream, back to our cozy place. I'm so spent that when Maximus stops for me to hitch onto his back, I don't mount a shred of fuss about it. All I want to do is get home in one coherent piece.

Home.

It's unnerving, how easily that designation pops to mind. Have I ever applied it to any place in my life? Such feelings were few and far between about the Beverly Hills mansion, despite growing up in the place. None of our vacation homes were that kind of a fit either. While the house I share with Kell is a little closer to the mark, the place still seems ... temporary. A very fancy dorm room with a great view, but never anything more than a home base to sleep, study, and hang out with my sister.

But here, in the smallest and most basic place I've ever

lived, *home* fills my head like a slipper that fits perfectly. Weirder, like it's just been there for years, not days.

The reason is already so obvious.

I'm here with the person who makes it feel that way.

Who feels even more like home once we walk through the door and he turns to lower me onto the couch. But I'm not ready to let go yet. This feels too good.

Maximus laughs when realizing I've turned him into a climbing tree with my rapid scramble around to his front. He follows with a wonderfully masculine chuckle, its vibrations resonating in the massive chest to which I eagerly mold myself.

He adjusts his hold, securing the new position of my thighs. I rearrange mine, one hand at his nape and the other against his scalp. He handles the shift with ease, so steady and strong. He hums into my ear, so intimate and inviting. He holds me tighter, surrounding me like an easy chair. And his scent is just as awesome. A mix of worn leather and sea wind. Comforting but intoxicating. Wrapping around so many parts of my heart and spirit…

"Thank you," I whisper into the base of his neck, though I lift my head the next moment. I need to look at him for this. Need him to see all the sincerity in my gaze, surging from my full heart. "Thank you for everything about today. Tonight too. Most guys would have told Arden to go screw himself earlier, if they believed him at all. But you—"

"I've learned to believe a lot of stuff that I never did before," he murmurs before lowering his lips to my nose. "But most of all, I believe in *you*. And I wouldn't have missed sharing today with you, every second of it, for all the nectar in Olympus."

The new husk in his tone speaks to deeper parts of me. I tilt my head back, offering my mouth to his again. As soon as he accepts the gift, erasing every millimeter of personal space remaining between us, my senses collide in wild celebration.

Our bodies press closer. Our lips mash with new passion. It's a kiss that makes me forget all others, even the ones from him. It's like we're crashing together for the first time, only all the familiar notes are still here too. How I pray he'll open my lips with his tongue. How I know I'll let him and pull in more of him with a long, needy groan. How his grip will turn just as critical, kneading my thighs until it hurts.

But I still want more.

And I'm telling him so by rolling my hips as much as possible beneath his demanding hold. By moaning once more, unable to ignore how even the tiny friction is like a torch to my sex. So many blissful shivers. So much impatient need. I long to scream in joy when his body reacts too. He's throbbing beneath my insistence. Surging toward me by hotter and hotter degrees.

"Perhaps ... I can interest you in another kind of nectar, Professor."

Maximus's low laugh is an aphrodisiac all its own. That and the aroused smoke in his hooded gaze. "Perhaps I like the sound of your buzzing bees, Miss Valari."

"Well." I quirk a small grin. "Perhaps just one. But she's a demanding little thing when she wants to ... cross-pollinate."

"Then let's not get on her bad side."

By the time he's done with that, my insides are humming like a honeycomb on crack. Not such a shock after the man carries me across the room to the plush rug in front of the fireplace, where I watch as he strikes a match to the kindling beneath the logs. Can I be blamed for my continuing stare as he grabs a blanket from the love seat and spreads it across the area with gorgeous grace?

At once, I dismiss the rhetoric as the noise it is. I'd dare every saint in the books to ignore the sight of this magnificent male in this exquisite moment, especially when he glances over and flashes a smirk that belongs nowhere near a holy altar. He's mesmerizing. Captivating. I could stand here all night in gawk mode and mark the time as a win.

But thank fate and all its fortune, my man isn't in basic gawk mode. "I hope this'll do as a nectar meadow?"

I follow the line of his downward glance and give in to a giggle. The blanket's design depicts flowers and ferns. "It's the most stunning meadow I've ever seen."

"And you're the most stunning woman I've ever known."

He paces back over, unfaltering about his intention. And oh my God, I'm riveted with desire. More so when I trace every play of the gold and orange light across his towering form and chiseled face. Even in his dark T-shirt and jeans, he's a mass of Olympus-worthy movement—and he's focusing all of it on me. My bloodstream zings. My core constricts.

"Look who's talking stunning, mister."

Thankfully, my vocal cords still work—at least until he steps in closer, now just a breath away. My throat constricts to the width of a pin as he delves his hands into my hair.

"Nothing like what you did today for Kell and Jaden." He extends his thumbs, stroking them along the crests of my cheekbones. "I'm never *not* proud of you, Kara. But everything today…it was next level."

I gulp hard, managing at least a few syllables. "Well, as much as I like the versatility of catsuits, nobody's lining up to fit me for a matching mask and cape." *Thank God.*

"This has nothing to do with watching you access your powers. It was knowing what you had to do beforehand. Pushing past so many fears and insecurities. And acknowledging that you actually could."

Everything he says is an affirming miracle. But I shake my head, unwilling to accept all the dazzlement. The truth here is too prominent.

"I did what I had to do, Maximus. I didn't have much of a—"

"Choice?" He stops his caresses. His gaze narrows. "That currency's not good right now. You very much had a choice—a lot of them, actually—and none of them easy. Best as I can tell, nobody got out a gun and pointed it at you for the decision."

"Nobody had to. Rerek was wielding the worse weapon. And we had no time to strategize an easier plan."

"Like there was one?"

I let his point stand. Theorizing an answer won't be of

any use now. "I'm just glad that Kell and J are safe." I smile again, thumping his chest in a celebratory rhythm. "I'm happy that we really did it."

"You mean that *you* did."

"No. I mean *we*." I slide my hands to the crooks of his elbows. "Without you and Arden, I probably would've been in a direct face-off with Rerek. Good chance that would've had me going catatonic."

He huffs. "I don't believe that."

"I do. And before all of that, just watching you two charge into the villa, all bold and brave and badass…it was the rocket boost I needed, at just the right time."

He slides a hand to the back of my neck and brings me closer again. "No pun intended, of course."

A sigh spills from me. I already know his intention, as clear as the cobalt rings that intensify around his irises. "You're my rocket fuel, Maximus Kane. The propellant for my flight. The wings to my spirit."

He leans over until our foreheads are pressed together. "And you're the bridge to my soul, Kara Valari."

As those words sink in, there's a burst inside my chest. A bloom of warmth that starts like so many others he's inspired, only to quickly become something different. Incredibly, almost frighteningly, different.

Just as suddenly, I track the change back to…him. There's a new layer to his aura, feral but beautiful, that's never been there before. Its energy prowls closer to mine, daring the corresponding parts of me to slip free.

Oh, yes. So good.

I press up on tiptoes, making sure more than just our foreheads have contact. Our chests press and pitch. Our groins notch and throb.

"And if I cross that bridge right now?" I rasp against his parted lips. "What will I find waiting for me?"

A rough sound rambles up his throat. He pushes in to take my bottom lip between his teeth. "*Not* a quaint little nature scene."

Air escapes me in shaky spurts. "Promise?"

There are no more words from him in response. Only actions that deliver on every syllable of his promise, in every way I crave. As he kisses me again, more references to honey push to mind, though I'm far from being a flitting bee about them. Not possible when I'm weighed by a barge of such heavy heat. It stunts my breaths and liquefies my knees. I drag him to the meadow blanket with me, and we're instantly tangled in each other atop the printed ferns and flowers.

The flames in the fireplace find their way into an air pocket between the logs. Sparks pop and light flares as Maximus sears his mouth to mine again.

He's inside me, exploring my tongue with his.

He's next to me, unhooking my bra and then stripping it off along with my dress.

He's atop me, peeling away his own clothes with more captivating motion.

And now he's here, fully bare and beautiful. Sinewy and striated. His gaze filled with necessity, his muscles clenching in all the best places.

All of them...along with one particular, and oh-so-vital, organ.

"Have to have you," he murmurs with more smoke than the stuff swirling off the logs. "Have to take you, right now. *Kara* …"

"Yes." It's barely an audible gasp, rushed out between my heavy pants. "Now … is really damn good. *Ohhh!*"

The breathy stutters are gone. My groan consumes my lungs as desire subjugates my senses. It's urgent and vibrant and a thousand kinds of hypnotizing. If that's really the case, I never want to be snapped out of the spell. I'll never have enough of this beautiful man, especially when he stares like he'll never have enough of *me*.

The edges of his elegant lips turn up, as if I've given him exactly that message with my thoughts. I almost expect one of his wry quips to temper my serious mush, but entirely different words are the entirety of his next husk.

"I love you."

"And I love you," I whisper at once.

He makes good on his word, truly taking me. One thrust and we're joined in full, rocking together in a rhythm older than the ages. Surely that was when the cosmos conceived the perfection of us as well. This fire is too pure, this need too complete. It feels too sinfully right to be this full of him yet craving more.

"Hang on, beautiful. This is going to be …"

"What?" I urge when the words are taken over by a heavy handful of his lusty breaths. At last, after his brow knits and his concentration steadies, he answers with one growl-infused word.

"Rough."

One *perfect* word.

I gouge ten grooves into his shoulders and hike my legs higher. He snarls sinfully into my ear, and I into his. Still, I pull together enough breath to give him a seductive answer.

"Promise?"

Unsurprisingly, we fall asleep in each other's arms in front of the fire. It's also not a shock to wake and learn Maximus is awake before me. I open my eyes to the sight of him drenched in early morning sunlight. His naked torso, rising from the blanket we've borrowed from the sofa, is better than a whole pot of coffee.

The best part of the sight is what the sunbeams do to his eyes. It doesn't hurt that he seems to be in a direct staring contest with the daytime star, and probably winning. The rings around his irises are nearly royal purple, contrasting with the sparks of blue fire seeming to spring from his pupils.

He's beyond beautiful. And more than mine.

I don't stop to question the conclusion anymore. It's my miracle to claim, and I'm no longer afraid to do so. With every conviction of my heart.

He's even more gorgeous while stretching an arm up and then beneath his head. While watching every mouth-watering moment of the action, I contemplate marauding him again. After the success of last night's acrobatics, I'm tempted to take up some rock climbing classes to hone my skills. Or maybe pole dancing. Why not both?

My growling stomach sabotages my plans for a surprise

mount-up. It's so obnoxious, I add a fast giggle to the symphony.

"Well, good morning to you too, Miss Valari."

"Sorry," I mumble into his chest because the chance to press flesh with his pectoral is *not* to be ignored. "I know you have that strict rule about snacks in class, Professor."

His chuckle sends delicious vibrations through my cheek. "I have even stricter rules about my woman going without nourishment for too long—and someone distracted me before I could get her properly fed last night."

"I blame it on the bee," I quip. "That's my story, and I'm sticking to it."

"Well, tell the bee it's time to go to breakfast." He punctuates with a light smack to my outer thigh. "I'm sure some tea with honey sounds good right now."

I don't disagree with him, especially when we arrive at the sala and I see Kell settling in with some fruit and coffee on the deck out back.

"Go ahead," Maximus encourages, already seeing the happy anticipation on my face. "Sister time awaits. I'm going to grab some java and head over to the barn. Check in on how everyone's doing over there."

I pull on the bottom of his messy bun to compel his lips down to mine. "Thank you," I whisper after our short but mushy kiss. "For the incredible size of your heart."

"Which you're still sworn to secrecy about once we get back to campus," he mutters for my ears alone.

"Yes, sir." I can't help a little grin. If only for a moment, it feels so good to be thinking about reading and essay deadlines instead of supernatural species riffs and honing my crazy witch abilities. "Mustn't have anyone thinking the Heathcliff of Alameda is actually a snuggly puppy guy."

"More like a tiger, fox, and horse guy, but you're still officially ordered to bite your tongue."

"Unless you want to do that for me?"

The rush of heat across his face almost has me turning around and dragging him...well, someplace other than here. I must admit, the library and its cozy vibes have already inspired a few nonliterary fantasies since we arrived.

Somehow, at least for now, we succeed in stowing our carnal cravings to approach the breakfast buffet. I'm not shy about plopping one, sometimes two, of everything on my plate. I'm also perfectly ready for Kell's sisterly commentary on the spread, issued as soon as I drop next to her.

"Holy shit." She huffs. "Knew I should've caved and grabbed a scone. Those look better up close."

"Which was why I grabbed two. You want cherry or lemon-lavender?"

"I have to pick?" Yet she greedily scoops up the lemon-lavender. "Beloved mother of carbs, this is breathtaking."

"But you still aren't gasping like you did for Arden last night."

Her gaze, a russet-infused color a second ago, goes nearly black. "I gasped *at* him. Big difference, darling. A huge one."

I tilt my head. "Huge? Are we talking the size of the diamond he threw into the ocean for you?"

She flings her pastry to her plate hard enough to cause

a soft *ching*. "Did you really want the lemon-lavender one? Is that why you're being a premium-level brat now?"

I flare my gaze. "Because I asked a simple question?"

She sniffs and reclaims the scone. "To clarify the point, nobody's doing anything for anyone unless it's Arden out for himself." Her side-eye is even more accusatory. "Tell me I don't have to spell that part out too. And for the record, your smugness is killing me worse than a scented candle shop."

Here's the point where I wisely choose to let her gain some mental footing. It's a good excuse to bite into my own scone, albeit with a lopsided smile.

"Well, as long as we're speaking on the record..." While brushing crumbs from the corner of my mouth, I make sure I've got her full attention. "I didn't tell you the full story about Arden's role in everything last night."

"Let me guess. He was the one who helped you fly up to the roof. He sprinkled you with dust made out of fairies' crushed souls."

"Interesting phraseology." I deliberately firm my spine. She's had her second to recompose; now she needs to see I'm serious about this. "Because he's the one who might be facing some soul squashing right now. When he first came here looking for me, Mother was with him. But there's not-so-fun history between the witches and her, and it was too hard for her to look past it to tell me anything."

Kell sits up straighter too. "History? Stuff so bad that she couldn't get past it? For J and me?"

"She was convinced she had other options."

"Ah. Sure," she grouses. "Like consulting her astrologist

or calling a press conference."

I reach for her hand. "To be fair, she was somewhere between off-balance and wrecked. And not in the grab-my-meds kind of way. I think it was really hard for her, just coming here in the first place. And I don't think it had anything to do with a bruised ego or damaged optics."

"You're kidding, right?" She pulls free to snatch up a strawberry and bite into it. "Everything's about optics."

"Not this time," I insist. "What I felt from her this time ... it was about ... trust. Well, a lack of it."

"So what happened then? If she ended up not telling you, did they just blow smoke and leave?"

She chuckles. I don't.

"Succinctly put, yes." I'm prepared for her to treat the berry as furiously as she did the scone. I'm not wrong. "But a few hours later, Arden found a way to circle back and return on his own."

"And Mother was okay with th—" Her gaze bugs wide. "Oh! She *didn't* know!"

Weirdly, I welcome the smack of her shock. It's not a rom-com matchmaker moment filled with the gleeful recognition of the enemies turned soft on each other—nothing about Arden Prieto will ever be that way—but at least Kell knows the whole story now. That in his warped way, he's trying to make things work. What that eventually looks like between the two of them is anyone's guess. I wish someone around here actually had the power of premonition, but even for Hecate, the future's a cloudy gazing ball.

"Kara?"

And speaking of our goddess leader ...

"*Kalimera*," Hecate says in the soothing tones that blend with her ever-present wardrobe bells. Today they're hunter green, adorning gauzy scarves around her waist and head. A light-green tank top and a colorful skirt complete her look. "It is a good morning, indeed, to see you and your sister better rested."

"Thank you, Goddess." I finish my murmur by giving Kell a hard knee nudge.

"Ow!" she grates, but then, "Uh. Yes. Thank you... um... Goddess. And... calamari to you too."

To my relief, Hecate emits a soft chortle. I bite my lip to avoid joining her. It doesn't seem right to be so amused by Kell's little gaffe. Thankfully, Hecate seems as ready to move on as me.

"Morgan's made up your morning elixir," she says gently. "So be sure to go grab it in the kitchen. We'll start morning enlightenment at half past the hour, as Circe and I must go over some feed requisitions with Kiama. That is, if you're feeling up to it?"

"Up... to it?" I hesitate saying anything more, wondering if I'm interpreting things wrong. But the new humor in her iridescent eyes confirms her purposeful pun, and I finally set a laugh free. "Of course, Goddess. Whatever *flies* best for the two of you."

Hecate tosses her head back with a good-natured groan. "Oh my, diamond. How you keep me on my toes."

She uses that as an affectionate parting shot, ensuring the sunny grin stays parked on my lips. I'm even beaming around a new bite of scone—until Kell's bemused stare turns into a force I can't ignore. She looks lost and found at the same time, darting her regard between Hecate's back and my face.

"What?" I manage before sloshing down the pastry with a swig of tea.

"She calls you *diamond*?"

"We're all called that." I shrug. "Guess it's like being in a sorority or something."

"Since when were you okay with being in a sorority?"

"Is that really your point?"

"No, actually." She only picks at her scone now. "It's just…this is so surreal. You're a *witch*. And now you're getting pointers about it from the goddess of magic herself, live and in-person at that goddess's secret ashram."

I can't avoid a laugh this time. "*Ashram?*"

"Tell me what else you call a place where breakfast is heralded with a Tingsha chime instead of a ranch triangle, everyone chugs 'morning elixir,' and there's food being ordered for the horses and goats?"

"And the fox and tiger," I add.

She whacks a hand to her forehead. "Now how did I forget them again?"

My giggle mellows into a wide smile. I still can't help it. It feels like I've lived the equivalent of a decade in the space of a week, but just for this moment, I'm the person I remember from before. A simple student just hanging out with her sarcastic sister over our morning caffeine.

"Fine. Your metaphor's sort of valid," I finally concede.

"Sort of?" Kell drawls.

"But does that change anything? Hecate and the others

have welcomed us here—clothed and fed us—and I'm beyond thankful."

"As am I," she offers with sincerity. "But that doesn't mean I've tossed my caution over the cliff. Nor that I should." She leans toward me by a few inches. "Come on, classics major. You know this material better than I. Hecate may be the coolest witchy OG there is, but she's still a *goddess*. And have you ever known of a god or goddess to drop their ethereal duties and mentor a protégé because their hearts are simply that pure?"

I shift a little. "Hecate hasn't exactly whipped out a contract and demand I sign it in blood, Kell."

"Good to know," she replies with a forced breeze in her voice. "I only hope she's not holding out for something more precious than that when she collects on the debt."

I scoff. "You're being paranoid."

"And I hope *you're* right on that one, sister."

CHAPTER 20

MAXIMUS

"AH! AS ALWAYS, YOUR timing is perfect," Kiama calls as I enter the barn. At the other end, there's a large truck piled with too many hay bales to count. "In the mood to sling some hay, Professor?"

"Knew there was a reason I inhaled three scones on the way over here," I reply with a grin.

Hers is a bright complement to her glowing skin. "See? I was right. You're also perfectly fueled up."

The delivery guy has already offloaded about a dozen bales. I breathe in, enjoying their sweet grassy smell. "Where do these get stored?"

"There's a storage loft to the left of where you just came in, but we have a portable elevator. Haul these outside. Liseli will show you how to load them on the hopper. Here are some spare hooks and gloves."

"What?" I tease, thankful that the gloves fit my massive paws. "You don't just whoosh it all upstairs with a spell or two?"

She flexes both arms. "We like to tackle a few things the hard way. Probably why it's always so fun."

"Speak for yourself." The source of that gibe, one slightly scowling sorceress who's quickly finishing a long braid of her thick hair, walks up and turns her focus to me. "Welcome! You have terrific timing."

"So I've been told."

"And also properly recruited. Good job, Ki." She winks in response to her friend's saucy smirk. "We're sure to get this done in no time."

She's right. With the help of the hay elevator, we get the bales into the loft with speed and ease. Having already inhaled my breakfast, I tell the two witches to head to the sala for their meal while I finish stacking the bales. Turns out Kiama's mind-set is contagious. It feels good to be working up an honest and productive sweat for the first time in a while.

After neatly placing the last big brick of hay, I straighten and use my T-shirt to wipe my face.

I'm ready to congratulate myself with a satisfied sigh, but the air stops short in my throat. There's extra noise in the barn, and it's not the goats getting amorous.

It's voices.

A pair that my instincts recognize before my logic does. Ergo, the gag order inspiration.

Circe and Hecate do *not* sound inspired to do the same. But just like yesterday morning, they're chopping their volume down with stubborn intent. They're so lasered on arguing with each other, none of the creaks from the hay loft have them tossing a single glance overhead. Not that I'm moving, let alone luxuriating in breathing, at the moment.

"Calm? You want me to stay calm despite everything you're implying right now?" Circe spits, only to earn herself the imperious iridescence of her leader's glare.

"I will not repeat myself," Hecate intones. "You heard me the first time. I have no idea—"

"You have *every* idea," Circe snaps. "And you know precisely what I'm talking about. You knew exactly when and where to find us yesterday, even after my cover story about needing to run down the hill to grab more medicine for the goats. That's because you knew it was a cover all along. Because you *already knew* what had happened to Kell. But you told me nothing. Why? Hecate, why didn't you say a single th—"

"Calm. Down. I insist on meaning it this time." Hecate's tone matches Circe's terse stomps, though her own steps are as queenly as ever. "You'll start agitating the beasties, not to mention Jaden and his extraordinary ears. If Kiama and Liseli don't come running back first, then—"

"Let them. Let *him*. Why not everyone else too? Maybe that's exactly what should happen now. Forget about letting *me* in on things. Maybe it's just time that *everyone* knows about this insanity of yours. What they're signing onto by continuing to declare fealty to you."

Damn. I mouth the word while pulling back, blending with the shadows, just in time. As Hecate drops her head back, her gaze hits the edge over which I was just leaning.

"Insanity? That's not what you were saying a few days

ago during Hera's freshest drama."

And now I wish I still had a full visual on them. *Hera*. I didn't hear it wrong, though I deeply wish I had. It's three degrees of separation, the Olympian version. The queen's name, on this goddess's lips, circles my mind back around to Magaera and her continued cavortings in this realm, disguised as Erin Levin. Clearly, the harpy isn't making a single move without Hera's consent—but why?

Hera's drama …

Something happened to set off Z's spiteful spouse …

Ten days ago …

Between one blink and the next, my brain aligns facts more succinctly than the hay bales behind me.

It was me.

Ten days ago was when Z found me and reached out to me. And by finding me, putting himself one step closer to my mother. The woman he clearly still has feelings for …

Circe's enraged huff hooks my attention again. I dare to lean out by an inch, watching her face pinch with matching ire.

"A few weeks ago—even a few *days* ago—I assumed Hera and Meg *were* the craziest ones in the acropolis. I didn't comprehend how you were chugging your own train straight toward the cliff…" Her cracking syllables send her head into her hands for a long moment. "And now you're about to crash it."

I'm able to catch the hitch of Hecate's shoulders, which does eerie things to the snakes tattooed there. The images seem to frown deeper along with Circe.

"But I'm still the locomotive," the goddess croons.

"Even after you've exploded at the bottom of a ravine?" Circe spreads her hands in an entreating sweep. "Goddess. Please. You're gambling on credit we *all* can't afford. If anyone, especially Arden, discovers that you were the back-channel source of intel to the *Hysminai*—"

"And how exactly would they learn that, my lovely lustre?" Hecate levels her stare. "While I'm certain that Rerek's started to harbor some theories, only two individuals know that little tidbit as fact—and I'm positive my favorite *Hysminai* lieutenant plans on keeping *his* mouth closed."

Circe drops her hands and pivots away. "None of that makes it right."

"From whose view?" the goddess retorts. "Are you really committed to the end result here, Circe? If so, then resign yourself with the means to get there and the timeline we have to accelerate. Our window to act is closing, and more rapidly than we thought."

Circe whirls back around, eyes encroaching on reptilian with their amber intensity. "But Kara—"

"Has to be shoved past her comfort zone at a less-than-ideal pace. As do we all."

"Well, *we all* weren't the ones soaring over Malibu last night."

Hecate pulls up her posture so regally, it's daunting. Even from up here. Circe is obviously affected too, her posture cowing like a subdued cobra.

"It was necessary," the goddess firmly declares. "Not the way I would normally go about such a test for a novice diamond, but urgent times call for bold decisions."

"So that's why you supplied Kell's exact location to the *Hysminai*?" Circe spits. "Because you wanted to throw some more activator fluid on Kara's abilities?" She doesn't wait for Hecate to finish with the regal nostril flare. "What if things didn't work out that way? If Kara never got word about Kell's capture?"

"Contingencies were in place," Hecate assures. "Though I must admit, Prieto behaved with heroism I didn't expect. And there I was, thinking I'd have to implant the girl with a hideous premonition."

"Well, of course." Circe doesn't pull the wallop of her sarcasm. "Because that wouldn't have taxed her circuits to their limits *before* having to do a controlled levitation onto a three-level Malibu villa protected by a chaos demon hex. Not too much to ask of her at all, right?"

"*Enough.*" A severe huff escapes Hecate. Her chin juts with defensive purpose. "Would you rather I told them to take the mansion's *housekeepers*? Tell me, how effective would that have been in motivating Kara? You think she would've pushed past her fear—the panic so great, she'd probably still be trembling at Rerek's place right now—to do what she did? And my stars, how she *did*. Come now, darling. Even you have to admit that it was glorious to witness."

"My impressions are of no matter here." Circe steps back again, though now it's to put her defiant flare on Hecate's captious prioress pose. "Kara's the one who should take center concern—"

"She does," the goddess insists. "She *is* my highest—"

"That so? So you've come clean with her? Told her about using her own sister and brother to speed up her progress toward witchy gloriosity? That you sold Kell out to Hades's forces as a means to that end? Have you let her ponder what would've happened if it had all gone sideways and her siblings were still in Rerek's hold?"

Hecate's steps, tracing an invisible oval in the middle of the floor, are no longer so regal. She's not in the corner but feeling like it. She's agitated. Aggravated. Unsheathing the claws.

"I wouldn't have let that happen, and you know it. To either Jaden or Kell."

Circe's sigh takes her energy in the opposite direction. She's resigned. Sad.

"No, Goddess. I *don't* know that. Not anymore." She doesn't flinch when Hecate wheels around, brandishing a full glower. "I hardly know you anymore. You're so obsessed with this scheme... Do you honestly not see the desperate danger of your actions?"

"Scheme?" the goddess chirps out now, wielding a high laugh. "So that's actually what you think this is?"

Circe rolls her head from one side to the next. "To be honest, I don't know what to think. Can you make the case for anything different?"

Hecate's lips twist. She rocks back with a blithe expression. "All right, then. Let's go ahead and call it a *scheme.* But what do I really know of schemes? You're the expert about all this, right?"

A tentative stillness from the enchantress. "What are you talking ab—"

"I mean, *I* never lured a whole battalion of soldiers to my private island and then spelled them into pigs. I also was never able to keep their pretty leader on said island for a whole year, feeding and bathing and gods-only-knows-what-else-ing him into compliance."

Circe's cheeks darken by several shades. The malachite in her gaze is now the shade of burnt copper. "Don't. You. Dare," she growls.

"Do what?" Hecate scoffs. "Play out the subject *you* started?"

"Odysseus stays out of this. He's an innocent too!"

"He's *dead*. A mortal who passed centuries ago. And if you want his descendants to live out their own lives as peacefully as he did, do your duty as an Olympian. Defibrillate that aching heart and check the steel in your spine. Only girders survive storms, lustre. Especially the one that we're about to bring."

The shallow breaths I've been permitting myself are again ordered to a stop, counterbalancing the small creaks beneath my feet as I angle for a better look at the troubled enchantress.

Come on, Circe. Don't go soggy hay on me. Challenge her! I need more details!

So many more details.

But mostly just one.

What the living hell is Hecate planning here?

But just like yesterday in the kitchen, the goddess wins again. Circe shuts off her fortitude like a light switch, demonstrated by the swift sag of her shoulders and the sharp dip of her head.

Which plunges me into the same clueless darkness as before.

"Forgive me, Goddess," she finally mumbles, though to anyone's ear the words are full of a different message. Something between *fuck you, Goddess* and *can I punch the wall now?*

"Nothing to be forgiven for," comes Hecate's maddening croon. "None of this is easy, but we must remain steadfast. Your heart is good, Circe, and it is bound to a true cause. In the end, you will see that with clarity."

It's a good phrase for them to leave on. I grab some much-needed breaths as soon as the witches exit the building, while wasting no time in blending the creaks of my new steps into the barn's groans from a new canyon breeze.

But my abundance of caution doesn't have me rushing down the loft's ladder yet. I can jump into action right from where I'm at.

Because with the new knowledge I've gained, sparse as it is, sitting still is no longer a comfortable option.

It's time to figure some shit out.

To do that properly, I'm going to need help.

Despite the resolution, I'm scowling as I swipe to the contacts page on my phone—and hit the name that shows up as most recent. I roll my eyes, hardly believing I'm doing this, but one of Hecate's silky one-liners actually comes in handy.

Urgent times call for bold decisions.

Though I'm still not sure if this is bold or just stupid.

"We really must stop meeting like this, darling," Arden croons over the line against a backdrop of heavy traffic.

"And either Veronica has found out what you did and thrown you out for it, or you were expecting someone else." I keep my voice below the caution line. If either Circe or Hecate lingered after their tiff, it's best that my murmur blends with the stirring beasts.

"Truthfully, neither," Arden says. "Hard as it is to believe, Veronica's working on her Zen-derful side. She's happy all three of the kids are safe and is even talking about throwing a thank-you bash with you and me as guests of honor."

"In what world does she think that's a great idea?"

"Insanity and brilliance often ride the same zip line."

I discreetly clear my throat. "Funny that you bring that up. The insanity portion, at least."

"Well, now I'm curious."

"Fine. Just tell me you're curious and close. To Iremia, I mean."

A rough hum escapes from him. "I can be. What's going on? Are Kell and Kara still safe?"

"For the time being, yes. And I plan on keeping it that way."

"So what do you need from me?"

"A fast and private way past Hecate's perimeter. Then a faster ride back into the city."

"Done. I can meet you and Kara at—"

"No. Just me. Kara can't know about this. Same goes for your betrothed. Not yet, at least. Hopefully all this leads us to absolutely nothing. If that's the case, I'll gladly wear a dozen eggs all over my face."

"I'll hold you to that."

It takes me a second to respond to his thoroughly serious line. "Just get here as soon as you can, fancy pants."

After telling me to wait for him at the old well near the barn, he quickly disconnects the call. But there's one more call I have to make before climbing down from here.

The other person who's crucial for this process.

The guy who picks up my call after half a ring.

"Well, if it isn't my favorite pain in the ass."

"Is that any way to talk to a colleague, Professor North?"

"When said colleague disappears for a couple of days and has me fearing the worst? Why don't *you* answer that?"

"And why don't I do you one better?"

"That depends. Are you bearing some bottles of Macallan or a pair of kinky twins?"

I laugh, which feels good despite the ape-sized stress that insists on riding my back. "How about an invitation to meet at the research library on campus?"

"*Hel*-lo. Do I get a vague hint of what it's about this time?"

"Only that we've got to do it quickly," I supply. "Something tells me we're working against a ticking time bomb here."

"Seriously? Less than a week after Mother Earth shook her sweet ass across the city?"

Another good-natured sound tumbles out. "Afraid so."

"Okay. Ticking time bomb. Aimed to blow up what, exactly?"

"If I seriously only knew, buddy."

CHAPTER 21

"OKAY, ADMIT IT," CIRCE challenges past her ear-to-ear grin—and the sweat-soaked curls that have escaped her high ponytail. "This is way more fun than you thought it would be."

I stop to catch my breath in the middle of the wild flower field she and Hecate brought me to a couple of hours ago. "Okay, okay," I laugh out. "Sure. Happy now?"

She cocks her head and retightens her hair. "Believe it or not, despite how soundly you just kicked my ass, yes."

I let out a longer chuckle and turn my face up to catch more of the sun. It permeates my skin, blending with my endorphins and kicking back some awesome euphoria.

Admittedly, I wasn't nuts about the venue change for this morning's enlightenment. I like *looking* at scenes like this, with the gentle slopes covered in sun-drenched daisies and poppies, but not tromping through it all in suede ankle boots and a strangely tied-off skirt in the name of a yet-to-be-clarified sorceress soul quest.

If that's even what this is.

Or maybe that's exactly what it is.

Maybe my two teachers have actually lost track of their souls—which would be no surprise, based on the friction darting like crazy electrodes between them. It now has me double-checking the status quo of mine.

Better yet, with the amazing being who's been entrusted with its safekeeping.

Just a few thoughts of Maximus in, and my day is already brighter and better. He has to be the most aptly named male in history. The syllables don't just reflect his formidability or sing about his beauty, they declare the strength that permeates both. The truth of who he really is.

But it's time to jump out of those particular clouds. Very clearly, we're not done with our training games. We began over an hour ago with an elaborate form of hopscotch, where we leaped fifteen feet between our designated squares. After that, we laughed our way through Pendragon, Hecate's cool update on Marco Polo, with boulders and tree stumps as safe spaces.

Now, despite Circe's easygoing acceptance of her defeat in the game's final round, I grow uneasy again. "Uhhh … what's she up to now?" I mutter, nodding to Hecate's tiny figure in the distance. "This is way too big a field for Red Rover, even the witchy version."

The enchantress tilts her head like a questioning cat. "Meaning what?"

"Ermmm … that if you two expect me to swoop all the way over there …"

"Is that how Red Rover is normally played?" She leans in during my long silence. "In a *swoop*? Or is the challenge better approached one step at a time?"

"Sure," I mumble. "I mean, I guess."

Her scrutiny intensifies. "Come now. You must've played as a child."

I toe the ground. "Our tutors didn't know those kinds of things. During the few years that Kell and I convinced Mother it would be good for us to have some *real* school memories in order to be more relatable as public figures, I was more into the library over the playground. And when I was coaxed out—"

"You had a lot of fun?" She lifts a sagacious smile. Or so she thinks.

"Not exactly." I hasten to address her jolt of new confusion. "I mean, it was cool feeling like just another normal kid...at first. That was before the boys realized that reading books didn't make me as weak as parchment. When they couldn't bend or break me like they first assumed, they got confused and mad. So did all the girls who had crushes on them."

I'm gratified to watch a wince take over her face. "Mmmph. I'm sorry about that. Doesn't sound too different from the peasants who couldn't decide between burning or worshipping me."

"At least the frog prince must've been grateful."

"For all of a few days," she mutters. "Which forced me to recognize what a waste of talent he'd been."

After a defined nod, she shores up her stance. The prouder demeanor has me doing the same, to the point that

I nearly forget the awkward swoops of my skirt and the sweat that makes my tank cling in too many uncomfortable places.

"So, did all that make things difficult for Kell and Jaden too?"

I laugh without mirth. "They were both smarter than that. They simply learned how to blend. Kell got in fast with every member of the fashionista crowd, while Jaden chose not to bother with school at all. That landed him an invitation to a clique all its own."

"Ah. Yes." A new nod from her is still confident, though in a new way. "Young Valari and his wild ways crew."

I throw a fast double take. Though that term was practically vernacular a few years ago with the press's overuse, it's been a while since I've heard it voiced out loud. Jaden's crazier dubs died when he decided to upgrade his extreme sports. *The wild ways crew* doesn't carry the same ring when it actually applies to a racing car pit team instead of a Valari on a nightclub floor with kohl-eyed groupies.

"You actually know about all that?"

Circe waggles her brows. "You think they break into *Hathaway Harbor* with alerts about *real* news?"

I chuckle again. This time it's genuine. "Winning point."

There's an answering quip in her bright-gold eyes, but it never materializes on her lips. Instead, she's back to sobriety that's a little jarring.

"But you ... never really blended."

Maybe more than a little.

Though it's not as if I haven't already admitted this

truth. *Long* before now. "Now you know why I liked the library so much."

Still no change to the gleam in her gaze—or the knowingness across her mouth. The certainty that solidifies as she continues to mull over my statement.

I heave a resigned sigh. She's not going to let this go until I confess everything.

"All right, I didn't fit in ... mostly because I didn't want to," I confess. "Living so much in the human world always felt like ..."

"What?" she asks, all the way invested now.

"Well ... like denying my demon side."

"And your grandfather along with it?"

She gets my fast but grateful nod. "But it was hard to figure out all the demon stuff too." I wince. "Really hard."

"Which is perfectly okay to admit, diva." The nickname is more like an endearment now, especially when coupled with a gentle grasp of my tense fingers. "*All* of it. You grew up with one foot in each world, though the ground in both probably felt like quicksand."

A dry chuff tumbles free. "Whatever it was, it was *not* easy to navigate in heels."

"And there's *your* winning point."

"Unless you count the part about being told I now possess a third leg." I nudge up my chin as she crunches a confused frown. "I mean, isn't witch DNA capable of that too?"

She snorts softly. "And there's your victory lap."

The wind, a typical gust of late-September air, blows

extra tendrils into my own face. I scrape them free with a defined scowl. "Victory also being relative?"

"To what?" She pushes in and grabs my hand. "What are you doubting here, Kara?"

Kara. I'm that to her now, instead of *diva.* The distinction makes me edgy again.

I pull my hand away, tangling it with the other in an obvious fidget. "*Doubt*...isn't exactly the right verb. I'm just...wondering, I guess. Perhaps questioning?"

"That's fair." She straightens a little. "And normal. Questions about what?"

"About...all of it."

I look across the meadow, trying to fill my face with apology. Can Hecate see it? Or even feel it? I'm supposed to be minding their instructions right now. Feeling the essence of my breaths and flowing that into my performance on these drills. So my timing for this existential crisis isn't the greatest. Or maybe it's happened exactly as it should. I hope for the latter before pushing on.

"I mean, I'm a witch," I finally say. "And obviously, that's not like discovering I'm double-jointed or have attached earlobes. But what *does* it mean? How does it define what my life is like from now on? Or not like? Do I even have a life expectancy? Am I...killable or not?"

"We are all killable, sweet one." Hecate's *whoosh* of new proximity is barely tempered by the affection with which she finishes. "Even I and every deity in Olympus. Granted, that would take a concerted effort and a celestial civil war, but it's not beyond the realm of possibility. As for your own annihilation?" She dips her head, managing to look perplexed and sage in the same moment. "That's a query we're all still trying to explore. Safely, of course."

"Safely."

It's unsteady in my throat but a necessity in my mind. The implications are already there.

Safely, because of the unknown territory into which I'm still tiptoeing here.

Safely, because it really has been just two days of lessons. Because maybe last night's success really was a mere fluke, aided by Hecate's presence as well as Maximus's and Arden's efforts with waylaying Rerek.

Safely, because even the goddess of magic herself doesn't know what she's dealing with in training me. But I'm certain that it's not because of my human DNA on top of my witch blood. Marie, Aradia, Kiama, and Liseli— probably even Morgana—were all mortal at one time and are fine now.

Undoubtedly, Hecate's more concerned about how my demon blood is influencing things.

A thought that, at the moment, screws with more than the plasma and platelets in my veins. The circuits in my brain are frantically flaring, and not with more admiration for the pastoral scene around us. Not this time.

What if...I'm still screwed here?

What if Hades surrendered me so easily to Hecate because he knew he'd eventually get me back? What if my demon DNA still ties me to hell, even by a thin thread? What if the goddess is aware of that too and is trying to prepare me better for that with all these witchy training sessions?

But who am I kidding about that?

Who are *any* of us kidding?

"Perhaps we're better discussing that over here." Hecate's suggestion, soft but concerned, is still a welcome one as she waves toward a pair of nearby boulders. "But also not until you've had some water. Circe, where are the canteens? She's as pale as pearls."

"I'm fine," I protest. "But I'll take the water anyway."

Neither of them look to be in believing moods, especially as I chug half the contents of a canteen without stopping.

"Must be hotter than I thought," I mumble. "But I'm ready to start again." And then jog up my chin and square my shoulders. "So what's the key for conquering this one?"

Because contemplating some long and crazy leaps across a meadow longer than a football field is way better than pondering when Hades might bend the rules and snatch me back again. And this time, there won't be a grimoire on hand to help me out of that awful dungeon.

Unfortunately, Hecate's had much more practice with her determined stance game. "I think, perhaps, this lesson is best saved for another day," she professes without a hitch.

But for all the certainty of her words, there's separate energy in her spirit. Feelings she can't veil from me because they're so fresh. A little frustration. A lot more disappointment.

"I think we can get it done today," I blurt back in an eager rush. But not the good kind of gusto. I'm pushing it out in desperation, the same sticky stuff I used to drag out with Mother. Back in the days when her opinion still mattered so much.

Too much.

No. This is different. It has to be. Hecate is nowhere near the same plane of existence as Mother. So why am I regressing like this? Could it have some Freudian tie to what happened yesterday morning? And if I'm realizing that with basic logic, why is my psyche allowing all my old tactics back in?

I'm better than that. Different than that. I have to be, for myself and for everyone here who believes in me. Especially these two incredible females. The ones who believe I'm a diamond of Iremia already. I have to show them that I can conjure—and control—the bigger stuff.

I won't freak out the kids on the playground either anymore.

I'm good enough.

I'm good enough.

I'm good en—

"If *getting it done* applies to a pizza run for lunch, then I'm totally in."

It takes me a long couple of seconds to snap my head up and around, riveting my gaze on the new arrival to our meadow.

"Just when a girl thinks she's safe from the sonar sibling…"

I trail it on purpose, hoping my tone will catch up with my sarcastic words. But Jaden's expression conveys that failure. I'm still too deep in my weird mire, craving every drop of my teacher's approval.

This is *not* me. It never has been. So what crazy rabbit hole have I fallen into?

I have no workable answer for that. But, at least for the moment, I'm not alone in the hole. A longer look at my little brother confirms it.

Jaden is in a noticeable muck of his own. He wasn't just out for a casual stroll. But he also wasn't purposely eavesdropping on our conversation. I sense he's here on a mini mission of sorts—looking specifically for me. The observation gives me the encouragement I need to change course with Hecate and Circe.

"Maybe you're right," I admit. "Holding off on the rest of this will give me something to anticipate for tomorrow."

Circe's grin is radiant. "Another winning point!"

Hecate pushes off her boulder and takes me into a hug that should be patented for its warmth and comfort. "You're remarkable, sweet one, even for how far you got today." When she pulls back, her gaze is as happy as her second-in-command's. She runs a gentle palm along my cheek. "We'll see you at the midday meal. And Jaden?" She gives him a tender wink. "I'll ask the lunch crew if they have materials for whipping up a quick pizza."

"Yesss."

My brother doesn't drag out the fist pump for long. As soon as Hecate and Circe stroll off toward the sala, he's gamboling toward the boulder chat area. "Hey, this is all pretty cool. Beats a stuffy classroom, yes?"

I fold my arms and wait for him to turn. "Chitchat is only effective on first dates and morning news shows. You should already know that, little brother."

"And big sisters shouldn't be so damn right all the time." In spite of the grouse, he cocks a casual hip to one of the big stones.

"Of course." I try to accent it with a laugh but get another long study of his profile. "But *right* doesn't mean omniscient, and the last time you looked this serious was when your gecko died. Jaden? What's going on?"

CHAPTER 22

MAXIMUS

ALAMEDA'S RESEARCH LIBRARY HAS always felt like a sanctum for me, but never more so than this afternoon. Probably because the place is quieter than usual as Arden and I enter through the sliding glass doors on the ground level. The university is only four days into McCarthy's two weeks of canceled classes, meaning even the most diligent students won't start trickling back in for another week.

The only signs of life we spot are a quick smile and wave from one of the research specialists at the desk and some soft coughs from the three national guardsmen who've found their way to the library's chess theory section. One of them plunks a curious gaze onto Arden and me on our way to the main stairwell, but he's the visitor in *my* stomping grounds, so I move on.

Arden scoffs with barely tamped disdain. "Ill manners certainly wait under any rock in the forest, hmmm?"

"Spoken like a guy who's only been on this campus for the fancy fundraisers."

A new grumble leaves him. "Do you think that churl's tendons will emulsify as quickly as Rerek's door hinges?"

I double my pace up the stairs, forcing him to keep up. "We've got bigger questions to address."

With answers more elusive than splinters in snow.

It's a gigantic risk, and I admit it. Leaving so fast from Iremia, without even telling Kara, was either really smart or really stupid. But I'm banking on the former over the latter. That I'll be able to return before Kara even knows I'm gone. That Hecate stays just as clueless. That I'll sneak back in and claim a long hike for aiding my trip on the perimeter alarms. Better yet, that I'll return after learning a totally innocuous reason for the goddess's secret hissing sessions with Circe. That I'll be making up for the melodrama tonight by pleasuring Kara under the stars, in the private area next to our little stream.

Thoughts I don't have any more time to indulge. *Game face* has never been a more applicable idiom for a situation: a conclusion I never thought I'd be embracing on this campus outside of orientation week. Few things can turn a roomful of students into a shiver of sharks faster than a professor who's off their game, and something tells me that Arden's instincts are even sharper right now. He'll get no blood in this water if I can help it.

I just wish that wasn't such a big *if*.

With perfect timing, the elevator *bing-bongs* as soon as we reach the landing. Before the doors are done opening,

I'm smiling. "What do we have here? No telling what the lift will drag up these days."

"Mmmph," Jesse flings back. "Missed you too, honey."

The sarcasm already gives him away. He means it more than he wants to admit, same way I secretly concede the same thing. The last five days have felt like a century for many reasons, but the top of that list definitely contains the sacrifice of barely seeing this guy. More confessions that have to be tossed aside. I settle for leaning in and clapping the guy's shoulder with brotherly brutality.

"Nice togs. Did you go to an early Halloween soiree and decide Miami-bound Davy Crockett was a good look?"

He chuckles. "Sorry not sorry. I picked up whatever was near. I think the shirt might be Misty's dress. Miss Marais is into some interesting role play."

"Marais?" I don't hide my double take. "She has a last name now?"

"Bigger questions to address, Professor Kane?"

I swivel and give Arden a thankful nod. "Touché, antiquities guy."

Slipping in the subtle respect gets me a matching mien from Arden—for the two seconds prior to Jesse's new comment.

"Antiquities?" he blurts. "*And* the *droll troll from the hills* accent? Holy shit. You stunt-joking me here, mister? Is this really him?"

I'm still figuring out what to say when Arden cuts in. "The *droll troll?*"

"Well, well, well," Jesse injects. "It is him. The incubutt, in the flesh. There's got to be a good story behind this."

"The *incubutt*?"

I grimace, hoping it serves as a temporary mea culpa. "Bigger questions, remember?"

"He's right, but I still want that story." Jesse maneuvers his wheelchair in a deft left turn, placing himself in front of Arden. "In the meantime, since it seems we're on the same team for Operation Ticking Time Bomb, the name's Jesse North."

"Arden Prieto." Before they're done shaking hands, he eyeballs me with new force. "Ticking time bomb? You mean different from the one we stopped last night?"

"Eh?" Jesse lashes me with a fresh gape. "What happened last night? And why wasn't I invited?"

Arden rolls his eyes. "Asks the gentleman wearing a leather muumuu for a shirt?"

"And why can't I figure out whether to punch you or salute you?"

"Focus up, gentleman. Please."

I nearly snarl out the last of that while wheeling on them with new steel in my posture. Behind them are the stacks that will become our investigative rabbit hole, if we're lucky and can figure out where to start.

"Focusing," Jesse assures, locking and loading with his own game-ready regard. "Let's get to it. Don't leave anything out of the brief."

I damn well don't.

I give them every single detail I can possibly remember. I start with Hecate and Circe's first frantic whispers in the sala, where references to rearranged constellations were finished by strategies of war. How their composures got no better when Arden brought Veronica for a surprise visit later that day. For Jesse's sake, just in case it means anything, I also give a fast account of our insane rescue mission at Rerek's Malibu place.

At last, I relay the latest confrontation upon which I spied in the barn a few hours ago. I include Circe's agitation and conflict, as well as Hecate's eerie zeal about a grander plan in the works.

A purpose that Circe referred to as an *insane scheme.*

A plot I'm no closer to fathoming, even after verbally laying it all out for these two men. But while my mouth has been busy and articulate, my spirit fights off a ballooning squall of frustration.

And desperation.

Maybe it's because neither of them looks ready with a working theory either. Two of the smartest—and, I'll admit, most devious—men I know, and they both look fairly ready to scratch their heads.

The best response I get is a half-cocked sigh from Jesse as he yanks out his trusty thinking toy from his chair's side pocket.

"Well, nothing like going for one's inner *generalista* over morning *huevos*," he mutters. "Or maybe war talk is a great caffeine substitute."

Arden's more demonstrative about his cluelessness. I let him have his moment to rise, pace, and slam his hands against opposing bookshelves. In honesty, I revel in it. It's surreal but satisfying to be sharing the vexation, more so with a male protecting his own Valari treasure. That still doesn't make him my friend, but for now, ally is good enough.

"Oh?" the incubus finally spits out. "So would that be with or without all the witchcraft fuckery in said coffee?"

"Okay, Sheriff Hellfire. We need a teeny slowdown at the hoedown here." Jesse flicks his wrist with an economic flourish, sending the long rubber rope out to smack the elevator's down button. And then the up. "Can you break that shit down in traceable logic for the rest of the room?"

Arden frowns. "You said Hecate referenced destiny? And readjusting coordinates because of it? The witches using their powers to do so?" As soon as I nod, he does too. "Okay. Right," he mutters.

"What is it?" My volley isn't so much of an order now. Far from it. "Just say it, all right? I wasn't blowing sunshine and C-14 at Jesse. We really could be dealing with a time bomb timeline here. But we won't know for sure until we know where to look for some clues. So, help a guy out? And maybe other people, like your betrothed's whole family?"

He slashes up an arm as if wielding a machete.

I fall into silence as if he's decapitated me with it.

"Fine," he grumbles while lowering it with the same ruthless *whoosh*. "The Iremia sorceresses…what it sounds like they did…Well, it wasn't an easy feat." His gaze darkens, and his lips compress. "Nor, for that matter, a safe one."

I pull in a heavy breath. "In what way?"

"You do mean way*sss*?" he emphasizes, laughing sharply. "The coordinates that Hecate referred to…more than likely, she was referring to maps of stars."

Jesse hitches himself straighter. "Now you're rolling into my neighborhood. What kinds of maps? If you tell me we're talking about separate galaxies, sign me up for the tour bus. As in, right the hell now."

A twinge of regret sneaks into Arden's expression. "I am referring to the same stars we have observed from this orb over the centuries," he states. "Except that certain witches, and likely Hecate herself, are simply able to observe them in different ways."

Jesse's already perking again. "In different ways…how? You mean like magnified shadows, refracted light, extended matter from supernovae?"

"Yes and no." Arden clasps his hands at the small of his back. I ignore his return to arrogant snob mode in favor of listening to the information he's readily dispensing. "They're able to see all of that, of course, in addition to the constellations themselves—only, their view is multidimensional. Better rounded out."

Jesse flings a puzzled frown. "Like how?"

Arden rocks back his head, seeming to deeply examine the ceiling tiles. "Have you ever been to the Pageant of the Masters, down in Laguna Beach?"

"Of course," Jesse replies. "The show where they use real people to recreate classic artworks."

Arden nods. "And because of the special lighting and makeup, you don't realize you're watching three dimensions instead of two."

"Until they turn the lights up and show you how it's done."

I return my friend's grin. "I remember the first time we saw that happen."

Jesse laughs. "Weren't we on a date with those twins from Pasadena? They thought we were such dorks."

"*You* were on a date with the twins. I was along to make things more respectable. And we *were* dorks, at least during that part of the show."

"Meh." The guy slides out a bigger smirk. "I turned it all around to my favor...later on."

Arden pushes past the point to make his. "Witches of a certain stature are able to look at the stars in the same manner. Because of that, they can use the stars as certain predictors of things." He tilts his head toward me. "Like love matches."

The intentional cock of his brow coincides with me jumping both of mine. "Like Kara and me?"

Jesse's grin blasts wider. "Written in the stars, my friend. That actually makes a lot of sense."

If we had more time, I'd be asking what happened to the guy who once sat in that chair, full of pragmatic purpose. But if I'm not the same man I was last month, Jesse's science-facts-first side has been fed with enough evidence to transform him too.

Besides...bigger questions to get to.

The topic of the day has me addressing Arden again. "So, assuming that's all a real thing, that the witches looked and saw our story, foretold by the stars...why are Circe and Hecate still stressing about it? Didn't everything happen the way it should have? I'm in love with Kara, and she with me.

And we're more than aware that we've got something special, so what's the issue with their scheming in the shadows?"

Arden rocks back on his heels and works his jaw back and forth. "Here's where we *do* get to the big questions. Clearly, there was more to their determination about your destiny than scratching some swoony itches. They even pooled the group's powers to ensure everything would fall into place."

Jesse surrenders his smile to a puzzled scowl. "So if the glitches aren't about *what* happened, they're with the *whys* and *hows*?"

"More specifically, the timing." As soon as I say it, I know it's the missing key for at least one of our locks. "Circe specifically talked about calibrating the coordinates differently. That if Kara and I had met next spring, it would've been 'more than enough time.'"

"Okay. For what?" Jesse prompts. "And what does *that* even mean, arranging the coordinates differently? Are we still talking about star maps here? If so"—he's not bashful about his bug-eyed gawk—"then this is now a discussion about messing with the cosmos itself. Even the possible screw-up of a bigger picture. Time itself."

The words are barely out before he's slamming back in the chair, as if his existential mic drop has become a detonation. I don't blame him. In a way, I even applaud him. There's still nothing but gibberish in my mind and larynx.

Thankfully, yet again, Arden's ready with words that make sense.

"So we're of the assumption that the witches have a

timeline for…something. A purpose that's been affected by recent events, somehow forcing their hand. They're clear about some strategic plan that involves Kara, and maybe you, in some way."

"Okay." Jesse whips up a hand. "Before I'm *some*'d to death, let's get moving on figuring out the answers, yes?"

I give a tight nod. "Affirmative."

Arden copies my action. "Just point the way. Which aisle for the paranormal and mystical studies?"

It's impossible not to join Jesse in a snicker. "You mean which *aisles*?" I point across the landing. "That whole section is practically devoted to the subject and its offshoots."

The incubus groans. "And I thought the library in Dis had a healthy catalog."

"Incubus for the valid point," Jesse says. "You sure about trying to tackle this, buddy? You know I'll be here for the ride, even if we have to suck it up and go over to Central, but—"

I shake my head so adamantly, my ponytail loosens. "Central's probably closed. That library was built in the twenties. Quake retrofitting or not, they're likely combing every inch of it for damage." I look up to make sure Arden's listening to my follow-up. "More than that, I've still got a shitty feeling about that ticking time bomb."

Arden expresses his agreement with the new tension in his spine. "An adversary isn't less of one because they're invisible."

"Which means it's time to start peeling off the disguises." I shore up my own stance. "I think we can do this with a three-pronged attack. Jesse, you start by cross-referencing astronomy, astrology, and even historical chemistry references to Hecate and her posse. That's going to include Morgana le Fay from Camelot lore, Marie Laveau of the New Orleans mysticisms, and Aradia of the Wiccan histories."

"Well, well, well, Professor." My best friend accents it with a low whistle. "You've been added to some interesting VIP lists lately."

Arden's still indulging him with a small smirk when I pivot around. "Prieto, I'll direct you to the classic arts section. Anything you can put together with cross searches will be appreciated. Any detail, however small, that you notice … whether it's in a caption or actually on an art piece, it might be a link we're missing."

"Understood."

"Maybe I'll hit on something to join with it from the literary and poetry angles." I rock on the balls of my feet, battling the bizarre urge to pump a fist and shout a corny line from a Dumas story. "Let's do this. Three routes but one road, my friends."

Too late. Dumas is either saluting or groaning from the grave.

"You know what I mean," I mutter. "Let's figure out this mystery."

Jesse hits me with a contemplative scrutiny. "And if we don't?"

"And I'm just being a paranoid dweeb who's overheard a couple of witches in all the wrong ways?" I allow myself a small huff. "That's totally something I can live with, buddy."

CHAPTER 23

Kara

"HELLOOO? GROUND CONTROL TO Captain Valari?"

When even my dorky humor doesn't snap Jaden into responding, I stomp over to practically face off with him.

"Hey. Head-in-the-clouds mode is my specialty, remember?"

At least he looks up for a second. "Yeah. Okay. Sorry. I was ... trying to figure this thing out."

I dip in with a chastising look, realizing I've probably channeled Mother in all the wrong ways. "A thing I might be able to help with, if I knew what it was."

He grimaces. It's not even the cute squinty frown he uses with the tabloids. "As they say in the greenroom, careful who you're lending that ChapStick to."

It's definitely my turn for the scowl. "I've never heard that in a greenroom."

"Because the last time you were in one was five years ago?"

I sigh and roll my head. The morning games were fun, but I'm going to be stiff from the newly stressed muscles. "Is this going somewhere besides us trading *Tonight Show* taping stories, or do you want to gloat again about how I broke a heel and face-planted in front of J.Lo?"

"Oh, sister, how I wish," he mutters.

Okay, this really isn't good.

The new tangle in my gut decrees it before I unravel enough of my senses to check on his. Sure enough, all I'm receiving is more tension and confusion.

Jaden glances over, conveying the wish that he could give me more, but that's the end of his effort. I'm getting nothing but more striations of stress.

Lots of weird, intense stress…

And voices?

Not the fuzzy echoes like from strong memories or dreams. This is different, perhaps clouded by our shared DNA, his anxiety, or both. It's not even like real sound, though it's more than simple vibrations. It's more like phonic globs, whomping and wobbling through my senses, instead of organized language.

This is so weird.

Was I expecting anything different after the last three weeks?

"Jaden." I grab one of his shoulders. "Out with it. What's going on?" I squeeze into his lean bicep, trying to bolster myself as much as him. To help with the words that well in my instincts. "Does this have something to do with what happened at Rerek's? Did he…do anything…to you?"

"You mean aside from what he did to you?" He pushes away and jams a hand through his mussed hair. "I've been trying not to think about that part, thank you very much."

"I don't follow."

"Of course you don't. Because that's the kind of heart that you have." He keeps his back to me but doesn't shield his tightening fist against the top of his head. "The kind that's likely forgotten why you went to Rerek's party to begin with."

"Okay, whoa." I step over and around, forcing him to look at me again. "You invited me because you love me. Well, at least decently *like* me."

He snorts out soft air. "Eh. You're all right, most of the time."

I smile but not in full. The guy is a balls-out committer to zip lines and skydives, but not the risk of full-hearted conversations. But that's what needs to happen now. "The point is, you assumed that Rerek didn't have any crazy trickery up his sleeves. Like a true friend, you trusted him—"

"And nearly landed you in hell forever."

"And I'm still not following," I volley as fast as I can. "J, none of it was your fault. Last time I checked, these supersonic side wings didn't come with crystal balls or divining rods." I demonstrate my topic by playfully tugging at his ears.

But when he lets me continue the teasing, the wad in my belly doubles. He's normally testy about anyone touching him there.

Where's his brain gone off to now?

He saves me from having to beg for that answer by grabbing my hands with firm purpose. "So, you're saying that friendship loyalty stuff isn't always the smartest choice, right?"

My brows push toward each other. "And here I was thinking I wouldn't have to force this point out of you."

"I'm getting there," he assures. "Just tell me you understand. Because you know who I really learned the friendship stuff from, right?"

I cock my head. "You throwing a spotlight or a gaslight?"

"Neither. Just a relatively objective observation."

"*Just* the one?"

I straighten out my sightline. But it doesn't bring the additional focus I hoped for. He looks and feels the exact same. All my senses burn with the same mix of his exhaustion and tension. And the sound is still there too. That same low-grade mix of jumbles and rumbles, intensifying my impressions even more.

"Come on, damn it. Just get it out, J. Your energy's chewing through me like raccoons on electric wires."

He sobers a little. It's not a casual comparison. He and I used to stay up watching the little furry bandits who sneaked into the backyard when the neighborhood fruit groves weren't satisfying their needs for the night. Instead they'd gnaw on the power lines to our pool and tennis court, leading to many grisly demises.

"I took a walk this morning. You know, because I could," he begins. "And at first, it was really great. I'd even say interesting…"

"Until?" I don't need any more prompt than his deliberation.

"Until it got *interesting.*"

"Meaning what?"

"That the things a guy overhears in a witch-filled ashram aren't like any place else."

"Oh God, *ashram*?" I *thunk* back against one of the boulders and fold my arms. "Not you too."

"Hey." He smirks. "When Kell's right, she's right."

His repartee isn't helping a millimeter of my focus. "Subject for a different time," I grouse. "Unless you've really tromped all the way out here, seeking me out, just to share some cute anecdotes about my new friends?"

In reality, my new extended family—but that's an assignment best delayed in conversations with him and Kell. Once they get to know everyone better, they'll understand. I hope.

"It'd be great if you tell me they *are* cute and nothing else," he offers. "Because, to be honest, I'm not sure."

"Why?"

He settles once more against the boulder across from me. "I couldn't see them, of course. But I think there were three people talking. One of them was definitely Morgana. Hard not to place a voice that sounds like it can summon Excalibur out of a lake."

"Right." But grilling him about the *who* of the exchange feels less important than the *what*. "So Morgana and… whomever…I take it their subject wasn't just the weather?"

"If it was, you know I would've tuned them out. But

they weren't exactly trilling about their bright-bright-sunshiny day. Usually that's even more of a reason to notch down my frequency—until yours and Maximus's names got stirred into their thunderheads."

"Okay." I use the tone more than the word, almost turning it into a question. "I mean, unless they were mapping out a plan to drive us into the wilderness and feed us to the coyotes…"

"No," he interjects. "It wasn't like that."

"So, what was it like?"

"The exact opposite."

I pull in a breath and make sure he sees. I'm trying to be the calming big sibling but have zero experience with this side of my brother. I have no idea how to read his Rorschach anymore.

"The opposite?" I ask. "In what way?"

"They all sounded…worried," he finally offers. "But more than that. Protective, I guess? No. That doesn't sound right either."

"Why?" I step back and scrape my fingernails around opposite elbows. "I mean, was there additional context to the conversation? Could you pick out anything else?"

And what am I going to do if all he heard were the globby sound clumps?

When Jaden fills a long pause with nothing but a taut expression, I begin to suspect exactly that—to the point that even his next words bring me bizarre relief.

"Well, that's where things got really wonked."

"Wonked." I examine his face, hoping the repetition

will draw out more of his intention. Not happening. "In a bizarro-scary way, or just a missing-essential-parts way?"

"Both." Jaden digs a hand into his hair again. "I know that doesn't help, but that's the truth."

"Well, get to the part where it does help. What were they saying?"

"The word I heard more than any other was…war."

My stomach isn't roiling anymore. Difficult for it to do that after seemingly sinking all the way out of my body. At the same time, my mind connects more recognitions to each other—most prominently, everything that Maximus spilled to me yesterday. He was in such a stunned stupor but was scarily clear about what he'd just overheard in the sala's kitchen.

Hecate reminded her…they're preparing to go to war…

"With whom?" I now demand from my brother, who looks close to being in the same kind of funk. "About what?"

Yes, I know the adage about insanity and doing—in this case, repeating—the same things. But maybe this time I'll get lucky with some solid answers to the demands.

But if so, will I still consider it lucky?

"They were playing some verbal dodge-and-weave," Jaden confesses. "Almost as if they sensed I was listening. At least afraid of being heard. So no, it's not like they were pushing around little figurines on their campaign board or anything. But if they did…"

His hedge has me scooting higher, throwing my most severe stare at him. If we were kids, I'd be a second away from grabbing my phone and outing him to his crush. Since he's been openly thirsting at Liseli since last night, he has to know I'm just as serious now.

"If they did…then what?"

"Then the figurines would look a lot like you and Maximus."

This time I don't flinch. It's not an unexpected revelation. What I need—and am wrenched about digging deeper for—are all the *whys* beneath.

"Because?" I ask anyway.

Jaden crosses his ankles and hurls back a pointed look. "You've got to know at least the first part of that answer, sister. You're not just a diamond among the sorceresses. You're something rarer. A human, demon, and witch hybrid. You're like a shard of stardust pressed into blood and bone and flesh. My guess is, that means something to a lot of someones, and they're not about to let a rare opportunity pass by."

"Opportunity?" I don't apologize for my new agitation. It's just a drop in the depths of my new conflict. An ocean too huge to be ignored now.

For all the kindness and care Hecate's shown to me, there's also the underlying details about her interactions with the rest of the world. With Mother and Arden and Hades…and even, sometimes, with Maximus. The careful thought before her words. The meticulous calm. The Zen that seems so unbelievable.

Is that because it isn't even real?

My heart yearns to scream *no*. And wants to be right.

My head fights back with too many unresolved issues. Irrefutable facts.

"What kind of opportunity?" I order him.

"Easier asked than answered," my brother replies. "Because *that's* a factor that they're obviously unified about, to the point they didn't have to name it directly." He waxes both hands across the air. "I know, I know, it breaks my chocolate bar the wrong way too—especially because that seems to be all they can agree on."

Again, not a shocking piece of news—but I'm more hesitant about replying to it. Maybe Circe's so addicted to soap operas because of the relatable bickerings. But if my own life has taught me one thing clearer than the rest, it's the exhausting pointlessness of all that.

Still, I force my head higher in order to keep up my side of the conversation. I can't let Jaden cut it off here.

"So, let me guess. Some of them think my enlightenment is going too fast. Others probably think I should be making the West Coast disappear by now."

He doubletakes. "Your enlighten-what?"

It feels good to give in to a chuckle. "An Iremia-ism for honing my magical side." Just as quickly, I sober up. "But there's no fancy way for expressing what the rest of them are likely thinking—unless they haven't filled me in on the code for *toss her out and forget about it*."

No brotherly whip-back on that one, though his narrowed glance comes close to the same message. "Not the words on anyone's lips—though slide over a little and you'll hit the hot button."

The second my mind does exactly that, my gut takes on new rocks.

"Maximus," I rasp, hating my brother's averted glance at that confirmation. "*Maximus?* They want *him* out of here? Why?"

Jaden drums a pair of fingers along his boulder. "*You're* the Valari with more tenure here."

"Right," I spit. "Enough to know that Maximus has been helping them feed their animals and clean up after their meals. That he's been humble, generous, and smart with everyone. More obviously, that he's way more fun to gawk at than me."

Jaden pushes back to his feet as if every one of my points has slapped him with physical force. Not hard, but firm enough to inspire his irked frown. "Makes more sense than where their conversation went next."

I'm liberal with my long groan. "You mean it got worse?"

"Let's just say I started to wonder if I should take notes," he states.

"About what?"

He turns and firmly plants his stance. "It's not Maximus the dude they're powering the lasers for. Their sights are fixed on his ... other stuff."

I shift my own weight, spraying pebbles in my urgency. "You mean because he's a demigod? Why would that matter? Their own leader is a child of Olympus—"

"Hecate's not the same," Jaden counters, "and you know it. How much time does she really spend up in Zeus's 'hood?"

"More than Maximus ever has!" I start to pace. I can't

help myself. "I'm sorry, but that's a weak take. They've got to have something more substantial for that garbage to stick."

"None of them flung it as garbage," Jaden counters. "Like Kell and me, they all think your guy is the real deal for uncompromising character. If he were just a regular mortal, we'd all be fighting about who gets to walk you down the aisle at the wedding."

I startle. As in, he might as well have lit a fire at my toes. "Who's talking about a *wedding*?"

Sure as hell not me. Not any hidden little girl inside me either. Not since I was told, from the age I could comprehend the concept, that I'd be marching down the aisle with a demon who'd be handpicked to deflower me. Like giants, beanstalks, and glass slippers, I've always known a fluffy white dress and harp-accompanied poetry are the stuff of my life's fiction, not facts. Jaden should be more than aware of that too.

"Okay, so your love shack buddy," he revises. "The main point is, nobody's denying they really like him. It's just his lineage that's a liability here, in one form or another."

"Or another," I echo in a bitter bite. "So how many forms are they trashing on?"

Jaden cocks his head back with such force, it's like he's auditioning for a hair commercial. "Somebody voiced concern about where Maximus's real loyalty lies. They talked about his recent reconnection with Zeus and even brought up the fact that Daddy Dearest popped in *here* when Maximus summoned him the other day."

I shake my head. "They didn't do afternoon tea or anything. Z was here for all of five minutes."

He throws both hands up. "Just relaying it like I heard it."

"And I'm thankful," I mutter. "Sorry."

"You're good," he soothes. "All of this has been more than the usual stress."

"You can say that again, but please don't. Just…go on. What else did they say?"

As he considers his answer, I engage in a fast gut check. Something's weird here. Something more than the strangeness that's already been here, at least. But it's not fully formed yet—and I don't want it to be. My heart's already racing, anticipating what it's morphing into.

I just know that I don't like it. Not by one awful shred.

"They talked a lot about payback—more specifically, the kind Maximus might mete once he learns how Hecate's positioning him as her pawn for the big play." He pinwheels one hand again. "And yeah, I'm direct quoting. *The big play* is what they said. When and how and why, I have no idea— merely that one person suggested he should be graduated to rook or knight, considering all the servicing he was providing for the Iremia princess."

My psychological gnat looms bigger now. "And they were serious?"

"Well, they weren't completely kidding."

Right away, I tell myself to slough off the comments as easily as I would any gossip reporter taking potshots at my love life. But I'm barely concerned about the last half of Jaden's account. It's the other stuff that stabs in the hardest. That now has me pacing the fastest.

"The big play." I twist it verbally, matching the torque with my coiling fingers. "What does that even mean? And why is Maximus a necessary part of it? And if they're wigging about his reprisal about it, why not mine too?"

"Maybe it's a compliment of sorts," Jaden ventures. "You're one of them now. Part of the squad. A fellow diamond and all."

"Not to the point that I'll turn against Maximus." I wheel around and scuff to a strict stop. "Not for Hecate. Not for any of them."

For a long moment, Jaden's still and quiet. The air itself goes just as taciturn. The pause is odd, as if dictated by a movie director. The birds are silent. The wind is dead.

I wish my psyche was equally acquiescent.

Even before his steady nod, I see that he gets it. *Sees* it. He knows even he and Kell are second priority to my pledge to Maximus. If anything, his salute seems stronger because of it. Imbued with respect that wasn't there before. But that's not enough to quell the rest of my havoc. The bridges that sprawl in my brain, alarmingly incomplete. Needing so many more details. For any kind of final conclusions—or feelings.

Except for regret.

That one's having no trouble clicking into me. A solid, sinister lock.

Why didn't I take Maximus more seriously yesterday? Why didn't I heed the anxiety in his face, the concern in his voice? Why did I insist he'd simply jumped to strange assumptions and that his misgivings were based on misperceptions?

Now...I don't know what to believe.

Do I still listen to the need to justify it all away? To assume that a quick conversation with Hecate will clear this up? To theorize that in Iremia vernacular, preparing for war is just a euphemism for getting ready for the grocery store?

Or do I listen to the voice from deeper inside? The whisper from the place quieter and more sacred than this meadow? The voice that prods at bigger parts of my psyche, chipping away at the support pillars to my devotion for Hecate?

At all the gratitude I still owe her...

I can't commit to believing either. Not now. Not yet. But I can't give up. I have to find a clear path. I *have* to figure this out.

To do that, I have to talk to Hecate.

But doing that feels impossible—even a little terrifying—without Maximus. Whatever has to be uncovered here, whether hilarious or harrowing, we have to do it together.

"Oh, fireballs."

The interruption wakes up the wildlife, along with Jaden and me. We jerk our stares around toward the blessedly familiar figure picking her every step through the tall grass.

"Damn. I should've brought some hand shears. This sage is so luscious," Kell mutters. Then, not too much louder, "What the hell are you guys up to now?"

"Obviously not as much as you, sister number two," Jaden replies. "Is that the basic blouse and leggings that Aradia loaned you? And has she seen them with your... creative touches?"

"What?" Kell volleys, brushing both hands along her outfit. "The Wi-Fi's more temperamental than my aesthetician during a Mars retrograde. I had to amuse myself. There was some fun fabric paint in the sala, and I custom cut some stencils. For your information, Aradia herself found the leather strips for me to braid into—"

She breaks into a harsh choke as I approach with a determined pace.

"Holy shit." Her wide browns start to water as she pinches the end of her nose. "You took a bath in fear on top of the stress, didn't you? What'd I miss? Have you two been escaping Sasquatch or something?"

"*Pffft.*" Jaden huffs. "That asshole only comes south of Seattle if there's a VIP room at the Kinky Rhino involved."

She ignores him, thank God, to push on with her interrogation. "So what's actually going on? K-demon? Talk to me."

"You first." But I say it more around her than to her, already trying to stab my stare through the trees and back to the sala's rear veranda. "Have you seen Maximus?"

"You mean lately? Now that you mention it, no. Not since he grabbed a paw full of scones and told us he was headed to the barn to help Kiama and Liseli."

"That's right." I rush it out with glaring relief. "Thanks. I'll head there first."

"And I'm right behind you," says Jaden.

I feel the knowing glance that Jaden exchanges with Kell before she speaks again.

"I'm in too." She falls readily in line on the footpath

behind me. "You think I'm going to give up on the mystery that easily?"

"It's not that huge of a deal, Stephanie Plum," I mutter. "At least not after I find Maximus and we figure this all out."

"Fine enough, darling," she quips back. "Just don't mind my sleuthy instincts for wanting to stick around a wee bit longer."

Wisely, she doesn't resurrect the remark once we arrive at the barn and find it empty of all life save the familiars and livestock. There's not a human to be found, even after we call out for Kiama and Liseli.

When we take the breezeway over to the farmhouse, there's still no answer for us in two-legged form. Adelfi, a sweet black Labrador that's more house mascot instead of active familiar anymore, barely lifts her head from the thick rug near the hearth as we walk through.

If only my racing nerves would learn some of Adelfi's game.

Instead, they pound harder with every passing second. There's a matching cadence in what's left of my stomach, which is not happy with me for this. Or, for that matter, any part of the last weird hour.

No.

If I'm being honest with myself...the last *twenty-four* hours.

Nothing's been settling right since Maximus walked into the cottage yesterday, looking like aliens had cruised by on the stream.

I almost pray for such an easy explanation now. But if

little green space-zoids were going to scuttle to our rescue, it likely would've happened by now. There are harder facts to face at this point, like pulling out my phone and punching Max's number is probably going to yield the same results as my first fifty tries.

Sure enough, I'm swiftly dropped to his half-mumbled voicemail greeting.

"Don't freak. He could be in a dead zone," Jaden murmurs, slinging an arm around my neck.

"Gee. What a shocker," Kell inserts. "Come on, chica." And then scoops up one of my hands. "Let's try the parking lot—or whatever it is in Iremia speak. Maximus told us he caught a signal out there."

"Yeah," I reply, brightening. "That's right. He did."

Though I can't be blamed for not booting up the memory right away. Not after the news Maximus took away from that conversation. Thinking about Professor Erin Levin is no help for my climbing anxiety levels.

Not when I theorize, even for a few seconds, that maybe *she's* mixed up in all this secret weirdness across Iremia too ...

Possible?

Perhaps. Witches and harpies have a lot of good reasons to band together, starting with their similar beefs with history. Both began as beautiful, helpful, and magical beings—brands that, thanks to centuries of hearsay and rumors, got shoved into descriptor boxes like spiteful, wrathful, and sinful.

But probable?

No. My intuition zings with the word. The parallels shouldn't, and don't, make them all sudden besties. If that amity were a real thing, why did Megaera run for refuge at President McCarthy's house, having to cloak herself as Erin to do so? Why didn't she head straight for Iremia instead and make peace with Maximus and me in the doing?

Magaera.

Drumming up the subject is no more fun now than a couple of days ago, especially because it's more sludge for my perplexity pile—which doubles in size once my siblings and I arrive at the gravel expanse that serves as Iremia's entrance pad.

"Mmmph." I glare at my phone. "I've got more bars, but he's still not picking up."

"Long shower?" With hands in his back pockets, Jaden shrugs. "Sometimes that's where I get some good thinking done."

I shake my head. "He showered last night. I'm a reliable eyewitness."

"Fun concept," he counters. "But not with you in the visual, sister. Moving on."

"Maybe it's time to try the locator," Kell suggests. "Even if the app is sketchy, it might give you a general idea of where he's hanging. Since it's definitely not there."

She indicates toward the truck that Maximus parked under some eucalyptuses when we first got here. The big vehicle's only twenty feet away but seems half its original size right now. I fight to ignore the incriminating feeling while acceding to her smart idea. If Maximus's signal shows him over by the cottages—my optimal wish—I'll head for our place by the stream. But if he's out on another hike, I'll hang with Jaden and Kell and all the nags of my impatience.

Either way, he couldn't have gone far ...

After the better part of a minute, those same words spill from me in a baffled mutter. But after circling the whole canyon with my finger, even in ultrazoom mode, there's no telltale ping on his phone. Not even one of those frustrating generalities stating he might be *in the area of*.

So what area *is* he in or of?

"This is ... weird." I gulp hard as punctuation, not daring to voice the other adjectives that bombard my mind. Things way worse than *weird*.

Like *troubling*. And *scary*. And *not freaking good*.

"Uhhh, yeah." Especially when Kell's undertone goes ahead and invokes all of them. "And so is that."

My gaze bugs as she pinches her fingers in order to increase the locator's search perimeter. At once, the boundary pings into enough new territory to fit a few small European countries. To the north, it encompasses Malibu, Thousand Oaks, and Point Mugu. On the southern side, it extends all the way to—

"Downtown?"

It spills from me like the ping really has just come from the middle of Croatia. Right now, at least to my mind, they're the same.

"What's he doing?" I don't even tap at the pulsing map pin, convinced it's going to vanish any second. "No. He can't be ... Okay, why is he ... And where is he ..."

"Alameda." Jaden speaks it as soon as he and Kell are fully flanking me. As she taps the pin, he translates the location on the downtown grid. "He's at the university."

"In the library," Kell finishes as soon as the map focuses down. "But now I'm as stumped as Kara. How'd he get there? And why sneak out like that?"

But *stumped* isn't me anymore. I demonstrate it by whipping up my head and letting a burning breath escape my clutching throat.

"He learned something," I state. "That has to be it. He's discovered something that we haven't. But not everything. That's why he took off."

"Sneaked off," Kell corrects.

"Accurate," Jaden says. "*Too* accurate. Dude didn't even say goodbye to you, K-demon."

"Because it was that urgent?" Kell queries.

I shake my head. "Because I was doing enlightenment out in the fields with Hecate and Circe."

Jaden's suddenly ashen. Kell too. I don't wonder about myself. The blood started draining from my vital senses before we left the meadow.

"Because..." my brother finally blurts, "whatever scoop he's after...involves her."

I don't indulge even a second of confirming that accuracy. Jaden's words confirm how certain he is of it, and Kell's victorious sniff conveys the same.

But she doesn't preen for long. Already roping her focus back in, she tilts an intense look my way. "So what's the call from here?"

For a second, I can only blink. This is unusual for us, since she's normally comfortable as the one with the priorities, plans, and decisions. But this time, the reins feel just fine in my grip. I take over with an eager and confident look.

"Well. I do see a truck with a hidden key box that one of us happens to know about."

And an invisible ashram perimeter that I no longer care about breaching.

For the time being, she and Jaden don't have to be apprised about that part. Not that either of them will be screaming at me to turn the vehicle around. A one-night canyon slumber party was about the limit for both of them, as they prove by rushing back toward the truck like superfans at a concert stage.

More vibes that might be smart to follow.

No matter how strongly I don't want to believe them.

No matter how much it hurts to be suspecting, more and more by the second, that maybe the perimeter isn't there for keeping the world out.

But why is it so important to control everyone who stays in?

I shake my head, still refusing to believe that's the whole case. That the goddess who rescued me from Hades's wrath with all that calm fortitude can also be such a desperate boundary setter. That makes no sense to any section of my heart or synapse in my head.

There's even littler logic to what I plan on doing now. If I really want all the answers to my dilemmas, it's more rational to stay in Iremia. But that also means more time apart from Maximus—perhaps a lot more, if Hecate decides to get more protective of me in his absence.

No. Not the right solution, on any level.

I have to get back to his side. If the last week has taught me anything with terrifying clarity, it's that forbidden love ignites the hottest crucibles—which forge the strongest survivors. Our kilns have become incredible fires in their own rights, but they're an unstoppable force only when bridged together. I'm better, in every single way, only with the love of my soul by my side.

It needs to happen.

The time is now.

CHAPTER 24

MAXIMUS

I AGREED TO RECONVENE with Arden and Jesse in a couple of hours, but after ninety minutes, my head is on the verge of pounding.

I rise and wander downstairs, hoping the coffee stand off the library's lobby has been kept open. Thankfully, there's basic black java and mini packs of ibuprofen available. I grab three of each, feeling vindicated about the call as soon as I return and spot them both.

"Oh *yesss*." Jesse raises both arms, *Hallelujah* style. "Come to papa bear, magical liquified beans."

Arden opts for a less effusive approach. "Thank you." But his calm gratitude is overtaken by a furtive glance around. "Am I missing the almond milk, by any chance?"

"By every chance," I correct. "New adventure. Go with it."

He grimaces. "You mean add it to the list of the other adventures?"

Jesse throws a wicked side-eye. "*Gasp.* Was that sarcasm, Mr. Prieto? Careful, one might think you're starting to enjoy this."

Arden's nostrils flare before his pewter-colored glare resettles on me. "There are countless artistic works created in Hecate's name since the fifth century. Naturally, I focused on common themes in pieces between that time and the Middle Ages, when the ancient gods and their religions weren't observed in public anymore."

"Sound theory," I commend. Out of the three of us, he probably had the most daunting job. Narrowing down his searches likely had to happen at some point.

"There are commonalities, of course. The most notable is that of the goddess in triplicate form, due to her affiliation with the moon and its three main phases. She's also the guardian of crossroads, so the multiple form allows her to watch out for travelers. There are usually torches in her grasp, further enhancing the protective theming."

"That thread runs through a lot of poetry and literature too," I add. "She's praised at great length by Hesiod, though a lot of scholars have taken exception to the gushing. Still, a Homeric poem from the same period refers to her as 'tender-hearted and bright-coifed.'"

"Well, I'm a real sucker for those bright coifs," Jesse murmurs. "How about you guys?"

Arden jogs a brow. "Was that *sarcasm*, Mr. North?"

I clear my throat and jump back into it. My instincts about our time limit, while unfounded, are still an incessant throb in my veins. "The ancients didn't have the corner on the mentions. She's brought up again in many AD texts. Ovid, then Shakespeare, are only two writers with stories that feature her."

"The Persephone angle," Arden supplies. "That has to be one of them. It's popular in vases, paintings, drawings... if the ancients knew how to mass produce T-shirts, it'd be on them too."

"Give me a minute." Jesse holds up his phone and begins thumbing in a search. "I'm sure there's *something* fun out on the interwebs..."

"Her connection to Hades's part-time consort is definitely one of them," I concede. "And the more well-known one. But there's another story that's just as intriguing. Hecate, who was originally the child of Titans, actually sided with Zeus in the gods' war with the Titans. She also fought on his side to help overthrow the giants in the Gigantomachy. Because of that loyalty, my father honored her with a high rank in Olympus and made sure that every deity in the place gave her the same respect."

"Which means she must have been thrilled to welcome you as much as Kara," Jesse says, still scrolling. "No wonder you know the tale so well."

I drop my head in an openly curious look. "So you'd think."

His thumb freezes an inch over his phone screen. "You mean Hecate didn't tell it to you? I mean, at least a dozen times?" He scoops Arden into his baffled moment. "Seriously, tell me if I'm wrong. Wouldn't she find a way to slip that into the convo at least once? Twice? Every *human* does it.

You wouldn't believe how many times I've had to hear about what a wild child my mom was in high school. I can give you every literal detail about her and Freddy G in the orchestra pit during rehearsals for *Once Upon a Mattress*—"

"We believe you," Arden cuts in, much to my relief. "But we still don't believe *you*." He jabs a finger in my direction. "Are you truly saying that Hecate didn't mention anything about her exalted standing with your father?"

I let my telling pause serve as an obvious answer. "To be honest, I'm grateful she left it alone. It's been rough to wrap my head around the subject as it is. Her trip down reminiscence road would've been…awkward."

In reward for my honesty, I get the *look* from Jesse. The one that instantly filets me, as if he knows exactly what part of my psyche to study for the complete truth. I glare back without hesitation. On this particular go-round, I have nothing to hide from the guy.

"Well, extra props to the goddess, then," he finally says. "She didn't have to go there for personal glory."

"Unless there were already other things on her mind."

I drop another indebted nod to Arden, acknowledging the statement that aligns our train back on the topical track. I wish my follow-up could surpass my gloomy mutter, but it doesn't. "Things we're no closer to figuring out than before." I pull out a chair, turn it backward, and drop into it with my arms folded across the top. "Seems Hecate's only been bested by Florence Nightingale, Mother Teresa, and Julie Andrews for global kindness icon."

"Kindness but ferocity," Jesse notes. "You want

something done to change the world, and even the stars, give the job to a determined female."

"Ferocity and determination—but not violence," Arden volleys. "Not things like war. I just looked at thousands of images of the goddess. And yes, in most depictions, she's brandishing torches or daggers. Many times, both. But not once is she in attack mode. Her weapons are there to help guide and defend. Her poses are proud and noble. Her expressions are neutral and collected."

As he says it, his own face goes for the opposite. I already envision the guy booking a three-hour facial to get rid of his scowl lines.

Jesse adds a similar grimace, without the please-suck-my-pores melancholy. "Well...bloody hell." He jogs his chin toward the incubus. "Pardon the pun."

Arden dips a diplomatic nod before walking over and rejoining me at the table. At once he drums the surface with a pair of agitated fingers. "So we're still no further to figuring this out."

Jesse sighs. "I really wish I could be the white knight here, kids. But all my research results don't add up to ten minutes from either of you. There's no constellation named after the goddess, though the Asteroid Hekate 100 was discovered in 1868 and is nearly a hundred kilometers in diameter. And Arden's statement is correct that the goddess is also associated with the moon, but most of those correlations only talk about the rituals of her worshippers when a new moon is coming. Random trivia? Her spiked head wreath is sometimes cited as the inspiration for the Statue of Liberty, though in some cases it's a crown of stars."

He probably has more than that one factoid, but Arden beats me to a blithe quip about an overall trivia challenge. Jesse pounces on it, ordering Arden to open his phone and look up the dive bar over on Eighth with the trivia console that he regularly beats me on.

But I'm already past the point of hearing them.

The buzz in my head has grown too deafening.

A rush of recognition that hits my brain like a falling comet.

An epiphany so extreme, I have no choice but to follow its silent, steady hail.

A crown of stars.

The words flash across my mind's eye as if the comet's now backing a marquee. They literally reload themselves as I watch, formatting themselves to fit the huge glowing sign.

A CROWN

OF STARS

I stare at my hands as they tighten on the chair's back.

Why do those words look so familiar? Feel so personal?

The battle for the recollection yields nothing. My knuckles get whiter. My breaths come faster. My senses are exhausted. It's only midafternoon, but the day feels like it started a year ago.

I get relief, but only for a second, when the connection clicks in.

"*Yes.*"

That's it.

That's it.

I don't realize all of it has tumbled out until I notice Jesse's puzzled scrutiny as I surge back to my feet.

"What's *it*?"

I circle around as if viewing my surroundings for the first time. That's how punched I feel about this revelation.

"I'll be right back." I feel safe about making the promise because I know exactly what I'm looking for. It's straight ahead, in the area where thousands of film and television scripts are stored for posterity.

Jesse gets a parting shot off before I get completely out of earshot. "You know, *eureka* moments are more fun when they're shared, buddy."

I pretend I'm too far away to hear, even down the aisle in which every one of my steps is prominent as a soldier's stomp, while closing in on the script archives.

Sure enough, less than ten minutes later, the object of my fixation is unhooked from its sleeve and spread open in my hand. My cheeks sting as an equally wide smirk takes over my lips.

Because here they are.

The words, on the title page, exactly as they sprang to my mind's eye.

A CROWN

OF STARS

Now, they're joined by another identifier. One that

doubles my pulse rate and grips my stare.

I pull out a chair while parking the script in an upright holder on the room's small study table. As soon as I turn on the little lamp, more of the library seems to fade away, turned into an inscrutable land beyond the glass enclosure walls. It enforces the instinct to keep the thing in here, at least for now. It simply seems weird to drag it out for a breezy table read with Jesse and Arden.

Definitely weird—and potentially wrong.

Who am I kidding? *Probably* wrong. This was a nutty move the first time, when it was more a hunch than a tactic. I got lucky and left the table with one of Kara's biggest secrets. I have to accept that I won't find all four leaves on the clover this time.

No matter how much more personal it feels. Almost... intimate. Like a friend has offered me their diary to read.

I smile once more at that friend's name. And then open to the third or fourth page, securely bound at the top of the thick paper sheaf. *Scene One* is there for me to read once more, hoping all my main memories about this plot are still accurate.

I take a deep breath. Before I begin to read, I whisper one earnest request into the air.

"Talk to me, Gio."

"Dude. *Hey.*"

I lift a hand instead of my head, using my other one to flip through the last pages of the script. I have no idea how long it's taken me to reread through this thing. Exponentially fast reading skills are a handy thing to have when a guy needs to read through a writer's whole backlog of scripts in a single afternoon, but as I've just learned, content retention becomes the sacrificial lamb.

The same one I've just sewn back together, stitch by painstaking stitch. Word by surreal word. Dizzy and dazed from the effort. Probably a lot of other things too, but I can't identify every feeling except for the grim shock that's still stumbling through every part of me. Trying and failing to escape the same buzz saw that hacked up my lamb.

"Maximus!"

I jog up my head higher. Slowly, Jesse's face comes into focus. "Huh? What?"

"*Right back* doesn't mean forty-five minutes, buddy."

"He's right."

To my surprise, though not unpleasant, the addendum comes from a new arrival to this end of the building. My reeling senses are thrilled about the solid ground of minding my manners, so I rise for the handsome woman who strides in, her proud posture looking professional even in crisp casual wear.

"President McCarthy. A pleasure to see you, ma'am."

"Same to you, of course," the woman answers. "We weren't going to be on campus very long but overheard chatter on a guardsman's radio that there'd been a Maximus Kane sighting in the research library. Imagine that."

I shake my head. "You'd think they'd have more important things to worry about."

"When one of my favorite professors is also my most

famous, that can take on a silver lining. Two birds and one stone, right?"

I chuckle. "Sorry if you had to wait. I just—"

"Lost track of time while reading?" She cocks her head back, showing off the simple but high-quality jewelry in her ears. "Would you also imagine *that*?"

Normally that'd get her a sizable chuckle from my end of things. But this isn't a normal circumstance.

Nothing near it.

Especially when I notice that McCarthy's *we* wasn't the royal version. She's really brought along a guest. One that, on everyone's first impression, exudes the same efficient aura as Alameda's president.

Everyone's but mine.

Because I'll never see Erin Levin as anyone—any*thing*— other than what she really is.

Since there hasn't been a spare second to brief Jesse on the professor's true identity, he's still turning on the charm with clear intent to impress her.

"No matter what, we're glad for the visit," he affirms to both women. "We were informed that you're settled into a home office until the guardsmen leave campus."

"Still the case," McCarthy returns. "But I haven't been back to campus since the earthquakes and felt a quick check on things was necessary. Professor Levin was kind enough to brave the drive with me."

"Which wasn't too strenuous, I hope?" Arden's insertion, earning him an appreciative smile from McCarthy, turns into an odd triangle once he assesses Erin. But it's not a leer or even a flirt. It's almost like he already sees through her.

"It wasn't at all," McCarthy answers, pausing just for a second as if scrolling a mental list of social contacts. "Thank you for asking...Mr. Prieto, is that it? We met at the Conquistador Crush gala. You were with Veronica Valari that night, yes?"

"Indeed." Arden's smile is smooth and easy. "You have an outstanding memory, President McCarthy."

"Doesn't take anything of the sort to recognize what a stunning couple you two are," she gushes, already pleased about her compliment. "Veronica's a lucky lady."

Before I have to focus too hard on stuffing down a chortle, Erin is the unlikely rescue officer of the moment. "Actually, I think Mr. Prieto has recently become engaged to *Kell* Valari."

"Oh?"

The woman's startlement is apparent, but the blazes in Arden's eyes are more than enough to send his irked message at Erin.

"Well, no matter what, it seems congratulations are in order, Mr. Prieto."

McCarthy again, saving the gloss of the conversation with her bright tone. It doesn't deter Arden from his incendiary stare at Erin, despite the refinement beneath his reply to Alameda's president.

"Thank you very much. But the news is still quite private. Can I ask how *you* learned it, Professor Levin?"

Erin wiggles her lips. Jogs her brows. "You're not the only one with lofty connections in the city, Mr. Prieto."

The next pause is worthy of every precommercial moment in the history of *Hathaway Harbor*. I just wish it gave me as much delight as the stuff dancing across McCarthy's face—or even, weirdly, on Erin's.

Or maybe...not so weirdly.

Before I can dismiss my instincts about that, I shuffle forward. "Sorry to bust in before the champagne is popped, but can I have a moment alone with Professor Levin?"

I'm ready with an assuring nod for the stabbing glances from Jesse and Arden. They'll get all the cake once I've figured out this whole recipe—which I'm hoping will lead to anything *but* cake.

At least not the one that's been baked around a knife.

The pointy bastard that I just found in Gio's screenplay.

As soon as the others leave the glass-enclosed area, I shut the heavy door all the way. As soon as the panel gives a defined *snick*, I snap back toward the cunning creature that has no way out except through me.

Not that she's getting that leave anytime soon.

Not that she looks like she wants it.

The bold shrew is so ready for this showdown, I'm even exposed to a few glances at her true form as she takes position on the other side of the study table. The eye color that shifts, turning bright and intense. The mouth that gives up its cultured smile in place of a calculated sneer. Most prominently, the birdlike abrasion that enters her voice.

"What are you doing here, demigod?"

"I work here," I bite back. "That's still questionable where you're concerned, *Professor*. So what are *you* doing here?"

She cocks her head, again too avian-zombie-creepy for my comfort. "I follow my queen's commands. They haven't changed. To keep you and yours out of the sacred halls of Olympus. You will never have access to its refuge or resources. They're not yours to claim!"

"Not what I'm after," I snarl. "And you know that, damn it. What I do want, and what you will give me, is an explanation about what I just read in here."

It's dauntingly satisfying to watch the harpy's gaze drop, following the jab of my finger against the final page of Gio's old script. Thankfully, Hera hasn't kept her that far in the dark. I observe that already, as the tension cranks tighter across her bony features. She absolutely knows what's in it. Probably every word, and probably better than I.

So she knows it's the plot for a movie that, over forty years ago, was unproducible and unbelievable schmaltz—but detailed absolutely everything that's happened across every supernatural landscape during this last week. That's likely because it's from the viewpoint of a beloved Olympian goddess with generosity in her heart and magic at her fingertips, who's pushed to the background as her king and queen vie for control of a shriveling, forgotten kingdom. It's the story of how that goddess takes definitive action about it… Decisions that will forever change every known realm.

Including the destruction of the humans' world.

Gio has spoken to me, all right. Really loud and really clear.

"Talk to me, Megaera," I order with a gut-deep growl. "Talk to me *now*. No detail deleted. When is Hecate officially declaring war on Olympus?"

CHAPTER 25

"YOUR DUDE'S PANTRY IS worse than Mom's."

I turn toward my brother, who's already embraced my offer of making himself completely at home. Maximus's apartment cupboards aren't proving to be J's happy snack source, but I'm smitten about the rest of his commentary.

My demigod.

That sounds really, really good.

Except for right now. When that magnificent male is causing me every variant of stress there is. Maybe a few new ones too.

I check my locator app again. The result is no better than it was when we got here. Maximus left the library, but there's been no new ping on his phone since. Not a bizarre occurrence with the tall buildings and scattered clouds likely screwing with the signals but one that still zaps my mind with a thousand possible what-ifs.

And surprise, surprise…none of them end with giant rainbows and sweet kisses.

It's not the only subject that's stirring my guts into stress stew. I turn around toward the living room, forcing myself to address the next biggest one head on. As if my sister and her glare are going to let me forget.

"I still don't think it's smart to split up," I state. But even from her place on the couch across the room, she's broadcasting peeved vibes about her preference for an alternative plan—and my fierce quashes on it. "Sorry, honey. But it'll take only one reporter or photographer to recognize any of us and then post it to the internet. How freely do you think we'll be able to move around the city then?"

"But Kell's also got a solid point," Jaden ventures. "Maybe splitting the paps' focus is a good thing. I mean, if what you've told us is true, that Maximus isn't trusted by Iremia nor wanted by Olympus, maybe borrowing a page from our mother's book is a smart idea. The mortal spotlight *is* where he's going to be the safest, at least for now."

"You mean after *we* can find him again?"

He flings a scoff at me. "You mean retrieve him? We *know* where he is, okay?"

I compress my lips, but not before jabbing a nail between them. I hate how much sense he's making, mostly because of the larger dilemma it now presents.

This whole afternoon and evening, my siblings have been my invaluable A-Team. But do I let them continue to help, even if it sacrifices their privacy—and very possibly their safety? Or do I order them to stay here in a passcodeprotected building that even the press isn't hounding right now thanks to the post-quake coverage frenzy? Moreover, a lot of practice has turned me into the family specialist at disguising myself as an ordinary Alameda student. With my practiced slouch and deep hoodie pout, I'll be able to slip across campus without a hitch. If I can find some earphone wires, even the library's front desk crew won't think of stopping me.

If Maximus is still there ...

My phone vibrates. The locator app has updated. But checking it has my throat squeezing in again.

The new ping isn't an anomaly. Maximus has officially left the library. And from the looks of it, he's now in a huge hurry.

He's already made it all the way off *campus*.

My stress spikes so high, I don't bother keeping that news to myself. My siblings' reactions are simultaneously comforting and aggravating.

"Headed where? What's he up to now?" There's the odd comfort, coming from Jaden.

"Before you find that out, maybe Jaden and I should head out and pull a few pied pipers with the press." And the aggravation, on cue, from my tenacious sister.

Jaden emerges from the kitchen with a bowl of mixed nuts and a canned protein shake. It's enough of an offering to make him dig in as soon as he sits at the dining room table. But his satisfaction aside, I'm stressing just looking at him now.

Next to his knee, in the hiding place that Maximus

found for it between the table's leaf extension lever and the tabletop, is Hecate's grimoire.

While a genius idea, the stash was never meant to be a permanent spot for the book. It was a quick fix for the moment, in which we were dashing from the apartment after getting the call about Kell in the humans' crisis center. The intention was to find a more secure location once we got back here with clearer thoughts and more strategic intentions.

That was five days ago.

Clarity and strategy still feel as reachable as getting my masters in metaphysics.

Worse, with my rising doubts about Hecate and the diamonds, I don't even know if I want to be *this* close to the tome anymore. It seems surreal, despite everything it's gotten me through. How it helped me focus my energy and get us out of hell. How it calms me whenever I'm simply holding it. How it speaks to me about amazing truths...

The power of Hecate, swelling in my DNA.

The manifestation of that force, drenching my veins.

The ringing of that calling, dominating my heart and mind...

But do I really want it all now? Or *ever*?

Or do I long to simply be free of it? From everything that associates me with...her?

And how do I know if that's even possible? Can I escape the absolute essence of my DNA? The stuff that's stitched into every seam of my being?

"Kara?"

The syllables are a distant warble in my senses. I shake my head, battling dizziness and nausea. I feel myself stumble, not knowing which way is up.

"Hey. I'm sorry. I didn't mean to upset you."

I look up, identifying Kell as the source. "I'm not upset."

But my sincerity doesn't serve the words. They spew out with much different intention, accompanied by a throb in my head and timpani in my stomach.

"Ah...whoa."

Jaden jerks back in his chair as if Kell and I have decked him. "What was that?" he demands, only to be checked by Kell's sharp glare.

"What was what? You mean the sound of you not helping your stressed-out sisters?"

"No. I—I mean, yeah. Sorry." He rushes to pull out chairs for both of us, but his actions seem rote, like he's doing it out of physical habit instead of mental care. His gaze wanders, searching the neighboring buildings like they're harboring snipers. "Seriously...neither of you heard that?"

Kell huffs. "Can you be a little more specific? That *what*?"

"It was like...it was in the damn room..."

"Hold up. *This* room?" I manage to stammer, though swinging around with an alarmed gaze only earns my equilibrium another whomping roil. A friendly neurological tidal wave joins it, meaning all I hear of Jaden's troubled mutters are hollow warbles and dark vibrations. "Ohhh... no," I groan out. "Ohhh...wow."

"You okay?" Kell mutters. "Come on. Sit down."

I acquiesce but only for a second. "Oh God." I get up, bracing my head with both hands. "That's worse. So much worse."

"What's wrong?" she pleads. "Can we get you anything? What do you need?"

I kick at the floor and anxiously twine my fingers. "Maximus," I finally rasp, trying but failing to hide my emotions. My whole being buzzes with this yearning for him. This need. It's turned into a visceral thing. It's an unfed hunger in my belly. An unassuaged ache in my bones. A restlessness that crawls through me like another creature, unmerciful even after I stomp out a bunch of laps between the living room and kitchen.

"Maximus," I blurt again. "I need ... *him*."

Jaden finally jolts from his strange stupor and snaps his head around. "Why don't you try calling him again?" he suggests. "What's the worst that could happen? More voicemail?"

I force back another terse answer. Voicemail isn't the worst option on that list. What if Maximus did answer, only to tell me he's someplace awful and painful? That he didn't leave Iremia willingly, and he's been captured or kidnapped? That something or someone beyond my rationale has gotten to him and is torturing him worse than Hades's hell soldiers?

I shudder without thinking. Or control. But I can't rule out the disgusting possibilities. I can't ignore the fear, now as much a part of me as instinct, whenever I know he's not near.

Until, suddenly, he is.

And the nausea recedes. And my head is righted. And my soul is bathed in a new flood of strength. Of courage. Of the pure, perfect fire that only he can bring.

That I rush for now, bursting with a laugh as I bounce back a reply to my brother.

"Screw the voicemail."

For that matter, screw everything else.

The post-hell trauma dreams. The fears about all the new rabbit holes of my life, big and small. The insecurities. The confusions. The worries about my family and their futures. Even the fuzzy picture of what my own destiny will be.

All I need to know about destiny is in front of me again. The man I'm wrapped around again. The tawny beard that scratches my neck and the warm breath that soothes my nape. The low growl that crosses the bridge to my soul, speaks to my spirit, and reaffirms everything I am.

His.

Today and now.

Tomorrow and forever.

Though the thoughts are like linked circuits inside, they make me squirm and ache. Even the knowledge of Maximus's approach isn't enough of a balm. It gets a little better during the two seconds that Maximus takes to pull back and kick his front door shut. But right after, he's back to doubling his grip on me.

I return the pressure in full. I can't get close enough to him . . .

"Little demon," he breathes into my hair. "Are you okay?"

Softly, I nod. My replying words aren't so tender. "Why did you go? And not even tell me?"

"I'm sorry." He tucks his head and presses his lips to mine with fervent intent. "I'm so, so sorry. But you were with Circe and Hecate. And I developed deeper...concerns about them."

"Concerns?" The challenge comes from Jaden, who chomps on a couple of cashews before rising again. "You're with family, man. Cut the niceties. They weren't *concerns*. They were suspicions."

Maximus may not share the same signal boost that punch up our abilities, but the purity of his intuition is as powerful to watch. He's already peering into my brother like he's a rare manuscript.

"You overheard them too?" he queries. "What'd they say?"

Jaden shakes his head. "It was some of the others. But there was enough verbal waltzing around the Hecate maypole that I walked away with some real...*suspicions*."

"And then he came and found me," I say. "And made me realize how callow it was for me to initially shrug off your worries..."

"Hey. Not all the way off." Maximus gently busses my forehead. "You just had a loyal pull to Hecate, and rightfully so. If you didn't, I'd have been equally uneasy."

"Uneasy? Or as totally bulldozed as you are now?" Kell cants her head and taps her nose. "Sorry. Can't be helped. The smell's pouring off you like twelve guys on a construction site."

Maximus hauls in heavy air. He shores up his own

stance to the point of releasing me from his side. Not all the way. One of his hands scoops around mine with purposeful strength. "You're probably right. But I'm definitely not sorry."

"Maximus?" I question as we head into the living room. I don't release him from my stare even as we lower onto the couch. "I tracked your phone when you wouldn't pick up my calls. We know you went to Alameda. To the research library."

"I figured," he says, securing my hand tighter. "I tracked you back and was relieved as hell to see you on approach to downtown. But that also means that we likely don't have much time."

I sit up straighter. Nail him with a frown. "Time? For what?"

"Did you leave Iremia without Hecate's clearance?"

"Ermmm…" I readjust my position, more as a lame excuse to process his answer-that-isn't. Not by one syllable. "To the best of my knowledge, yes. I mean, without Circe to run a cover story or Arden to do—well, whatever he magically does—"

"Not this time."

"Huh?"

I'm unsure if I'm reacting to his interruption or the action that comes with it. No way did I expect, in this moment at least, to watch him sheepishly glance away from me.

"Afraid I might've claimed the Prieto VIP ticket," he mutters, looking to Kell and Jaden as they drop into the leather easy chairs to either side of us. "He got me to Alameda in record time, which resulted in some strange and optimal timing."

Jaden wraps his hands around the edges of his chair. "Now I'm almost afraid to ask."

Secretly, I second the disclosure. What am I supposed to think as Maximus uses the moment to wrap his other hand around both of mine?

"Arden helped Jesse and me with an informational deep dive about Hecate. None of us found anything that would logically link her to all these backroom talks about preparing for war—until we had a pair of visitors in the library."

Now I'm the one tightening my grip. I'm not comfortable with the nervousness that climbs through his own composure. It leads me to an awful conclusion. One I can't ignore any more than the creature who first inspired these feelings in both of us—just three nights ago.

"Megaera," I blurt. "It was her, wasn't it?"

He gives me a small smile. "You *are* my perceptive little demon."

I push out heavy air through my nose. "It was McCarthy, wasn't it? You said visitors, plural. So she was tagging along with the university's president."

A full nod from him this time—except his head's notably weaving in my vision. I squint in wonder, trying to determine if he's playing one of those marble-in-the-hole games, only along the grooves of his brain.

"It actually turned out to be a good thing. Okay, not a

good thing, because that termagant is one giant handful of strange venom, but—"

I jerk back despite dictating myself not to. "There's a but in here?"

Maximus calms me with the steady force of his deep blues. "But during the five minutes I forced Meg to tell me what's going on, instead of everything Hera's not going to let me do about it, I got every confirmation I needed from her."

"Confirmation?" Kell cuts in. "For or about what?"

"More like an *account of*," Maximus clarifies. "In the form of a screenplay I just reread."

I startle again. "One of Gramps's scripts?"

Maximus's stare intensifies. The cobalt gains new depths, like direct sunlight in Caribbean tidepools. I know—and adore—this shade. But I haven't seen it for a couple of days, since we waved goodbye to Gramps at the mansion.

"Once again, your grandfather has given us all the details we need. They're there, poured out in one of his old screenplays. It was probably something he'd overheard, simply playing the part of the nonchalant writer wallflower in hell, but he turned it into a story, and it's becoming a full-fledged prophecy."

I spend a long moment in jaw-dropped silence. The same look crosses Kell's pale features. Jaden's the one breaking the mold, already leaning forward with elbows on his knees and keen gold glints in his gaze.

"A prophecy...about a war," he murmurs, getting a fast answer in the form of Maximus's next nod.

"A war declared by a Titan who was then turned into a goddess, only to be slowly and steadily neglected through the years. A goddess who witnessed the same fate befalling all of Olympus and quietly vowed to do something about it. But in order to do that, she needed a special plan. And to make that plan happen, she needed a special weapon."

"Holy. Shit."

Jaden rolls back to his feet. He moves around the room with energy I haven't seen since he was a teenager landing his first movie part.

"Kara," my brother blurts, his gaze twice as scattershot as before. "*She's* the weapon. A blend of three races and of all their powers..."

"The races that Hecate needs to unite," Maximus states, "in order to take back Olympus from the king and queen who've messed it all up with their bickering and backstabbing."

Jaden stops, hands on his hips. "She wouldn't be wrong."

"But she's not totally *right*." Kell surges up from her chair too. "Fixing Olympus isn't going to happen by ravaging three of the four other realms, even by grooming a chosen one as their figurehead like this."

"Okay, stop." I stand to face off with them. "Groomed? How did some encouragement and enlightenment get translated into *groomed*?" I sweep a hand down, showcasing the smudged leggings and dirty tank that I've been wearing since this morning's exercises in the meadow. "And what about any of this looks *groomed* to you?"

Jaden rocks back on one heel. "Sorry, ashram girl, but

your fellow diamonds have gone and rearranged stars to make your story happen. All of this—you, Maximus, all these revelations and adventures—it's part of an altered narrative now. A world order that Hecate's orchestrated down to the inch."

I throw my hands up. "But it's insanity. Doesn't she see that? Chosen ones are a fictional trope for a good reason. Because they can't be *reality*. True change won't take a revolution. It'll take *generations*. A shift throughout *a lot* of time. Hecate needs so much more than me for this!"

I'm ready with more, so much more, but my rant peters out beneath the force of my siblings' stares. Their *scrutiny*. Looks that penetrate beyond the normal sisterly side-eye or brotherly frown. I feel…examined. Studied in ways that make me step back and clutch hands to my opposite shoulders.

"What?" I finally spit. "Come on. You two are freaking me out. *What is it?*"

I don't know why I'm thankful that Kell speaks up first.

"Generations," she echoes with slow, soft care.

"Bingo." Jaden's tone, while more decisive, is no less creepy for my nerves. "I should've realized…that sound I heard right after we first got here… Oh, *Kara*."

"And now I can't smell anything else," Kell rasps. "It's just not a combination I get to experience every day."

It's the sheen in her big browns that finally makes me tremble from head to toe. *Tears*. Kell *never* lets herself well up like this. *What. The …*

I don't realize it has stammered out of me until my

brother and sister stop me from completing the phrase, gripping me on each side with strength that borders on possessive.

"The sound I heard earlier was a heartbeat," Jaden states. "And it wasn't mine, yours, or Kell's."

"Okay. So, it was probably Maximus's."

"It wasn't his either," he cuts in, as if anticipating my skeptical protest. "Because it's fast. Really damn fast."

I park my hands on my hips now too. "Which means what?"

"Which means it's new," my brother murmurs carefully.

"New?" I stammer.

"And you don't smell a thing like dirt or sweat, sister," Kell offers from my other side. "All I'm getting now is talc and milk and strawberries."

I frown. "Strawberries? And *what*?"

She throws a dismissive hand into the air. "Don't ask me to explain it. All I know is exactly what it means."

And strangely, somehow, in this frightening but extraordinary moment...so do I.

But I don't say it. I *can't*. I just stand here, breath held and heart roaring, until Jaden utters what we all know now to be the truth.

"Kara...you're pregnant."

HOPE
of
REALMS

BLOOD OF ZEUS: BOOK FIVE

Keep reading for an excerpt!

CHAPTER 1

MAXIMUS

SINCE THE DAY OUR fingers first touched, Kara Valari has changed my life in a hundred incredible ways. A million surreal moments.

But never so much as this one.

I'm still in my own apartment, surrounded by all my familiar things—but my world is upended. Catapulted to someplace far different than the hell I traversed to rescue her or the magically cloaked ashram in which we both tried to recover from the ordeal.

My mind battles to grasp an announcement that overshadows both those experiences. Larger than falling in love with her in the first place, and then the moment I learned, from the king of the gods himself, that I'm his bastard son.

That was all before learning everything about *her*.

That nearly from the second she was born, she was promised in marriage to another. An incubus who'd help her make more demons for the glory of Hades and the underworld. But, because of the extra element in her blood, she was saved by her witch sisters for another destiny.

The path of falling in love with me.

But she and I didn't need the help.

I'm sure of it, down to the marrow of my bones, as I gaze at her now.

Her beauty has never sucked away more of my breath. Her hair shines brighter in the late afternoon sun streaming through the big windows. Her skin is practically glowing. The edges of her lips, caught by uncertain quirks, have never been more captivating.

Even as they open to stammer out words at her brother. The exact same words screaming through my mind.

"*Pregnant?* Jaden. Come on. This isn't a fun way to take revenge for the fantasy pony decals on your Daytona car."

"You think that's what I'm doing right now?" he volleys, glaring through thick swaths of his hair. "About a subject like this?"

Good point. One that has my legs finally giving out, sending my ass down to the cushions of my couch. With one hand, I beckon Kara to join me. As soon as she does, I look back up at Jaden.

In the same sweep, I include Kell, who's communicating more with her silence than any vocal message. Like Jaden, the woman has extrasensory abilities imbued by her demon DNA. Clearly, Kell's able to smell something extra about her sister while their brother hears it.

No. Not something extra.

Some*one* extra.

A new life, growing inside my woman this very second.

The concept feels too large to fathom. Too miraculous to embrace. It crowds my senses, huge and hot and looming, tempting me to roar aloud from the pressure.

I've never been so grateful for the self-containment skills that have been like a sixth sense since childhood. They've never been more useful than now, as I return Kell's and Jaden's gawks with determined purpose.

"We need the room, you guys. Please. If you want to stick close by, Jesse's probably home by now. He's three floors down, basically the same unit location. Look for the door knocker that looks carved by a depressed German viscount."

"That supposed to make us feel better?" Kell snaps.

"Well now I'm intrigued," Jaden adds.

Either way, I'm grateful they're already headed toward the door. I'm even more glad for the warmth of their sister in my arms.

But like before, that only scrapes the surface of what I'm truly feeling. *Glad* is reserved for when Jesse and I finish grading term papers. It's the satisfying conclusion of a good book. The gratitude for sunshine on the beach in the middle of January.

This...is far beyond all that. At least a thousand words past that hill and the twenty behind it.

This is the build-up of all those words behind the massive knot in my throat. It's impossible to whisper everything I planned into Kara's ear. Nothing feels right enough. Vast enough. Life is suddenly a panorama of possibilities, made even more beautiful by the vision of sharing them with this amazing female.

The center of my soul.

The bearer of my child.

Continue Reading in:

Hope of Realms
Blood of Zeus: Book Five

ACKNOWLEDGMENTS

What a journey this one has been! Beyond grateful to so many people for helping with this book.

Most prominently, I cannot thank you enough, Meredith Wild. Your creativity, mastery, and insights have helped me learn and grow in my craft. More importantly, thank you for believing in me when few others did. Your steadfast support and encouragement are such treasures in my world.

Equally indebted to the incredible Scott Saunders and the entire editing, formatting, and proofreading teams. You are truly the A Team, responsible for catching the little things that truly saved us from stepping into some huge, horrifying puddles. THANK YOU!

Many thanks to the entire Waterhouse Press team for your passion in supporting the work: Haley Boudreaux, Amber Maxwell, Kurt Vachon, Jonathan Mac, and Jesse Kench.

My profound and passionate love for the friends and colleagues who held my hand through the twists and turns of creating this one: Victoria Blue, Rebekah Ganiere, Katana Collins, Helen Hardt, Martha Frantz, Carey Sabala, Shayla Black, and Stacey Kennedy. I treasure you all so much!

Thanks to my mom: you have been my emotional glue, and I will never find enough ways to repay you for your unconditional love and support.

Most importantly, thanks to the readers who believe in this series and in Maximus and Kara's story. You are all so wonderful for following the journey. Thank you for your love and support!

— Angel

ABOUT MEREDITH WILD

Meredith Wild is a #1 *New York Times, USA Today,* and international bestselling author. After publishing her debut novel, *Hardwired,* in September 2013, Wild used her ten years of experience as a tech entrepreneur to push the boundaries of her "self-published" status, becoming stocked in brick-and-mortar bookstore chains nationwide and forging relationships with major retailers.

In 2014, Wild founded her own imprint, Waterhouse Press, under which she hit #1 on the *New York Times* and *Wall Street Journal* bestseller lists. She has been featured on *CBS This Morning* and the *Today Show,* and in the *New York Times,* the *Hollywood Reporter, Publishers Weekly,* and the *Examiner.* Her foreign rights have been sold in twenty-three languages.

Visit her at MeredithWild.com

Photograph © Sharon Suh

ABOUT ANGEL PAYNE

USA Today bestselling romance author Angel Payne loves to focus on high-heat romance starring memorable alpha men and the women who love them. She has numerous book series to her credit, including the action-packed Bolt Saga and Honor Bound series, Secrets of Stone series (with Victoria Blue), the intertwined Cimarron and Temptation Court series, the Suited for Sin series, and the Lords of Sin historicals, as well as several standalone titles.

Angel is a native Southern Californian, leading to her love of being in the outdoors, where she often reads and writes. She still lives in Southern California with her soul-mate husband and beautiful daughter, to whom she is a proud cosplay/culture con mom. Her passions also include whisky tasting, shoe shopping, and travel.

Visit her at AngelPayne.com